HOPELESS
ROMANTIC

Praise for Georgia Beers

Flavor of the Month

"Beers whips up a sweet lesbian romance...brimming with mouth-watering descriptions of foodie indulgences...Both women are well-intentioned and endearing, and it's easy to root for their inevitable reconciliation. But once the couple rediscover their natural ease with one another, Beers throws a challenging emotional hurdle in their path, forcing them to fight through tragedy to earn their happy ending."
—*Publishers Weekly*

"The heartbreak, beauty, and wondrous joy of love are on full display in *Flavor of the Month*. This second chance romance is exceptional. Georgia Beers has outdone herself with this one."—*The Lesbian Book Blog*

One Walk in Winter

"A sweet story to pair with the holidays. There are plenty of 'moment's in this book that make the heart soar. Just what I like in a romance. Situations where sparks fly, hearts fill, and tears fall. This book shined with cute fairy trails and swoon-worthy Christmas gifts...REALLY nice and cozy if read in between Thanksgiving and Christmas. Covered in blankets. By a fire."—*Bookvark*

Fear of Falling

"Enough tension and drama for us to wonder if this can work out—and enough heat to keep the pages turning. I will definitely recommend this to others—Georgia Beers continues to go from strength to strength."
—*Evan Blood, Bookseller (Angus & Robertson, Australia)*

"In *Fear of Falling* Georgia Beers doesn't take the obvious, easy way... romantic, feel-good and beautifully told."—*Kitty Kat's Book Review Blog*

"I was completely invested from the very first chapter, loving the premise and the way the story was written with such vulnerability from both characters' points of view. It was truly beautiful, engaging, and just a lovely story to read."—*LesBIreviewed*

The Do-Over

"You can count on Beers to give you a quality well-paced book each and every time."—*The Romantic Reader Blog*

"*The Do-Over* is a shining example of the brilliance of Georgia Beers as a contemporary romance author."—*Rainbow Reflections*

"[T]he two leads are genuine and likable, their chemistry is palpable... The romance builds up slowly and naturally, and the angst level is just right. The supporting characters are equally well developed. Don't miss this one!"—*Melina Bickard, Librarian, Waterloo Library (UK)*

Calendar Girl

"*Calendar Girl* by Georgia Beers is a well-written sweet workplace romance. It has all the elements of a good contemporary romance... It even has an ice queen for a major character."—*Rainbow Reflections*

"A sweet, sweet romcom of a story...*Calendar Girl* is a nice read, which you may find yourself returning to when you want a hot-chocolate-and-warm-comfort-hug in your life."—*Best Lesbian Erotica*

The Shape of You

"I know I always say this about Georgia Beers's books, but there is no one that writes first kisses like her. They are hot, steamy and all too much!"—*Les Rêveur*

The Shape of You "catches you right in the feels and does not let go. It is a must for every person out there who has struggled with self-esteem, questioned their judgment, and settled for a less than perfect but safe lover. If you've ever been convinced you have to trade passion for emotional safety, this book is for you."—*Writing While Distracted*

Blend

"You know a book is good, first, when you don't want to put it down. Second, you know it's damn good when you're reading it and thinking, I'm totally going to read this one again. Great read and absolutely a 5-star romance."—*The Romantic Reader Blog*

"This is a lovely romantic story with relatable characters that have depth and chemistry. A charming easy story that kept me reading until the end. Very enjoyable."—*Kat Adams, Bookseller, QBD (Australia)*

"*Blend* has that classic Georgia Beers feel to it, while giving us another unique setting to enjoy. The pacing is excellent and the chemistry between Piper and Lindsay is palpable."—*The Lesbian Review*

Right Here, Right Now

"The angst was written well, but not overpoweringly so, just enough for you to have the heart-sinking moment of 'will they make it,' and then you realize they have to because they are made for each other." —*Les Reveur*

"[A] successful and entertaining queer romance novel. The main characters are appealing, and the situations they deal with are realistic and well-managed. I would recommend this book to anyone who enjoys a good queer romance novel, and particularly one grounded in real world situations."—*Books at the End of the Alphabet*

"[A]n engaging odd-couple romance. Beers creates a romance of gentle humor that allows no-nonsense Lacey to relax and easygoing Alicia to find a trusting heart."—*RT Book Reviews*

Lambda Literary Award Winner *Fresh Tracks*

"Georgia Beers pens romances with sparks."—*Just About Write*

"[T]he focus switches each chapter to a different character, allowing for a measured pace and deep, sincere exploration of each protagonist's thoughts. Beers gives a welcome expansion to the romance genre with her clear, sympathetic writing."—*Curve magazine*

By the Author

Turning the Page

Thy Neighbor's Wife

Too Close to Touch

Fresh Tracks

Mine

Finding Home

Starting from Scratch

96 Hours

Slices of Life

Snow Globe

Olive Oil & White Bread

Zero Visibility

A Little Bit of Spice

Rescued Heart

Run to You

Dare to Stay

What Matters Most

Right Here, Right Now

Blend

The Shape of You

Calendar Girl

The Do-Over

Fear of Falling

One Walk in Winter

Flavor of the Month

Hopeless Romantic

Visit us at www.boldstrokesbooks.com

HOPELESS ROMANTIC

by
Georgia Beers

2020

CREDITS
EDITORS: RUTH STERNGLANTZ AND STACIA SEAMAN
PRODUCTION DESIGN: STACIA SEAMAN
COVER DESIGN BY ANN MCMAN

Acknowledgments

More often than not, my path to a new story idea begins with the question "What if?" Not that long ago, my niece Mikki got married, and I was lucky enough to be included in all the planning (holy cow, is there a lot of planning!). About two months in, she decided to hire a wedding planner to help, and it was one of the smartest things she did. The wedding planner took so much off her plate, it was hard to believe. I was fascinated by the organization she had, the scheduling she managed, the contacts she kept handy. As much as I helped Mikki with her choices, I also paid close attention to the wedding planner, simply because I found her job super interesting. And then one day, it hit me. The "what if?" I thought, "I bet she's seen a lot of these marriages go south. What if she's become jaded and doesn't even believe in marriage anymore?" We ask the "what if" question, and then we run with it. So, that's what I did, and you're holding the result in your hot little hands.

Thank you to Radclyffe, Sandy Lowe, and the entire staff at Bold Strokes Books. This publishing a book thing could be really difficult and stressful, but you all make it run so smoothly and easily, and I consider myself very lucky to be on board.

My editor, Ruth Sternglantz, is now in charge of making me the best writer I can be, and I'm already learning so much from her. Eagle-Eye Stacia Seaman, my copy editor, picks up the rest, and between the two of them, I actually look like I know what I'm doing. I'm forever grateful for that.

Big thanks to my friends who make up my support team; I don't know what I'd do without them: Melissa (who often helps me see things from a different angle), Carsen (who holds me accountable to my daily word count), Rachel (who checks in to make sure I'm still alive and eating), Nikki (who makes me laugh), Kris (my chart expert), my family, and more. These are the people who get me, and there is nothing in the world more comforting than having people who understand you. I've said many times that I'm an introvert who enjoys being alone. Writing is the perfect career for me. But if I need advice or a joke or somebody to help me out of the corner I've written myself into, knowing my gang is a mere keystroke away makes everything okay.

And then there's you. My readers. What can I say that I haven't already said before? You keep me writing, and I could not be more grateful for that. Thank you, thank you, thank you.

Chapter One

G oddamn it."
    The key wouldn't turn in the lock.

"God*damn* it," Teddi muttered again under her breath—which she could see, thanks to the unseasonably cold October morning. She was so not ready for fall because fall meant winter and she hated winter, but fall was most certainly here and announcing its presence by freezing her fingertips.

And, apparently, the temperamental lock on the front door of her shop.

"Goddamn it." She left the key in the lock and blew on her cold hands.

You've got to finesse it, Preston always told her. *Be gentle. Coax it and it'll open.*

"Finesse it, my ass." She turned the key again. Still stuck. As if to mock her, the wind kicked up, blowing her hair away from her ears, leaving them vulnerable to stupid October and stupid fall and goddamn it, why couldn't something go right for her? Just once? "Okay. Okay. Fine. Finesse it is." Teddi stepped back, set her shoulder bag down on the sidewalk. She shook out her arms, tipped her head from one side to the other, bounced on the balls of her feet like a boxer preparing to fight.

One big inhale.

One slow exhale.

Relax. Be gentle.

She stepped up to the door calmly, grasped the key, turned it.

Nothing.

"Goddamn it!" she yelled and stomped her foot. Actually stomped her foot, balled her hands into fists. Like she was five. She'd felt a little like that for the past two-years-plus, though. Angry. Toddler angry, like she couldn't have what she wanted and the only way to make her frustration known was to stomp her feet. Maybe fall to the ground and roll around a little, pounding her fists and crying.

Teddi stood at the door and leaned forward enough to let her forehead drop against the glass in defeat.

"Are you manhandling the lock again?" The voice of Preston Lacosta, her assistant ever since she'd opened her business, was both a relief and a frustration. Relief because he'd get the damn lock to open. "What did I tell you about being gentle?" He let his coal-eyed gaze rest on her face, reached for the key, and turned the lock with no resistance whatsoever. "See?" Yeah, and frustration because he'd get the damn lock to open.

"I hate you." Teddi picked up her bag and pushed through the door.

"You hate me because I'm beautiful," Preston called out as he bustled through the shop and past the counter, not affected in the least by her foul mood. Probably because it came standard lately with Teddi, and Preston understood it, had almost become used to it. It wasn't like she'd given him a choice. He told her over and over that time was the best thing for her, that eventually, she'd be back to her old fun, cheerful self. But it had been over two years and she was still...what was the right word? Angry. Yeah, that was it. Teddi was mad at the world. And Preston was a fixer, a problem solver, but she knew he wasn't sure how to fix that for her. After all, she'd earned that anger fair and square. She could see it on his face often, though, that it squeezed his heart to see his friend so broken.

"You're not wrong," Teddi called back as she headed through the shop and to the rear where her office was, mentally counting to ten and forcing herself to chill the hell out. Preston didn't deserve her snark. Nobody did. *Well, that's not exactly true.* "Nope. Nope, not going there right now," she said quietly into the empty office, then clicked the lights on, dropped her stuff onto the desk, and flopped down into her chair with the exhausted sigh of somebody who'd just walked several miles. Uphill. Carrying a bag of rocks.

It had become a ritual of sorts on those days that started off stressful, like today with the damn lock. She made a mental note to call a locksmith even as she began her breathing exercises, hoping to avoid a panic attack. She hadn't had one in quite a while, not since her therapist had taught her that the best way to harness her anger and frustration, to keep it from eating her alive on a daily basis, was to control her breathing. Teddi was skeptical of something so simple— her feelings were certainly not simple. They were beyond complicated. They were a whirlwind, a jumble, a bowl of noodles all tangled up in each other. Surprisingly, though, the breathing exercises helped, so she did them. After a few moments, she felt better. Sorting her things—bag, snacks, phone, tablet—also helped, and by the time she was ready to walk back out into the shop and face the day with Preston, she felt almost like herself.

"What do we have today, kind sir," she asked of Preston as she set her things down behind the counter. Preston was in the spot they called the Refreshment Corner, where the coffeemaker, the mini fridge, and all the snacks lived.

He doctored his coffee as he said, "First things first, I'm calling a locksmith. I'm worried I'm going to show up for work one day and there will be a Teddi-shaped hole in the glass."

Teddi scrunched up her face and nodded. "Okay. But get a quote first, please? I don't want to pay a million dollars."

"Well, a million dollars for a new lock would certainly be extravagant." He pulled a second cup of coffee out from under the drip, added cream and sugar, and carried both cups to the counter.

"Bless you, my child," Teddi said, reaching for the mug with the giant yellow smiley face on it and holding it in both hands to warm up, ignoring the irony of the imprint. Preston's mug shouted *Fabulous!* in bright rainbow lettering. She'd given it to him for Christmas last year, and he drank out of it every single day. "What else?"

Preston sipped his coffee as he scrolled on his tablet. The man *was* beautiful; Teddi had known him for nearly ten years and not one day had gone by when she hadn't had that same thought: *gorgeous*. Right up there with Idris Elba, if her clients were to be believed. From his mahogany skin, which was smooth and blemish free because his skincare routine rivaled that of any woman Teddi had ever met, to his perfect dark hair cut in a fade, to his too-fit-to-be-fact body, he was an amazing specimen of the male figure. *Damn gay men. Why are they always so much prettier than me?* Teddi grimaced but wiped it back to a pleasant expression of curiosity when Preston looked up at her.

"I've got to meet the caterer with Johnson and then help Meyers with her bridal party dresses. You've got three meetings today with potentials."

"Three?" Teddi felt her eyebrows rise up toward her hairline in pleasant surprise.

"Yep. Land 'em, would you?"

"I will."

Preston turned his head her way, a brilliantly white smile cutting across his face. A genuine one, not the artificial one he used when he pretended to agree with a bride's insistence on a hideous choice of fabric/color/flowers. "That." He pointed at her. "That's the Teddi Baker confidence I like to see. I've missed it."

"Me, too," Teddi said honestly. Seriously, the last twenty-five months—no, wait—the last three years, really, had just been brutal for her. And even though she still had moments like the lock on the front door, they were just that, moments. They were no longer hours or days or weeks. That was progress, right?

She sipped her coffee, tasted the deep richness, the sweet creaminess, and allowed herself to smile as she took in the shop before her.

Wedding planning was something she had sort of fallen into when her mad organizational skills had made her the go-to person to help first a college friend and then a cousin with planning their weddings. Before she knew it, they had told friends and relatives about how much Teddi had eased their minds and their workloads when it came to their nuptials, and all of a sudden, she was getting a dozen calls a month from strangers offering to pay her if she'd help them organize their weddings. She somehow managed to work her regular job at a print company *and* plan weddings on the side. The best part wasn't even the money, though that was a definite bonus—it was that she enjoyed it. No, that was a lie. She *loved* it. She loved spreadsheets and phone contacts and the relationships she'd begun to develop with vendors. Teddi was made to run the show, to be in charge. It's what she did best. Then one night, after finishing up her umpteenth wedding, she and her girlfriend at the time sat down with her father the CPA, and they hashed out a plan. Teddi would quit her job and open her own business.

That's how Hopeless Romantic was born.

Not many wedding planners had actual storefronts, but Teddi was very successful, had a sterling reputation and five stars on Yelp. In fact, for a while she'd had three storefronts in three different areas...

Nope. Nope, not going there right now.

It was a mantra and she used it. A lot. But it worked. Her brain diverted from its path and looked for an alternate direction. In a display of perfect timing, the phone rang, and she snatched it up before Preston even got close.

"Hopeless Romantic wedding planning, this is Teddi. How can I help you today?"

CHAPTER TWO

A little late.

That was going on her tombstone, Leah Scott was sure of it. *Beloved daughter, wonderful sister, always a little late.* Her tardiness used to drive her family and friends kind of crazy, but at some point, they'd mostly gotten used to it.

I'm going in. Get here!

She could almost hear the panic in her little sister Kelly's voice as she read the text and checked her watch. The appointment was for four o'clock and it was barely four fifteen. She pulled her Lexus into a parking spot three doors down and across the street from Hopeless Romantic, the wedding planning place that Kelly had talked nonstop about for longer than Leah could even remember. She'd been so thrilled to get an appointment with Theodora Baker, the owner, the woman Kelly called the "brilliant mind behind the fantastic designs all over Pinterest." She'd gone on and on about the colors and the hanging muslin and the tablescapes and the unique flower arrangements, all of them coming from the incredibly creative mind of Ms. Baker. Leah had spent the past too many months nodding and smiling and working hard to keep her eyes from glazing over as her sister went on. And on. And on. Interestingly, she'd said at one point, Ms. Baker used to have three locations across the city, but two had closed within the last two years or so and now there was only the one Kelly had been stalking. She'd been following Ms. Baker's work for nearly three years, since the moment she realized Dylan was The One and she would marry him. Leah had been instructed to periodically check Kelly's own Pinterest board, which was an enormous array of designs and dresses and locations and food, all the things she wanted for her own wedding. Which would take place in exactly eleven months, one week, and three days.

Not that Leah was counting.

Except of course, she was. Because while Kelly's intensity around her wedding slowly grew in strength—and annoyance, if she was being honest—it didn't matter. Kelly could be as intense as she wanted and Leah wouldn't mind at all. No, she couldn't be happier. Her baby sister had found the love of her life, and that was the most beautiful thing in the world. She'd look at all the Pinterest boards and flower varieties and tablecloths Kelly wanted her to. This was a big deal—a *huge* deal—and Leah was thrilled to be a part of it all.

Where are you?! Another text.

"I'm not even that late," she muttered as she grabbed her purse, got out of her car, and took in the place. The storefront was neat and classy, with *Hopeless Romantic Wedding Planning* scrolled in elegant gold lettering on the glass over the top of an absolutely breathtaking window display. Well, that Baker woman was certainly showing why she was the most expensive planner so far.

With a shrug, she crossed the street and pushed through the door.

"There she is." Kelly's voice hit Leah just before the lovely smell of—was it lilacs?—did. Her gaze followed the sound to her left where Kelly sat with a brunette who had such an instant effect on Leah, she couldn't move. *My God...* Her heart began to gallop. Any and all moisture left her mouth until her tongue stuck to its roof. She blinked way too much. And she just stood there as if her feet had grown roots. Stared.

Put together was probably how most people would describe Ms. Baker, at least that's what Leah thought. Elegant. Classy, maybe in her early forties, and a little intimidating because of the combination. Her features were very dark—dark hair that fell a little past her shoulders and looked like she'd used a wide curling iron on it; the darkest brown eyes Leah had ever seen, accented by liner and mascara that only increased their intensity; super tan skin. She wore a simple black skirt that ended just above her knees and a creamy ivory lightweight sweater with a low neckline and three small gold buttons decorating the front.

She did things to Leah. On a physical level. Weird things. Weirdly sexy things. What in the world was going on with her?

"Teddi Baker, meet my eternally late sister, Leah Scott."

Kelly's words unstuck her somehow, thank the good Lord above. Leah tried to shake off the strange feeling that had rendered her paralyzed. *Move your feet, Leah. Stop acting like a weirdo.* Hand outstretched, she put on her best professional face and crossed to the table. "I'm so sorry I'm late."

"It's great to meet you," said the woman through full pink lips that shined with a hint of gloss, and her grip was firm, her hand soft and warm. Teddi held on a little longer than necessary, with her hand as well as with her eye contact, and Leah was totally okay with both.

What is happening?

A loudly cleared throat. Leah's gaze shifted to Kelly, whose eyes were slightly wider than usual, and she used them to gesture to a chair. Leah sat.

For the next half hour, the three of them talked weddings. Colors, designs, venues, food, music. Leah was no stranger to what went into planning a wedding, but she'd never been smack dab in the middle of it like she was with Kelly. It was daunting, yes, but she'd never seen her little sister so happy, her hazel eyes constantly bright, her radiant smile part of everyday life now, and if helping Kelly pay for the wedding of her dreams was going to keep her that way, Leah was all for it. Their parents had little money. Well, their mother had little money. Their father had some but was by no means wealthy, and Kelly didn't have a ton of interest in asking for his help. *He's never been there for us. Why would I expect him to start now?* was her very valid reasoning.

Bright. Excited. A little fidgety in her chair. All being displayed by Kelly as they talked. Yeah, this was the planner for her. Leah could feel it. They'd seen three others, none of whom had impressed Leah a whole lot, though Kelly liked one of them quite a bit, but Hopeless Romantic was going to be the one.

"So," Teddi said as she wrapped up her pitch and slid a pale pink folder toward Kelly. Teddi smiled, and Jesus, Mary, and Joseph, the *dimples*. Leah swallowed hard. "Why don't you take this information home, look it over. Talk with your sister." Teddi's gaze shifted her way, and her eyes were the darkest Leah had ever seen. She was pretty sure she could get lost in them. "Check out the gallery on our website—see what we've done. It's a great way to pick up ideas. Then give me a call or shoot me a text and let me know what you think."

None of that will be necessary. Leah almost said it out loud but was able to stifle it under a grin. Kelly was practically vibrating in her seat, and Leah stood, hoping Kelly would follow so she could stop wiggling around like a five-year-old on too much sugar. She did, bouncing up as if the chair had ejected her.

"I will." Smile wide, energy high, Kelly held out a hand and shook Teddi's. "Thank you so much. I'll definitely be in touch."

Teddi let go of Kelly's hand and turned to Leah. "I hope to see you again soon." Teddi was a couple inches taller than her, and those dark eyes captured hers, held them, as Leah put her hand in Teddi's and didn't want to let go.

"Same," was the only word Leah could manage to push out.

Kelly held herself in check until they were out of the shop, across the street, and standing next to her car. Once there, she squealed in delighted excitement, hands fisted as she bounced on the balls of her feet.

"Well, you managed to last seventeen seconds out the door," Leah teased.

"Oh my God, I love her so much."

"Not news," Leah said with a grin.

"I want to hire her." This time, Kelly was tentative and uncertain. "I know she's more than the others…"

Leah swore she could see dollar signs floating above Kelly's head. Yeah, this was going to cost her. But she didn't care. Kelly deserved it. "Doesn't matter. You're worth it."

Another squeal of delight and Kelly was in Leah's arms, hugging her like she used to when they were kids. It didn't happen often now. After all, Kelly was a grown woman of thirty-one and Leah was disturbingly close to forty. But that didn't mean she couldn't remember being eleven and carrying three-year-old Kelly around, teaching her, protecting her. She was tiny then and she was tiny now—only five one. Granted, Leah was not tall by any means, but at five three and a half, she was still the Big Sister in every way. She closed her eyes and held tightly, waiting until Kelly let go first.

"Thank you so much. I'm going to go through this and do some more online searching. I've already been through their whole gallery, but I didn't want to say so and look like a crazy stalker of some kind."

"You let me know when you've set up the next appointment, and I'll be here."

"I bet you will," Kelly said, her voice laced with a teasing tone.

Leah raised her eyebrows in question.

"Mm-hmm. Don't play dumb with me. I saw the way you were looking at her."

Leah clenched her teeth and made a face. "Not so subtle after all, huh?"

"Please. I know you better than anybody."

"True." Leah opened the car door for Kelly to slide into the driver's seat.

"Not that I can blame you. That woman is *hot*."

Leah felt her eyes go wide. "Oh my God, right?"

"Maybe she plays on your team."

"Her? A woman who plans weddings for straight girls? I don't think so." But she'd certainly felt *something* from Teddi. Some kind of signal? Pheromones? Leah was by no means an expert in the ways of women dating women, but she knew when a woman might be into her. And Teddi Baker had sure given off that vibe.

Kelly hit her hip with a playful smack. "She does gay weddings, too, pessimist."

"Yeah?" That was new information. Leah let it roll around in her head and find a comfy spot.

"Yes." Kelly buckled her seat belt. "Go, before you get run over standing there with my door open." She made a shooing motion. "I'll text you later."

Leah shut the car door, and moved around the car up onto the sidewalk, watched Kelly pull into traffic and drive away. Hands shoved into the pockets of her black wool coat, she stood there for a moment, her head a jumble of emotions. Love and happiness for her sister. Financial logic regarding the expenses to come. Arousal around Ms. Teddi Baker…Yeah, that was the biggest one.

She cast a glance across the street toward Hopeless Romantic, and her breath hitched as she saw Teddi standing in the window. The second their eyes met, Teddi looked down at the table in the window display and fixed one of the place settings, adjusted a few things, then hurried out of sight.

Leah grinned, then lowered her head against the chilly breeze that had picked up, and headed up the street to her car.

❖

"Teddi Baker? Hmm." Tilly Scarsdale scrunched up her nose and furrowed her brow as she looked into her phone and at Leah. Her thinking face. "It sounds vaguely familiar, but I can't place her."

It was late. Not *late* late, but after midnight and later than Leah should be up. She made it a rule to try to get at least six hours of sleep each night if she could, but tonight? Wired. Utterly, completely wide awake. Like she'd had an espresso or five before giving up on the rom-com she was watching and heading to her bedroom.

"Yeah, she didn't ring a bell for me either. I mean, it's not like I know every lesbian in the city, and I don't even know if she's gay. But she was definitely feeling it, so I thought maybe she plays on *your* team." Leah lifted the glass of Cabernet she'd carried down the hall to the bedroom with her, and took a sip, felt the wine's warmth as it hit her system.

"I don't know all the bi or genderfluid women in the city either. Sadly."

"Yeah."

"But I can ask around. Who knows? Maybe I'll meet that certain someone." Tilly said the last two words in a dreamy, breathy voice.

Leah squinted at the screen of her phone and feigned suspicion. "Are you trying to get out of our pact, missy?"

Tilly let out an exaggerated gasp of horror. "How dare you?"

"I'm just saying, I'm going to be forty not long after Kelly's wedding. Almost a year from now. And then we'll both be forty, and you promised that if we were both unpartnered by the time we hit forty, we'd get married. Don't you dare back out now."

"I would never." Tilly went off screen but kept talking, and Leah could picture her very tall, very androgynous form changing into her pajamas. "We still have a whole year to find our persons, right?"

"Right."

"Don't give up, babe. She's out there."

"Yeah, yeah." Leah sipped again, reached out to pet Lizzie, who was rolled into a feline ball next to her, purring as loud as Leah's vibrator. She stroked the soft tiger-striped gray fur once, went a little too close to the off-limits underbelly area, and got a claw swipe for her trouble. "Ow, Lizzie, be nice to your mommy."

"That cat is evil," Tilly said, returning to the screen in a blue-and-white-striped pajama top that buttoned down the front. "Only too happy to bite the hand that feeds her."

"She is not evil. She's just particular and is in charge of her own life. Huh, honey?" She made kissy sounds toward her cat, who paid her zero attention. "That's why I named her Elizabeth Bennet."

"She's the devil. And that's why I *renamed* her Lizzie Borden. She's gonna kill you in your sleep one of these nights."

"Pssh." Leah waved her off, turned her focus back to the FaceTime call. "I love your Mike Brady pj's, by the way. Are there matching pants?"

"Is that a real question? Of course there are." Tilly moved her phone so Leah could see the striped bottoms. "You're just jealous."

"I totally am." Which was a lie because Leah couldn't imagine sleeping in so many clothes. An old Coca-Cola T-shirt and bikinis made up her sleeping attire, and only because it was chilly in the house tonight. Chances were, they'd end up on the floor before morning. She'd get annoyed and feel tangled and trapped and strip them off in the wee hours. It happened more often than not.

They chatted for another ten minutes about cases they were each working on before signing off with a promise to text the next day.

Leah plugged her phone into its charger and set it on the night-stand. Tilly was her touchstone, helped ground her when she felt like she was floating off into the ether. And she'd definitely felt that today, though it had taken her by complete surprise. Next to nothing. That's what she knew about Teddi Baker. But damn if that woman hadn't run through her brain, messing things up, disorganizing the organization she depended on. She really needed to focus on important things.

"Like, oh, I don't know…my *job*, maybe?"

Outside, the wind picked up, newly fallen leaves rustling along the pavement, clicking softly against the windows. Leah slid into bed. Sheets cool and soft, comforter just heavy enough. *Might be time to dig out the flannel set.* Winter would arrive in no time, and she tried to concentrate on that, the weather, which turned out to be laughable. Impending snowflakes and upcoming holidays were quickly replaced with much more pleasant things.

Like dark, dark eyes, olive skin, and dimples.

CHAPTER THREE

"So, the DiMarco-Jensen wedding is Saturday, right?" Harlow McCann bit into her cheeseburger and hummed her delight.

Teddi nodded, stabbed a chunk of cucumber and a tomato from her salad, and tried not to let her cheeseburger envy show.

"Just get the burger next time." Harlow shot her a wink. Harlow was her best friend and the most confident, cheerful person Teddi had ever met. Harlow loved life and everything about it. Gusto—Harlow was the epitome of it, and Teddi envied her more than she cared to admit. To herself or anybody else.

"That," Teddi said, waving her fork up and down to indicate Harlow's black floral-print dress and black leather jacket, "is fabulous, by the way. What I wouldn't give for half your fashion sense."

"Please, you always look amazing. You're sophisticated. I can't pull off sophisticated. I have to settle for edgy."

She did it well, there was no denying it. Edgy. Trendy. Hip. Harlow was all those things. Teddi always took mental notes but just didn't have the same level of style as her BFF. "How's Rashim?" Harlow and Rashim had been her very first clients, their wedding simple and beautiful.

"My boo is great. Working too much, but that's nothing new." Something passed over Harlow's face then. If she hadn't known her so well, Teddi wouldn't have caught it.

"What's up?"

Harlow sighed, sipped her Sprite. "I'm just a little annoyed by everybody asking us when we're going to start a family. Even my mom. Especially *his* mom. *It's been almost ten years. Where are my grandchildren?*" Harlow did a perfect Pakistani accent when imitating her mother-in-law.

"You guys don't want kids."

"*I* know that. *He* knows that. Nobody else seems to even consider that as a possibility." She groaned, then waved a hand. "Talk about something else. Please. How's my boyfriend, Preston, the beautiful, beautiful hunk of a man?"

Teddi sipped her drink and grinned at the familiar question. "He's good."

"Still gay, huh?"

"Afraid so. Also, you're married."

"Listen, I have fantasies. You can't stop me. They're totally allowed."

"They are." God, she loved how Harlow could make her laugh. Shifting gears, she said, "I got a new client last week. Wedding's next September."

"Oh, good. And not a last-minute one. Nearly a year. That's a nice change."

"Right? I meet with her again this Friday. I'll give her your card." Harlow was a photographer and a damn good one. Teddi sent all her clients Harlow's way, and not one had ever been dissatisfied. Not in ten years. "Her name is Kelly, and she came in with her big sister, Leah."

Harlow popped a French fry into her mouth and nodded as she chewed.

"She seems to hold at least some of the purse strings," Teddi said.

"The sister?"

"Mm-hmm. Kelly seemed to run things by her, looked to her for approval. I don't know what she does for a living, but she didn't seem to be worried about what I might charge. I wonder if it'll be different as things progress. Whether it'll be an issue."

"With *the sister*." Amusement. Teddi detected it in Harlow's tone immediately.

Teddi swallowed. "Yes." Felt herself flush.

"You're blushing." Harlow took another bite of her burger. Satisfaction was all over her face. Harlow knew her well. Too well. "Spill."

"Damn it." Teddi hung her head for a second, annoyed at her apparently fantastic impression of a piece of glass. Harlow saw right through her.

"You have a thing for the sister." Again with the amusement, the self-satisfaction.

"Shut up. You don't know everything."

Harlow grinned widely. "I know you have a thing for the sister."

"You annoy me."

"It's my life's work. Now tell me all about her." Elbows propped on the table, hands clasped near her chin, body leaning forward, Harlow was settled in.

Teddi blew out a breath, resigned, and sat back in her chair. "There's nothing to tell, really. I mean, we spent about half an hour together."

"But she affected you if you're still thinking about her a week later, yeah?"

"She did." *She really, really did.* Teddi didn't add that part. Didn't add how she'd watched Leah walk Kelly to her car or how she'd kept watching until Kelly had driven away and Leah had turned toward the shop. Had she seen her? Teddi had done a terrible job of pretending she'd been in the window to fix the display. No way was she going to tell Harlow that. "So, I stared at her when she left. I stood in my own window like a stalker and stared." Teddi closed her eyes in defeat. It was impossible to hide things from Harlow. Impossible.

"She must be hot." Harlow's grin said she was enjoying this way too much.

"Stop grinning like that." Torn between shame and humor, Teddi reached for the glass on the table, turned it slowly with her fingers.

"I'm sorry." Harlow's tone said she was, as did her reach across the table and the way she squeezed Teddi's forearm. "It's just been a really long time since I've seen you notice anybody. It makes me happy, that's all." Once Teddi let herself smile, relief crossed Harlow's face. "What does she look like?"

That face was not hard to recall. It had invaded Teddi's mind and stayed there for days. "She's blond, hair just past her shoulders. And I've never seen eyes so green, my God. They were intense. Deep. She's a little shorter than me. She was in a suit, so she must be some kind of businesswoman."

"Pants or a skirt?"

"Pants. And pumps. Black pantsuit with black pumps and white shirt underneath with tiny black dots."

"Interesting. A slick professional suit, but polka dots under it. She's playful."

"You think?"

Harlow laughed and held her hands palms up. "How the hell would I know?"

Teddi joined her laughter as any tension bled away. "She adores her sister—I can tell you that."

"I wonder what their story is."

Teddi nodded, not admitting to Harlow that she hadn't wondered much else since the meeting. Those eyes… She cleared her throat and lifted one shoulder.

"I guess maybe you'll find out on Friday?"

❖

Fast paced, immersive, jam packed, and crazy busy—words that described every Friday before a wedding in Teddi's business. Hopeless Romantic had always had a reputation for excellence and still did, despite their few recent bumps in the road.

"T.J. is on line two," Preston told her as she hung up from a heated debate with a caterer.

"Carlson's trying to jack up his pricing at the last minute. Put a note in his file for me. We'll think twice before recommending him again." Teddi swiftly changed lines. "T.J. the DJ. How's the music business today?"

The morning flew by like it had a jet engine and someplace very important to be. She and Preston sat down over a lunch of subs and chips and went through their lists for tomorrow's wedding. Amelia DiMarco was marrying Todd Jensen at a vineyard about an hour away. They were a sweet couple and Teddi was looking forward to it.

"This should be a nice one," Preston said as if reading her mind. "No bridezilla. No douchebag groom. I think they'll make it."

"Same. What's our average now?" Since they'd begun working together, they'd predicted the future of each and every couple they'd dealt with—who'd stay together, who'd be divorced within a year, and everything in between.

"We are disturbingly accurate," Preston said, then took a bite of his roasted veggie sub.

Teddi grinned. "Okay. I've conferred with the caterer, the florist, the DJ, and the delivery guys."

Preston glanced at his tablet, scrolling a bit with one hand while he held his sub in the other. "Venue, Harlow, limo, videographer. Check, check, check, and check."

"Fantastic. We are a well-oiled machine, my friend."

Preston high-fived her across the table.

They ate in silence for several moments, decompressing from the busy morning and bracing for the rush of the afternoon.

"You have newbies coming in later?"

Teddi nodded as she swallowed. "At four. Kelly Scott. Seems like a nice girl. I'll get more detailed info from her today, then let you know what we're looking at."

"This is the one that came in with her sister, was it?"

"Yeah, an older one. Leah. I don't know where the mother is or if there is one."

"You'll find out." He wasn't wrong. Being a wedding planner was weirdly like being a bartender. People just *told* Teddi things. Secrets. Hopes. Fears. She knew about unannounced pregnancies. She knew about last-minute affairs. She knew when a woman wanted to get married more than anything in the world, and she also knew when a woman thought she might be making the biggest mistake of her life. She got it all, never by asking, and she was used to it by now. Preston's perfectly shaped eyebrows met at the top of his nose. "Leah Scott? Why does that name sound familiar?"

"I'm pretty sure that's what her sister said. I don't think she's married." Objection. Rejection. Irritation. Her reactions to the idea of Leah being married. *Ignore them. Ignore them all.*

Preston tapped a manicured finger against his lips, then shook his head. "Nope. I can't place it. I might be thinking of someone else."

Teddi popped the last of her turkey sub into her mouth and crumpled up the wrapper. "Ready for round two?"

Preston mimicked her cleanup. "Let's do this."

They stood together, fist-bumped, and then headed in separate directions to conquer the battle that was a Friday afternoon at Hopeless Romantic.

Is it four o'clock already?

The question flew through Teddi's head a while later when the electronic ding-dong that meant the front door had opened hit her ears. She heard Preston's greeting and knew Kelly Scott was here. Was Leah here, too? It occurred to her that she wasn't sure. She kind of hoped so—she could admit that. She stood up and glanced in the mirror that hung in her office. She had fixed her hair, repaired her eyeliner, and was adding a quick coat of lip gloss before she registered what it was she was doing. *Oh my God, you're primping. You're actually primping. Stop it!* With a shake of her head, she took a deep breath, let it out, then left her office to meet her client.

❖

"Say something," Leah demanded of Kelly as they pulled the door to Hopeless Romantic open and a pretty little electronic bell sounded.

Kelly squinted at her. "What?"

Leah feigned shock, tapped the face of her silver watch with a finger to punctuate each word. "I. Am. On. Time."

Kelly stopped dead halfway through the door. A super tight hug followed, one that surprised Leah but made her laugh. "You *are*." The door eased shut behind them, and Kelly let go of her but didn't step forward.

"You okay?" Leah asked quietly.

"I'm nervous." Kelly turned wide eyes to her. "Is that weird?"

Looking at Kelly transported Leah back many years. Just for a moment, she was twenty-three and Kelly was fifteen, getting ready to go out on her first date, gazing at her big sister for reassurance as she told her how nervous she was. Leah had felt protective then and she felt protective now. As she tucked an errant strand of hair behind Kelly's ear, she smiled tenderly. "It's not weird at all. I think hiring a wedding planner is a thing that sets it all in motion, you know? Forward, full-force. No turning back. Of course you're nervous. Totally normal."

Semi-convinced. Leah could tell by Kelly's expression. But Kelly gave one nod. "Okay."

"You must be Kelly Scott." One of the handsomest men Leah had ever seen walked toward them with a hand outstretched. Judging from Kelly's deer-in-the-headlights look, she felt the same way. "I'm Preston

Lacosta, Teddi's assistant manager. It's lovely to meet you." He shook Kelly's hand.

"Isn't Ms. Baker going to be here?" The words were out of her mouth before Leah even knew she was thinking of saying them. She rolled her lips in and bit down on them.

"And you're the sister. Leah, is it?"

Those deep, richly dark eyes of his probably mesmerized a good chunk of the women—and probably some of the men—who came in here.

"Kelly. Leah. Good to see you both again." Teddi Baker materialized from somewhere in the back, and just like that, the ground that had felt shaky and uncertain under Leah's feet seemed to stabilize. Weird. Teddi shook hands with Kelly, her smile wide, dimples on full display. When Teddi turned to Leah, those dark, dark eyes seemed to reach out and collect her, cradle and hold her within them. Their hands clasped, and Teddi's smile softened as she greeted Leah with a soft "Hi."

"Hey." Leah had never believed in things like instant connections or soul mates or any of that hokey crap, but there was something here. Something undefinable. Something sharp and heavy and strong. Did Teddi feel it, too? She wanted to know so badly, but how exactly did you ask that of a virtual stranger? *Yeah, keep your mouth shut. You're here for Kelly.*

That shook her back to reality. The spell broken—or at least temporarily set aside for now—they moved to the same table they met at last week and took seats, Preston joining them. There was a white mug half filled with coffee and bearing a pale pink lipstick print.

Teddi grabbed it and held it up. "Can I get anybody coffee?"

"I have had more caffeine than I need today, but thank you," Leah said. Kelly shook her head.

"You've met Preston?" Teddi asked, and at their nods, she went on. "He's my right hand around here. I will be your point of contact always, but if for some reason you can't get ahold of me, don't hesitate to call him."

"I have access to everything Teddi does," Preston added, his smile revealing the perfect white teeth Leah expected. "Files, vendors, your details, any emails. It's unusual for Teddi to be completely out of reach, but if she is, I can usually get to her."

"It's true. I can't get away from him." Teddi exchanged a look with Preston that told Leah they were yin and yang to one another, their fondness obvious.

The down-and-dirty came next. Leah listened but let Kelly take the lead. Casual observer was the role she took on, and she couldn't help but smile as Kelly became more animated. Teddi watched her with a soft expression, probably humoring her. There was no way Teddi hadn't heard this stuff a million times, but she never rushed Kelly, never interrupted her, and seemed to understand every single thing Kelly said.

And Teddi was beautiful. Leah took in the ivory sweater dress Teddi wore, a classic contrast to her olive skin. Gold bangle bracelets jingled softly when Teddi moved her hand. Her hair was down, a soft brown that looked like it might be a shade darker underneath. Subtle brown eye shadow accentuated the deep dark of Teddi's incredible eyes, and her full lips shone with the glimmer of a coat of lip gloss, just a hint of pink.

And it wasn't odd at all that she noticed Teddi's impressive posture, right? Her spine was straight, her shoulders squared the whole time she spoke, twisted, moved her arms. Teddi wasn't tall—maybe two inches taller than her—but she seemed it. The way someone carried themselves said a lot about them, her mother used to say, and nobody in her recent memory illustrated that point better than Teddi Baker. Her presence said: *Yes, I'm attractive. I also run this show and will snap you like a twig if I need to.*

Leah felt the corners of her mouth tug up at the thought.

"What are you smiling at?" Kelly's question took her by surprise, and Leah sat up a little straighter. Teddi's eyes were on her as well, and Leah swore she could feel them, straight down to her—

"Just happy to see you so happy," she replied, pulling an answer out of her ass so fast she even impressed herself. Teddi's gaze stayed on her for an extra beat. It did things to Leah.

Shoulder bumps were Kelly's signature move of affection, and she leaned into Leah with one. "Can you give Teddi the deposit?"

"Oh. Of course." Leah fished her wallet out of her purse and pulled out her Visa card.

Preston took it from her hand and slid it through the Square he'd plugged into his tablet. "Leah Scott," he said as he watched the transaction on the screen. "Your name seems familiar to me."

"Pretty common name," Leah said.

"She's a lawyer," Kelly said, pride in her tone.

"Oh yeah?" Preston turned the tablet around and pointed. "Just sign here with your finger."

Leah hated signing with her finger, always felt like a five-year-old trying to sign her name in crayon, and she squinted, certainly signing as slowly as one.

"What kind of lawyer?" Preston asked.

Leah hit the green button that read *Done*. "I'm a divorce attorney."

A heavy coffee mug had to hit the ground just right in order to shatter, and Teddi's apparently had, the sound of the crash startling the other three enough to make them each flinch in their seats. Leah's head whipped toward Teddi, who sat wide-eyed and seemingly shocked, a Rorschach inkblot of a coffee stain blossoming on her beautiful ivory dress.

"Oh my God, are you okay?" Kelly sprang into action, her kindergarten teacher reflexes kicking into high alert as they did any time something was spilled or broken.

Teddi stood slowly, head down, her focus seemingly on the puddle of coffee and pieces of mug scattered across her hardwood floor. "I'm fine. I'm sorry. Clumsy. I'll just..." She pointed over her shoulder, blinked several times, never meeting Leah's eyes, then turned on her heel. "Preston, set up the next appointment, would you?" In the next three seconds, she had disappeared into the back.

A full five seconds of silence passed before Kelly and Leah exchanged looks. "Um, is she okay?" Leah asked Preston, whose head was turned toward Teddi's exit.

"Uh, yeah. I'm sure she's fine." He turned back around. Uncomfortable. It was the only way to describe him. "Let's get your next appointment on the schedule."

Ten minutes later, Leah and Kelly stood at Kelly's car, almost mirroring the first time they left Hopeless Romantic. It had been a beautifully crisp fall day, but now the crisp had kicked up and the beautiful had pulled back. Leah put her hands in the pockets of her long coat.

"That was so weird," Kelly said, pulling open her car door and slipping inside.

"Right?" Such a strange reaction to a broken mug. Leah looked back at the storefront. "Do you think she cut herself?"

"Or she's allergic to divorce attorneys." Kelly chuckled and started the car. As if sensing Leah's confusion, Kelly said, "That's when she dropped the mug. When you said you were a divorce attorney." With a snorted laugh, she asked, "You didn't handle her divorce or something, did you?"

Leah blinked at her.

Kelly's smile faltered, no longer lighthearted. "You didn't, did you?"

"I..." Leah wrinkled her nose and shrugged. "Is she divorced? I mean, I guess it's not out of the realm of possibility."

"Oh, great." Kelly let her forehead fall against the steering wheel, then immediately lifted it up again. "Well, we've paid a deposit and she's the best in the business, so let's hope, if you did, we can all just remain professional."

"Yeah. Okay."

"She *got* me, Leah." Pleading her case. Thrilled and happy. Excited anticipation. Leah loved seeing these things on her sister's face, hearing them in her voice. "She got everything I mentioned. I felt so comfortable with her."

"I know."

"I don't want to unhire her. She's exactly what I want."

"Then we won't." Leah swallowed the twinge she felt at that last line. "We'll work it out. Don't worry." Words she'd said to Kelly their entire lives, and she'd always made it so, no matter how much of a pretzel she'd had to twist herself into. She always worked it out. For Kelly.

Kelly held her gaze for a beat. "Okay. I love you."

"Love you, too." Leah slammed Kelly's door and watched her pull away. One last glance at Hopeless Romantic. No Teddi standing in the window. "Well, that's a damn shame," she muttered, waiting an extra moment or two, just in case. Then she turned away and headed toward her car.

She had information to find.

CHAPTER FOUR

So, I had to do some searching, but I finally found her." Leah sighed, stabbed a hunk of salmon with her fork. "Theodora Baker. I represented her ex, Julia Bingham, in their divorce."

"And who got the better settlement?" JoJo Gonzales asked, then took a sip of her iced tea. Her almost-black hair was in a French twist, and she wore her navy blue suit with what she called her power-red silk blouse underneath, as she'd had court that morning.

Leah cocked her head and arched an eyebrow. "Seriously?"

"I can't believe you actually asked her that," Tilly said, feigning insult. Her short white-blond hair was a little spiky on top but tamer than it often was, and she tucked a bit over an ear.

Nearly twenty years. Was that right? Leah did the math in her head. *Holy shit, it is.* She'd known Tilly and JoJo since they'd been thrown together in a suite in law school. They'd been lucky enough to hit it off—not all their classmates had—and they'd been a trio of besties ever since. They called each other almost daily and made an honest effort to have lunch, dinner, drinks, or all three at least once a week. It didn't always happen, but they tried.

Back to the subject at hand, Leah said, "It wasn't a difficult case, really. Together for eleven years, married for almost seven. My client kept the household running financially while her wife got her business up and running. Once it became a success, my client quit her job to study...ceramics and pottery, I think it was? Met someone, fell in love, asked for a divorce. They fought over the property division—Teddi said she'd been paying all the bills for years and it wasn't fair."

"But it was," JoJo surmised.

"I mean, yeah. But"—she grimaced, stabbed some more salmon—"I did some research, and Teddi had to close up two of her three locations so she could cover the settlement."

"Ugh, that sucks." JoJo shook her head.

"Nature of the beast," was Tilly's comment. Emotion had no place in law. That's what she always said. "Who'd she have?"

"Dennison."

Tandem groans came from both friends.

"No wonder," Tilly scoffed. Tilly hated Tim Dennison, thought he was a hack who took shortcuts so he could make the most money for the least amount of work. She wasn't wrong. "Guys like him are the reason there are lawyer jokes."

"I hate the idea of Teddi being repped by that dick." Leah shook her head, her appetite dwindling a bit.

"So much for *feeling it*, huh?" Tilly asked, making air quotes.

"Wait. Feeling what?" JoJo looked from one to the other. "Am I out of the loop? Again?"

"You are," Tilly said. "Loopless, as usual."

JoJo snorted. "Listen, loops are hard. Talk to me when you guys have two kids, a mother-in-law moving in, and a husband who has no idea how the dishwasher *or* the washer and dryer work. Now, fill me in."

"It seems that not only is this Ms. Baker the only wedding planner in the world for Kelly, but she had some serious chemistry going on with our friend Leah here."

JoJo's big brown eyes got even bigger as she did an exaggerated turn of her head toward Leah. "Oh, *really*?" She drew out the last word comically.

"Well, it's all shot to hell now, so it doesn't matter." Leah tried not to sound as disappointed as she felt. Potential. That's what she'd allowed herself to feel around Teddi. Possibility. Hadn't lasted long.

"Yeah, her dropping her coffee on the floor when she heard you were a divorce attorney is a pretty big clue." Tilly wiped her mouth with her napkin, then gestured to the waiter across the room that they were ready for their check. "Do you think she'd been trying to place you?"

"Maybe my name. We never met in person. Everything was handled outside of court."

"Fucking Dennison," Tilly muttered.

"What did you do last night when you figured it out?" JoJo, too, finished her lunch and tucked her napkin alongside her plate.

"I watched *Notting Hill*." Leah shrugged like that made perfect sense. Which it did, to her.

"I'm standing here in front of this boy—"

Tilly didn't get any further before Leah cut her off with an upheld hand. "No. Absolutely not. You do not get to butcher one of my favorite films by getting the lines wrong. Just stop."

JoJo tsked, shaking her head in dismay. "Oh, Matilda. You'll never learn."

"Ms. Joellen Gonzales, would you care to correct Ms. Scarsdale?"

"I would love nothing more, Ms. Scott." JoJo made a show of turning to face Tilly and cleared her throat. Hand pressed to her heart in a display of the utmost sincerity, she recited, complete with the proper pleading emotion, the actual line from the movie perfectly, even adding in the correct pauses and inflection.

"Bravo," Leah said, clapping.

"Thank you." JoJo took a bow from her seat. "Thank you very much."

"Only one of the best romantic lines of all time, Tilly," Leah said.

"Agreed." JoJo nodded.

"Ugh. Sap. That's all it is." JoJo and Leah gasped in unison, and Tilly laughed and shook her head. "You two. It's a good thing I love you both."

"It is," Leah said while JoJo nodded.

It was an age-old disagreement the three of them had, and at this point in their friendship, they used it for laughs. Tilly was a horror movie fan. JoJo liked a wide variety of movies. And Leah watched every romance she could get her hands on—she had, ever since she was old enough to know what a romance was. Her library was extensive and included a few classics, several from when she was a kid, and many current films. At first Tilly had made fun of her and JoJo had piled on, but after their friendship deepened they began to understand what those movies were to Leah. When they'd finally begun to understand that, despite having a front row seat to the bitter divorce of her parents, despite her career choice, Leah actually believed in happily ever after, craved her very own with everything in her heart, they eased up on her.

The waiter dropped off the check, which Tilly scooped up almost before Leah'd even registered its arrival. "My turn this week."

"So what are you going to do?" JoJo asked, her gaze on Leah. "About Kelly?"

Leah shrugged. "She wants Teddi as her wedding planner. She did her due diligence. She met with three others. She says Teddi gets her."

"Are you worried it'll be awkward?" JoJo clenched her teeth, made a face.

"All I can do is hope we can maintain a professionalism for Kelly's sake. You know?"

"Leah did her job. It wasn't personal." Tilly. Matter-of-fact.

All Leah could do was nod. Tilly was right. She'd done her job and she'd done it well. But she was pretty sure Teddi Baker didn't look at it that way.

❖

While June was still the most popular month for weddings, September and October had moved up the ranks. Hopeless Romantic was busy, something Teddi never took for granted. Any time she felt like complaining that the schedule was too hectic, she made herself remember how hard she'd worked to come back from the verge of bankruptcy, thanks to Julia and her lawyer, Leah Scott.

She'd gone through her filing cabinet the previous night, looked up her divorce papers, found Leah's name on them, confirming what she already knew in her heart. Her intention had been to give herself the evening to be angry. Leah Scott was the one who'd gotten Julia such a ridiculous settlement. Leah Scott was the reason Teddi had had no choice but to close not one but two of her three locations in order to pay Julia what she wanted—what she *deserved*, if you read the documents. Teddi was bitter. Absolutely, she was. Who wouldn't be in her situation? So she'd gone home right after her meeting with the Scott sisters, Oxy-cleaned the hell out of the coffee stain in her favorite dress—another thing she'd likely lose, thanks to Leah Scott—and stomped around her house in the foulest of moods.

Yeah, still pissed. That was her first thought when she opened her eyes the next morning, so she'd allowed herself another day to just be mad. Preston had watched her stomp around the shop, speak rather curtly to her vendors, rip open her mail with more force than necessary. Smartly, he'd given her a wide berth, and when she'd come in the day after that, she was back to her old self again. A week had gone by. Two weeks. Teddi felt better, felt like her old self, finally.

Until today.

Because today, she would be seeing the Scotts again.

Really hoping any history you may have with my sister won't affect our working relationship, Kelly Scott had texted her the day after they'd met last time. *I feel like you understand exactly what I want for my wedding, so I hope we can continue to work together.*

"I was kind of hoping she'd bow out," Teddi had admitted to Harlow on the phone that night. "Like, she'd feel awkward and decide maybe it was better to find another wedding planner."

"Except you can't be turning away clients," had been Harlow's very accurate response.

"Exactly."

"Can I say something you're not going to like?"

"It's adorable that you pretend I have a choice."

"Funny. I just want to make sure that you know, if you need to blame somebody, blame Julia, not Leah Scott. She was just doing her job. It wasn't personal."

"I know," Teddi said. And she did. She understood that. She also understood that it had been *very* personal for her.

And so, here she stood, behind the counter in her shop, piles of emails to return and calls to make, just minutes away from another meeting with the Scott sisters.

"You okay?" Preston asked as he made himself a cup of coffee from the Keurig.

Teddi saw the slight concern in his eyes. "Sure. Why?"

"Because you've been staring out the front window for about..." He checked the gold watch on his wrist. "Seventeen minutes now."

Forced smile. Straightened posture. Teddi tipped her head from one side to the other, feeling the satisfying pop in her vertebrae. "I'm good."

"Nervous?"

"A little, I guess. Which I hate."

Preston crossed to the counter with the coffee and surprised her by sliding it across to her. It was in one of the to-go cups they kept a supply of. She grinned at him. "No spilling or dropping, okay?"

"What about throwing?"

"No throwing."

Teddi sighed dramatically. "Fine. Fun killer."

"It's really okay. All right? It's business. Income. Pretend they have dollar signs tattooed all over them."

That brought a tiny bubble of a chuckle up from her lungs. "I'll do that." It had been a short and sweet pep talk, but it helped and she was grateful.

Through the shop's window, she saw Kelly Scott slam her car door and hurry across the street toward the door. Maybe it would just be her today, no Leah. One could hope, right?

"Here we go," Preston said, then took up residence behind the counter to take care of email and answer the phone while Teddi was busy.

The door swung open, letting in the chilly fall breeze that seemed to be the new regular thing lately. Kelly bustled in, smiling and cheerful, as she'd been both times Teddi had met with her, and Teddi *really* looked at her for the first time, noticed she was a shorter, slightly plumper, less sleek version of her big sister. While her hair was a touch lighter blond than Leah's and her eyes were more hazel than Leah's arresting green ones, their bone structure was similar—high cheekbones, rounded jawline—and you could tell they were siblings. Today, she wore comfy-looking jeans, a light blue sweater, and white Chucks. A picture of her sitting cross-legged on the floor reading to small children needed no conjuring. It just *was*.

"Kelly. Hi. How were the kids today?" Teddi greeted her client with a smile and an outstretched hand.

"A little wild," Kelly said with a half grin. "Halloween is close and the excitement levels are off the charts."

"I bet." Teddi put away anything that wasn't work-related. In a box. Marked it *not important right now*. Put it up on a high shelf in her brain. It was time for business. "Is Leah coming?" Oops. Okay, so that slipped out.

"Supposedly." Kelly said it with the smile and acceptance of a person used to the tardiness. She took off her jacket and draped it over the back of a chair, then sat.

How did they plan weddings before the internet? Teddi asked herself that question almost daily. Even when she'd first started out nearly ten years ago, she'd had so much at her fingertips. Finding colors, choices, designs was super simple and there were too many, really. Luckily, most women planning a wedding—or who even hoped to eventually get married—tended to have a Pinterest board where they pinned anything and everything that sparked some kind of interest. Wedding gowns, bridesmaids dresses, tablescapes, venues, color schemes…it was all there for the scrolling. Part of Teddi's research on a client was to check out her Pinterest board. Incredible how much you could learn about someone just from scrolling through the things she liked.

"Okay," she said to Kelly as they settled in. Teddi slid her chair around so she sat next to Kelly rather than across from her. Touching the screen on her tablet, she said, "Let's take a look at your Pinterest board."

They'd been at it for about twenty minutes, scrolling, brainstorming, Teddi getting to know Kelly a bit better, when the door swung open.

"I know, I know," Leah said. Her heels clicked on the floor and she crossed to the table and the empty chair on the other side of Kelly. She seemed breathless. A little frazzled. "I'm late. Not news. I'm sorry." Annoyed with herself, definitely, Teddi could see that. Leah opened her trench, slipped it off her arms to reveal a smart black pantsuit with a silver silk shell underneath the jacket. Her blond hair was pulled partially back, the rest hanging down in gentle waves that cascaded over her shoulders. She took a seat, glanced up at Teddi for a split second, then quickly back down.

She's as nervous as I am.

She could be wrong, but it seemed pretty clear that Leah had also figured out their connection and was a bit uncomfortable. *Well, good. She should be.* Vowing to make as little eye contact as possible—because Teddi was twelve, apparently—she instead watched Leah's hands as she pointed to different things on the tablet Kelly held. How had she not noticed what beautiful hands Leah had? Small. Fine-boned. Her nails were manicured, the polish white—the latest trend, and it looked unexpectedly sophisticated on her. *Oh my God, stop it! This is the woman who helped take two-thirds of your business!*

"What are your thoughts on that?"

Teddi blinked, looked up at Kelly, who'd asked the question. "I'm sorry?"

Kelly pointed at the screen. "I really love these chairs."

Focus, Teddi. A clear of her throat. A moment to return to business mode. "Well, they're nice chairs. They also cost more to rent. We haven't gone over your budget yet, but you'll need to decide what's important to you. What's worth spending extra on, and what's not. Where are you okay laying out a little more, and where does it make sense to cut some corners?"

A big sigh. "That's what Leah keeps telling me."

"Mm-hmm," was all Leah said. Teddi could feel her eyes on her but didn't meet them.

"But look how pretty they are." Dreamy voiced, Kelly traced a finger over the twirly back of one of the chairs in the photo.

"Tell you what—let's talk numbers first." Teddi took the tablet and set it aside. "We'll revisit the chairs. I promise. I have a warehouse where I keep all the larger supplies I've collected over the years, including several different kinds of chairs. We'll come back to them, okay?"

"Fair enough." Kelly gave one nod, then turned to her sister and waved a hand as if conceding the floor to her. "All you."

They were surprisingly good at talking business, she and Leah. It was something she noticed right away. Leah was solid, had a budget that was generous but not ridiculously so, and spoke with a confident certainty. Teddi addressed any cons she saw, concerns they might run into—not many—and finally gave a nod.

"All right," Teddi said, setting the tablet aside and waiting for Kelly to meet her eyes. She was acutely aware that Leah's eyes were also on her, but she addressed the bride-to-be. "I am here to make your wedding planning run smoothly. To take any stress off you that I can. I can make any recommendations you ask for. I can even make calls for you. I have a large variety of vendors I've cultivated relationships with over the years. I know who will be able to fill your requests and who might not. And come the day of your wedding, I will be there running the show so that you don't have to. Bottom line: I am here for you. Never hesitate to call me. No question is stupid. We can work as closely together or as loosely casual as you want. Okay?"

Happiness. Excitement. Relief. Lots of that last one. Teddi was used to the emotions that played out on the face of a bride-to-be when she essentially took much of their worry off their shoulders. All of them ran across Kelly's face before she opened her mouth to speak.

"Closely," she said with a grin that bordered on embarrassed. "I want to work closely because I have no idea what I'm doing."

"Oh, I don't know about that. Your Pinterest board is pretty thorough." Reassurance was another thing brides-to-be often needed, and Teddi had become a pro at offering it. "I'd say you do have an idea what you're doing. And I'm looking forward to helping you put it all together."

"Good. And with my mom's schedule being crazy and unpredictable, Leah's going to be my right hand in all of this." Kelly smiled at her sister, squeezed her hand. "So the three of us will be working together."

There was something in the way Kelly said it, something in the way she looked from Leah to her and back again, something said but not spoken. Kelly was reiterating what she'd said in her text without actually saying it. Fine. Enough. Teddi would say it.

"Listen, I'm a professional." She kept her tone calm, did her best to allow no snark or anger or bitterness to seep in. "The history I have with your sister is just that. History. Do I wish the circumstances were different? Of course." Teddi could feel Leah's eyes on her, wanted desperately and inexplicably to meet them, but forced herself to stay focused on Kelly. She didn't think she could keep a grip on the calm if she looked at Leah. "But the bottom line is that I want you to have the exact wedding you want, to be the happiest bride you can be. I'm sure your sister wants the same thing."

"Absolutely," Leah said, though Teddi still didn't look.

"So we'll put our differences aside and focus on that. Okay?"

"That would be great," Kelly replied. Teddi hadn't realized that Kelly might actually be as worried as her sudden relief seemed to imply, but when her smile grew and her shoulders relaxed, it was clear. "That's all I want. After all, I *am* the bride."

The meeting wrapped up, Teddi sending Kelly home with a

few assignments, things to think about or explore online, and they scheduled to meet again in mid-November. This time, Kelly forewent a handshake and threw her arms around Teddi instead. Not unusual. Brides-to-be often ended up as Teddi's friends, at least for the duration of the planning. But Leah was standing right behind Kelly, so Teddi had nowhere else to look. Leah's tiny smile was hesitant, and she looked away quickly as Kelly let go.

"Ready?" Kelly asked Leah as they donned their jackets. Leah nodded and didn't glance Teddi's way again.

Teddi found that unnervingly disappointing. Karma? For doing the same thing to Leah the whole meeting?

Once the door closed behind them and Teddi stood alone in the middle of the shop, Preston said, "You did great." A slight relief. Teddi heard it and felt it. "I was glad you addressed things head-on."

Teddi inhaled and let it out. "Yeah."

"Don't hate me for saying this, but man, that girl can pull off a pantsuit."

Teddi turned to him, not even trying to hide her admiration. "God, right?"

❖

Were bacon and eggs the ultimate in comfort food?

Leah often wondered that as Lizzie twined around her legs, purring, waiting for a handout. She pushed the down lever on the toaster and thought of other things that might qualify, as she flipped her eggs. Macaroni and cheese. Mashed potatoes…

Her phone interrupted her thoughts. Tilly. Leah answered, hit speaker. "Hey, Stretch."

"You are so original with the nicknames. Because nobody ever calls the tall one *Stretch*."

"Shut up. I'm tired."

"What are you frying? I hear sizzling."

"Eggs."

"Tell me there's bacon."

"There's bacon."

"Is it that turkey crap?"

"It is that turkey crap."

A disappointed groan from Tilly. A laugh from Leah.

"It's late for you to be having dinner," Tilly commented. Nine thirty-seven. She wasn't wrong. "You work late?"

"Yeah, I went back to the office after meeting with Kelly and the wedding planner."

"Oh, fun times. Did she yell at you? Sob uncontrollably? Tell you that you ruined her life? Tell you bad lawyer jokes?"

Leah thought back to the meeting at Hopeless Romantic, how it went smoothly and also made her kind of sad. "It was fine. I mean, she never made eye contact with me, but it was fine."

"Seriously?"

"Yeah, but it's...whatever. Kelly's happy and that's all I care about." Mostly true.

"Why does it sound like you care about more?"

Leah sighed. "I don't know. I mean, this is what happens, right? It's part of the job. The lawyer always gets the blame."

"But it's bugging you this time."

She hated that Tilly knew her so well sometimes.

Leah took her plate and the phone into the living room and sat on the couch in front of the TV, which was already tuned to the Hallmark Channel. "It is. It bothers me that Teddi is holding something professional against me personally, but I don't know why, and that's bothering me even more." This was par for the course of being a lawyer in pretty much any capacity. It was not news. Not to Leah. So why was she edgy about Teddi refusing to even look at her? Why couldn't she just blow it off like she would with any other person?

"I've got an idea. It's kind of out there. Brace yourself, okay?"

"Fine. Braced. Hit me."

"Maybe you and her could, oh, I don't know, talk about it?"

"What? Where do you come up with these weird-ass schemes?"

"I don't know, man. They come to me in dreams."

Leah laughed. Lightening things up was Tilly's specialty.

"I mean, you've gotta work with her on and off for the next, what? Year?"

"Pretty close to that, yeah." Leah poked the yolk of her egg so it ran, then dipped the end of her bacon into it and took a bite, thought about earlier. "She kind of brought it up as we were leaving."

"Yeah? What'd she say?"

"Just that our past history shouldn't affect the current business."

"History? She called it history?" Tilly gave a snort.

"Yeah. I mean, it kind of is."

"You never even met the woman. Your history is a few pieces of paper with your signature on them, Lee. That's it."

Leah blew out a breath. "I know. It's fine. I just want things to be okay for Kelly. If I need to spend the next year's worth of meetings avoiding eye contact, so be it."

"Yeah, I guess." Comfortable silence reigned for a moment before Tilly said, "All right. I'm gonna go watch a movie. What's on your TV? *She Returned to Her Small Clichéd Hometown and Realized Love Had Been Waiting There All Along*?"

"Yes, that's exactly the one. What will you watch? *Idiot Teens Spend the Weekend in a Cabin in the Woods and Are Killed One by One*?"

"You know that's my favorite."

"I do."

They said their good nights. Leah finished her dinner and nibbled on the last slice of bacon. Tried to focus on the movie. Kept having her thoughts interrupted by the gorgeous brunette who wouldn't look at her.

Maybe Teddi hadn't looked at her, but she had certainly looked at Teddi. Even surrounded by the icy exterior she'd crafted, Teddi was still beautiful. She'd had her dark hair pulled back today. Black pants and an emerald green top had given her a sleek, sophisticated air that made her seem almost untouchable. But, God, did Leah want to touch her.

And there it was.

Yeah.

It wasn't like she didn't know, right? It wasn't like this was a surprise to Leah. She found Teddi Baker devastatingly attractive. The pull was nearly magnetic. That was a fact. And nothing would ever come of it. Also a fact.

"Okay, Ms. Bennet," she said to her cat, who'd climbed up onto the back of the couch and lain down directly behind her head, one paw on her shoulder. In love or warning? *I love you so I touch you* or *If you don't share that bacon, I'll open your jugular*? Leah played it safe, held some bacon up for the cat. "I just have to accept this. Yes, she's gorgeous. Yes, she might play on my team. No, it doesn't matter because she hates me now." She turned to look into the enormous green eyes above her. "Right?"

Lizzie chewed, flicked her tail, looked off into the middle distance.

"Right." Leah snuggled into the couch and went back to watching the television. She'd lose herself in the romance on her screen, like she always did, like she always had, and she'd stop thinking about Teddi Baker.

After all, she didn't have to see her again for a couple weeks. That would definitely help her clear her head.

CHAPTER FIVE

Leah whispered the last line of the movie along with Julia Roberts as the end of *Pretty Woman* played out on the big screen. The theme song of the same name started up, and a few people in the theater applauded. Leah smiled. She'd never clap in a movie theater. Ever. But she loved that the film gave somebody enough joy to want to.

She inhaled deeply and let out a very satisfied breath. *Pretty Woman* was a definite favorite. A classic. She waited for another moment before she stood up, gathered her things, and strolled up the aisle, feeling lighthearted.

The Classic Theater was one of her favorite places in town—they knew her by name there. Next door to the theater was the Classic Café. Leah didn't always stop, but they had amazing desserts, and the enticing aroma of freshly brewed coffee tickled her nose, tugged at her as she passed the concessions counter, then the box office. A glance out the front doors told her the November wind had kicked up, ready to bite right through her olive green jacket, which was super cute but not nearly heavy enough to actually keep her warm out there.

Decision made, she turned and allowed her nose to lead her through the large archway that led from the theater into the café so patrons didn't have to go outside at all. The small line wasn't at all a surprise. While the theater rarely drew a huge crowd on Classic Night, they had a steady contingent of loyal patrons, and it seemed like the brisk weather had convinced more than Leah not to go home just yet. She put in her order for an Irish coffee and a slice of cherry chocolate cheesecake, took her receipt, and had turned to scan the space for an open table when her breath caught.

Teddi Baker sat alone at a table for two, large mug near her left hand, phone in her right as she scrolled. Dark hair down. Black sweater that looked thick and soft even from a distance. Leah stood frozen, uncertain. Run? Should she do that? Just bail? A glance at the door, debating. A glance back at Teddi.

Snagged.

Teddi was looking right at her, expression unreadable.

When people said time stood still? Leah never understood it until right then, until she locked eyes with Teddi Baker across the Classic Café and couldn't move. Couldn't look away. Interestingly, Teddi didn't either.

The spell was broken when someone jostled Leah from behind.

"Excuse me," he said, though his tone made his annoyance clear. What he probably wanted to say was *Stop staring, lady, and move it, you're in the way.*

Leah blinked rapidly, glanced around at the occupied tables. The only seats available were single stools at the counter. *Whatever. I can sit there.* But when she tossed one more look Teddi's way, Teddi was making a rolling come-here gesture with her hand. And though part of Leah suddenly thought the stool might be the safer option, her feet started moving as if she had zero control. In four seconds, she was standing at Teddi's table. She noticed that in addition to the sweater, there were light blue jeans and black ankle boots. Yeah, so Teddi Baker rocked casual just as well as she rocked sophisticatedly dressy. Unsurprising.

"Hi." Leah's voice was a croak, so she cleared her throat and tried again. "Hi."

"Hey," Teddi said, then waved to the other chair. "Sit. Doesn't look like you have much choice."

"Thanks." Leah pulled out the chair, sat, and looked around the room. Why, she wasn't sure. Was she going to run to another table if one opened up? *Stop it. Be polite, at least.* She shifted her gaze to Teddi. "Come here often?" she asked. Winced immediately.

Teddi surprised her by barking a laugh. "I guess being in the Classic Café warrants using a classic pickup line."

Leah grimaced. "I didn't mean—"

"Relax, Leah. I'm kidding." Teddi picked up her mug, took a sip.

Kidding. Okay. Unexpected, but okay. Leah would take that. "What are you drinking?"

"It's a London Fog. Earl Grey tea with frothed milk and a little bit of vanilla syrup. It's perfect for this kind of weather." As Teddi glanced over her shoulder out the window, Leah wondered if the waves in her hair were natural.

"Here you go." They were interrupted by a café employee who delivered Leah's Irish coffee and cheesecake. "I brought two forks, just in case," the girl said, then smiled as if she knew something they didn't and left.

Leah raised her eyebrows and held a fork toward Teddi, who hesitated, her uncertainty clear. Leah added a gentle smile. "Help me?"

A visible swallow. A blink. Two. Teddi reached for the fork. "Maybe a bite."

Thrilled. Alarmed. Awkward. All of those things raced through Leah as Teddi slid the fork from her fingers. She inhaled quietly, deeply, slid the plate to the center of the table, then pushed her fork through the end of the cheesecake. "I was serious when I asked if you come here often." She snapped her eyes up. "Not a pickup line."

Teddi followed suit with her fork. "It's not far from my apartment, so yeah. I like it here." She put a bite into her mouth and her eyes closed briefly, a soft hum coming from her throat. Leah stopped chewing, took a moment to watch. "You?" Teddi asked when she opened her eyes again. Those deep, dark eyes of hers.

Leah nodded. "Yeah, I always come if they're showing a romance, especially a classic. Tonight was *Pretty Woman*."

"What's not to love about Julia Roberts, am I right?"

"You are very, very right." Did the mood lighten? Just a smidge? "Plus, they have the best cheesecake in town."

"I agree wholeheartedly with that." Teddi cut another bite of the cheesecake. "Thank you for sharing yours."

"Listen, I do not need to eat this entire piece on my own." She pointed her fork. "I mean, don't think that I can't. 'Cause I totally can." Teddi grinned and Leah felt things lighten again. "I just don't *need* to, see?"

"I do see. I understand completely and am happy to share your burden."

"You are a kind and noble person."

"I'm a giver." She took another bite. "God, this is sinful."

"Right?" A beat went by, two, as Teddi seemed to people watch and Leah had an internal debate. Finally, she made a decision. She slowly forked another bite, her eyes on the cheesecake as she spoke. "You know…" Bite in her mouth. Chewed. Swallowed. "You know I was just doing my job, right?"

Teddi blinked at her. Stared as she ran her tongue over her teeth.

Leah waited, heart pounding. Why was this important? She'd had hundreds of cases by now. Lots of people blamed her for their situations—she was positive of that. Why did it matter to her that Teddi Baker understood?

It was like Teddi rolled that around for a moment, like she'd never thought about it from that angle, even though Leah knew she must have. She was a smart woman.

Finally—*finally*—Teddi exhaled a large breath, almost like it was in defeat. "Yeah. Yeah, I do know that."

One nod. Okay. Leah had actually been braced for an argument, she now realized. Or maybe a snarky retort of some kind. Not complete agreement.

There was a shift. She felt it.

"Okay. Good."

"It was a very bad time for me." Teddi's voice was quiet. Leah almost didn't hear her over the din of café customers. Teddi's face clouded just for a second before she yanked back control. Leah saw it, was learning her. "Yeah. It was a rough time."

"I can imagine. Divorce is hard on everybody. That's been my experience."

"Harder on some than others, though…" Teddi's statement seemed to dangle, as if not a statement at all, but an unfinished thought.

"True." Leah couldn't disagree with that.

"I bet you've seen some meltdowns." Teddi picked up her mug, sipped her tea, her eyes fixed on Leah's over the rim.

Leah nodded. "Yeah, but a lot of my cases don't even make it to court. Often, I never meet the other party." She set down her fork. "I'm done. So full." An attempt at a subject change.

"Like my case."

Leah nodded, picked up her own mug to have something to do with her hands, something to look at.

"Am I making you uncomfortable?" It was a bold question, but the tone had a slight edge of…Was Teddi teasing her? Elbows on the table, mug in both hands, eyes tracking Leah's every tic.

Leah didn't really get nervous. All her time spent in the courtroom in front of judges and clients and galleries, she was used to being front and center, focused on. But somehow, honesty seemed in order here. "Yes." Leah allowed herself a nervous chuckle as she admitted the truth to this woman she barely knew. "A little bit."

"Mm," was all Teddi said to that.

Leah narrowed her eyes just a bit. "Are you playing with me?"

Dark eyes caught hers again, held them. *How does she do that? How does she keep me prisoner with just her eyes?* Leah'd never experienced such intense eye contact as she'd had with Teddi, more than once now.

Teddi set down her mug, broke the spell. "Maybe just a little bit."

The relief that came along with Teddi's gentle smile was big. Bigger than Leah expected, and she wasn't sure she liked this, liked feeling that what Teddi thought of her was important. Leah was strong. She'd had to be. But now, here she sat with this woman who barely knew her, yet her sense of worth and acceptance suddenly seemed tied to Teddi.

That would not do.

Nope.

"Well." Leah smiled, took one last sip from her mug, then set it down. "I'd better head home."

If Teddi was surprised or thought her exit seemed abrupt, she hid it well. In fact, she seemed perfectly happy to continue to sit and enjoy her tea. "Better bundle up. That wind is brutal."

Leah did, buttoned up her jacket, pulled her gloves from the pocket. "Thanks for letting me crash your table."

"My pleasure. Thanks for sharing your cheesecake."

Leah didn't give herself permission to smile, but smile she did. "Anytime." With a quick wave, she made her exit. Had to get out of there, though she wasn't entirely sure why, or what was making her flee. Because that's what she was doing. She was fleeing, absolutely.

Teddi hadn't been kidding about the wind. The November night slapped Leah right in the face when she pushed through the café doors, and she stopped dead. Needed a moment to catch her breath. Then, head down, she walked into the wind toward the parking lot.

What was supposed to be a relaxing evening of a rom-com and some cheesecake had turned into something completely different and unexpected. Leah felt like she'd just stepped off a merry-go-round and was having trouble keeping her balance, walking in a straight line. Or like Teddi had walked by, messed up Leah's hair with both hands, and kept walking. She was out of sorts. Off-balance. She only knew one thing for sure.

Teddi Baker had gotten under her skin.

Chapter Six

It had been a little over a week since the shared cheesecake at the Classic. More than enough time for Teddi to scrub the evening from her mind, to erase the picture of casual, movie-going Leah Scott from her memory banks. No, she much preferred to think of Leah in a suit—not that that was a bad thing—in lawyer mode, destroying the lives of unsuspecting spouses whose exes were trying to take more than what they deserved. It was easier because when she thought of Leah in those terms, in those clothes, she didn't have to deal with the weird feelings and niggling interest that Casual Leah had unearthed in her.

Today was another meeting with the Scott sisters. Kelly had chosen a venue, so they needed to sit down and talk about that, go over some details, make a plan for the next things on Kelly's list.

She heard the door open before she saw it, but when she looked up, it wasn't Kelly Scott or even Leah Scott. It was Harlow.

"Hey," Teddi said, setting aside the notes she'd been working on. "What brings you by?"

Harlow crossed to the counter and slung her messenger bag up onto it. She wore a black wool peacoat with a bright red scarf and a matching red beanie. "I had a shoot down the block, so I thought I'd swing by and say hey, see if you had time to grab coffee."

Teddi pointed a finger at Harlow, moved it up and down in front of her. "This is snazzy. And the way you've got your hat off to the side a bit? The epitome of jaunty."

"Jaunty is exactly what I was going for. What do you say? Coffee?"

"Ugh. I wish I could. I've got the Scotts due in any minute."

"The Scotts?" Harlow's entire face lit up. "As in the sweet bride-to-be and the big sister that nearly sent you into bankruptcy?"

"The very ones, yes."

"In that case…" Harlow unbuttoned her coat.

"What do you think you're doing?" Teddi arched an eyebrow. Knew very well what her friend was doing. Hanging out. She wanted to lay eyes on Leah.

Before she could protest further, the door pushed open, carrying in the chilly air, the smell of impending winter, and Kelly Scott, and Harlow shushed her, then winked.

"Hey, Teddi," Kelly said, her usual smile in place. *I'd want her as my kid's kindergarten teacher.* The thought was random, but true. Kelly Scott exuded gentleness, calm, joy. "It's cold out there," she said as she unwrapped the blue-and-white striped knit scarf from around her neck. Static electricity, ever present in the fall and winter months, lifted some of her blond hair, kept it floating.

"Did you knit that?" Harlow asked, crossing toward Kelly.

"Kelly, this is my good friend and amazing photographer, Harlow McCann." Teddi waved a hand toward the two of them. "Harlow, Kelly Scott. My client."

They shook hands as Kelly nodded. "I did. I'm new to knitting so haven't done much more than scarves, but…" A shrug.

"I love it." Harlow rubbed the end of the scarf between her fingers. Kelly blushed. Teddi shook her head. Putting people at ease was a specialty of her BFF's.

Teddi grabbed her file, set her calls to be forwarded to voice mail, as Preston was at an off-site meeting, and headed toward the table where Kelly was already settling.

"Just so you know, Kelly, Harlow is the photographer I recommend to people who don't have one or don't know where to look. Yes, she's my best friend, but she's also the best wedding photographer in the city. And I would say that even if we hadn't known each other for years." She took a seat and Harlow stayed standing.

"Really? I don't have a photographer yet." Kelly shrugged out of her coat.

"No pressure," Harlow said as she set a card down in front of Kelly. "My website has a ton of weddings I've shot. Take a look."

"I'll do that." Kelly was tucking the card into her purse when the door opened. "Look at you, practically on time," she said with a grin.

Teddi looked up as Leah seemed to literally breeze in, as if the outdoors had blown her through the door and into the shop. While she was happy to see the sight of straight-from-work Leah, Destroyer of Businesses, today in a navy blue skirt and blazer with a silver and white pinstriped blouse underneath, Teddi still found herself missing the Casual Leah from last week at the café. Skinny jeans with holes in the knees and a long cream-colored sweater. Brown leather boots. Blond hair in a messy ponytail...

"Maybe I'm turning over a new leaf." Leah's voice yanked Teddi back to the moment.

"Good luck with that," Kelly said, a note of gentle ribbing in her tone.

"Hey, have a little faith." Leah slid off her coat and draped it over the chair, then met Teddi's gaze. "Hey, you." Softly. Not quite intimately, but it wouldn't take much for Teddi to get to that.

"Hi yourself." Teddi cleared her throat. Harlow was giving her a look—she could feel it.

"What'd I miss?" Leah asked as she sat.

"You missed meeting Harlow," Kelly said and introduced them. "She's a photographer, and I'm going to check out her website tonight."

"Cool." Leah shook hands with Harlow as Teddi took a seat.

"I'll let you guys talk shop," Harlow said, then pointed at Teddi. "I'll call you later."

Teddi knew what they'd be talking about, and it made her grin. "You know how to find me." The door closed and Harlow was gone.

"I like her," Kelly said.

"Most people do. She's amazing," Teddi agreed.

"She's Teddi's best friend," Kelly informed Leah.

"Oh, I see." Leah nodded.

"Can I get you girls anything? Coffee? Tea?"

"Cheesecake?" Leah said, then winked at Teddi, who blushed, she was sure of it.

"What does that mean?" Kelly asked, looking from one of them to the other, like the kid who'd been left out. Teddi felt bad and filled her in.

"Your sister and I ran into each other last week at a café."

"There was no place to sit, so Teddi shared her table with me."

"And Leah graciously shared her cheesecake."

"Were you at The Classic?" Kelly asked, then turned to Leah. "What did you see this time?"

"*Pretty Woman*," Leah said.

"Aww, I love that one." Then she quoted a line from it, her hazel eyes bright. Leah quoted the next line. *They do this a lot.* It was a realization that had Teddi feeling warm inside. Cozy. Turning to Teddi, she asked, "Did you see it, too?"

"Oh no. I was just in the café."

"You'll probably see her again if you go. She practically lives at that theater." Not teasing at all. Kind. Tender, as if this was a part of Leah's personality that Kelly loved. Maybe it was.

"Only when they're showing a rom-com," Leah corrected.

Kelly leaned over the table toward Teddi and said, lowering her voice, "She's a little bit addicted. She'll watch nothing but the Hallmark Channel until after Christmas."

"Really?" This was news. Leah liked rom-coms.

"She's got the Hallmark Christmas movie schedule on her fridge," Kelly said, then bumped Leah with a shoulder. Being playful.

"Stop," Leah said, but she was smiling. "We're not here to discuss my television habits."

For the next hour, they discussed wedding details. Luckily, Teddi had been wedding planning long enough that she could listen to her client and think about other things at the same time. And right then, she was thinking about the dichotomy that was Leah Scott.

What kind of a divorce attorney watched silly, cheesy rom-coms? How did that make any sense? Leah had to have seen what happened to love, how destructive it was, how it could break somebody, shatter them like glass, leave them flattened, hollowed out, hopeless. How could she come home from seeing that all day long and then shift gears to happy, joyful, romantic?

Teddi liked things to make sense. Leah Scott? Didn't. She made zero sense. From the divorce lawyer who watched romances to Teddi wanting to hate her but also finding her physically magnetic, it was all wrong. It didn't fit.

"Teddi?" Leah's voice. Concerned. "You okay?"

Several blinks and Teddi pulled herself back. "Yes. Sorry. Yes, I'm fine. Good."

Leah's green eyes fixed on her. Intense, a little worried. "You're sure?"

A nod. A smile. "Yes. I'm good."

They finished up. Leah's eyes were on her. She could feel it. Didn't mind it. *What is happening?*

Being simultaneously relieved to say good-bye to the Scott sisters and also sad to watch Leah walk out the door was beyond confusing. She tried to shake it away as Preston came in.

"I'm back. Miss me?"

"Desperately," she said, grateful to have somebody else take her focus.

"I figured." He went behind the counter, shed his coat, opened his bag. "My meetings went well. I think we can add these two caterers to our list."

Something practical. Something businessy. Thank God. That's what she needed. She'd been standing next to the table but sat back down.

"Show me."

❖

"Do you have time to grab a drink?" Kelly asked once they were on the sidewalk in front of Hopeless Romantic. "Or do you have to go back to work?"

Kelly had that look. Leah was familiar with it. Soft eyes, somewhat hesitant smile. It wasn't begging or pleading. It wasn't to guilt her. It was genuine. Hopeful. It said that Kelly really wanted to spend time with her, but she'd completely understand if Leah had to bow out to work. And also, that she expected the latter.

Disappointing Kelly was not something Leah enjoyed doing, though she did it more than she cared to admit. For that reason, she smiled and nodded. "As a matter of fact, I do have time."

A Christmas tree. An airport runway at night. The way Kelly's face lit up was total joy, and Leah loved it.

"Great. There's a cute little wine bar around the corner toward the lake. How about there?"

"Perfect."

They hopped in their respective cars and within ten minutes were seated at a cozy table for two in an adorable little place called Vineyard.

"Hi, ladies." The waitress was blond and smiled warmly as she set two glasses of water on the table, then handed them wine lists. "My name is Lindsay. Don't hesitate to ask any questions you might have." She gave them some time as she left to take care of a group of three women that had just walked in.

A few minutes later, they had wine—Malbec for Leah and a Riesling for Kelly. "So," Kelly said, sipped her wine, looked at her sister, "do you plan on bedding my wedding planner?"

Leah spluttered on the wine in her mouth. Dabbing her face with a napkin, she asked, "What?"

"You heard me."

Leah stared. Slight concern. A lot of amusement. She saw both on Kelly's face. Leah scoffed, did her best to sound like that was a ridiculous notion, but not to overplay it. There was a balance here. It had to be perfect. "Of course not."

"I mean, you *did* share your cheesecake with her. That's big. You don't even share your cheesecake with me."

"That's because I don't really like you." Leah went with a joke. Tried to steer her away. Didn't work.

"But you like *her*…" Kelly sipped, let the sentence dangle.

"Kelly. I represented her ex. Remember?"

"Yes, but she let you sit at her table, and she ate your cheesecake, and she knew then that you repped her ex."

It was a valid point. Leah could admit that. She took a sip of her wine and scanned the wine bar, not really focusing on anything. "It's not something I'd apologize for, though. You know?"

"Who says you'd have to?" Elbows on the table, Kelly leaned in. "Look, you have a job, a calling that came from your childhood. I get that. You get that. And you know what? I think she'd get that if you wanted her to."

"Who says I want her to?" A little snarkier than intended. Why was she so defensive all of a sudden?

"I'm just saying." Kelly usually knew when to back off, but she pressed a little more first. "It's been a while since you dated, and that first time we met with Teddi? Before the whole divorce attorney thing came up? She was into you. I could see it. And you were into her, too. That's all. I'm shutting up now."

Leah snorted to demonstrate how much she believed that last statement. A half shrug, a sip of wine. "What can I bring to Thanksgiving? Have you decided yet?"

Kelly made a tiny groaning sound. "No, I'm still menu planning. And I'm so nervous."

Subject successfully changed. Satisfaction hidden behind the rim of her wineglass, she said for what was probably the twelfth time, "You have nothing to be nervous about." Kelly and Dylan had been living together for over a year, much to the dismay of Dylan's parents. This year, they were having Thanksgiving at their place with both Dylan's parents and Kelly's mother as guests, along with Leah.

"It's the first time Mom will meet Dylan's parents. What if she hates them? What if they hate her?" Kelly's eyes were wide. It was real, her worry.

"Nobody's going to hate anybody." Realistically, Leah couldn't be sure of that. Dylan's parents, from what she'd heard, were ultra-religious. That was totally fine with Leah, except Kelly said they could also be judgmental. They frowned upon divorce. And other things. "All that matters is that you and Dylan are happy. That's all any parent wants for their child. It's all any big sister wants for her little sister."

"They'll probably hate you." Kelly winked when she said it, but it was likely reality.

Leah shrugged. "It's whatever. I'm going to be there for *you*, not them."

"Imagine if you brought a date." Kelly's eyes were bright with mischief.

"And you introduced me as your gay sister and her gay date?"

"Yes. Exactly. I wonder if their heads would explode. Seriously, what decade is this again?"

Leah lifted her glass and touched it to Kelly's. "I will come stag. No worries." And then a weird image materialized in her brain, like a ghost appearing out of the fog: Teddi sitting by her side at Thanksgiving, the two of them grinning at each other over inside jokes that only they got, Leah touching Teddi's knee under the table…

Oh my God, stop. Just stop.

Why was this happening? Why couldn't she get Teddi out of her head? She really needed to.

Didn't she?

❖

Teddi adored her little townhome.

No, it wasn't the kind of place she'd pictured herself inhabiting a few years ago. She remembered spending Sundays with Julia early in their relationship, looking at houses along the canal, fantasizing about how they'd be able to afford one of those someday. And those fantasies had come closer and closer to reality as time went on and Hopeless Romantic became successful. It was interesting, though, how her happiness with Julia—or, more accurately, Julia's happiness with her—was inversely proportional to the success of Teddi's business. The more successful she became, the more distant she'd felt from her wife.

When everything fell apart for Teddi, she wasn't sure what she was going to do. Julia wanted to keep their house, and honestly, Teddi was fine with that. She didn't think she could bear to live there after everything that had happened. But where would she live? What could she afford after Julia took half of everything she had?

Luckily, Harlow's brother Eddie was a Realtor, and he decided to make it his mission to find his little sister's best friend an amazing little place, and he had come through with flying colors.

Her place wasn't big, but it had tons of charm and was close enough to Hopeless Romantic that she could walk to work. She'd taken her time choosing colors, painting, going to estate sales to find furniture to add to the new stuff she'd purchased and the few items she'd taken with her when she moved out. It had taken some getting used to, coming home to a place that nobody else lived in. She and Julia had moved in together within their first six months as a couple, so ending her workday and walking into an empty house had clobbered her for the first few months. But gradually, so very gradually, she began to settle in. To start to embrace that the townhouse was hers. That everything in it was hers. After having so much taken from her, possessiveness had made a place in her brain. But now, after so much time, she'd begun to love her home.

The galley style kitchen was roomier than most. It still needed some updating, and Teddi planned to replace the counters after the holidays, but it was more than functional. She dropped her bag, shed her coat and gloves, took her boots off, and headed straight for it, specifically for the small table in a corner that she referred to as the bar. Various bottles of liquor, a martini shaker, and a corkscrew were enough to qualify it as such, as far as she was concerned. Anyway, who cared? She just wanted a Manhattan.

Who'd have thunk a person could find solace in mixology? It had started as a passing interest a few years ago, but Teddi found she liked the precision, the methodology, the little bit of chemistry. It relaxed her, helped her clear her mind.

And did her mind ever need clearing.

Rye whiskey went into a mixing glass. She added vermouth, then opened the small bottle of bitters and gave that a shake. She'd made enough Manhattans to know she liked slightly more than a dash. Added ice. Stirred—not shaken—and strained into a rocks glass, garnished with a cherry, the golden red color the thing she liked most about it.

In the living room, she flopped onto her gray microfiber couch—not a material she'd get next time, but the one she'd been able to afford when she'd moved—and sipped, absently wondering what she wanted for dinner. Her phone saved her from that dilemma, and she glanced at the screen.

Harlow. Right on time.

"What do you want?" Her standard line when answering a call from her best friend.

"Your undying love and devotion." Harlow's standard reply.

"Done."

"What's tonight's cocktail? Old-fashioned? Martini?"

"Manhattan."

"Oh..." Harlow drew out the word. "Yum."

"It's not bad, if I do say so." Teddi admired this quality of Harlow's. She never went directly to the subject of the call. She made small talk first. *How was your day? Nice weather we're having. What are you drinking?* All before *Let's talk about the hottie that is your client's sister.*

"How'd things go with your meeting?"

"Which one? I had four today." Teddi loved to play hard to get with Harlow.

"Stop it. You know which one."

"I assume, because you're a nosy gossip, that you're referring to the meeting with Kelly Scott."

"And her hot sister, yes."

Teddi mentally gave herself a point for calling that. "It was fine."

A scoff. "Fine? No. The meeting was not fine. You know what was fine? The sister. The sister was *fine*." She made the word sound almost dirty.

Harlow wasn't wrong. That was the thing. "She is."

"Oh, so you're not blind. Good. I'm relieved." Teddi could hear Harlow's TV in the background. "What is *The Little Mermaid*?" she shouted.

Jeopardy. "Are you winning?"

"I'm kicking these contestants' collective ass, so yes." Without missing a beat, Harlow went right back to the original topic and said, "When will you ask her out?"

"Ask who out?"

"Oh my God, do you do this on purpose? Do you play dense just to drive me insane? Is that your grand plan?"

"Maybe." Teddi grinned and took a sip of her Manhattan. "I'm not going to ask her out."

"Why not? She's hot. She seems intelligent. She's into you."

A snort from Teddi this time. "She is not into me."

"Please. You should have seen things from my seat. Trust me. She's into you."

"Don't you think our history makes a pretty good obstacle?" She was admitting that she'd thought about it, thought about a date with Leah, what it would be like, where they'd go, what they'd talk about.

"Honey, obstacles are made to be conquered."

"I lost so much because of her." Voice soft. Emotions close to the surface.

"No." Harlow was suddenly gentle. "That had nothing to do with her and everything to do with Julia. You've got to shift your way of thinking around that, you know?"

Teddi gave her head a shake. "I don't have to have this one. There are lots of other fish in the sea."

"Yeah? When's the last time you went fishing?" A little firmer this time. "Because—and feel free to correct me here—as far as I know, you haven't been on a date since your divorce was final."

God, was that true? Teddi blinked.

"What's it been? Two years now? Two and a half?" Harlow asked.

Teddi hated to admit that Harlow was right, but she was. She'd tried to do some online dating not long after she moved out of the house, but that was more about being rebellious than trying to find somebody to click with. Once the divorce had been finalized and those papers arrived in the mail, Teddi found she had exactly zero desire to be with anybody. Maybe ever.

"Yeah. Around that."

Harlow let a beat pass and Teddi could almost picture her reining herself in, telling herself to ease up. Harlow had the habit of going at something she was adamant about at full speed, and sometimes, that could shut down the person she was talking to. "You deserve to be happy, Teddi."

"I was."

"You deserve to be happy again."

Do I? It was a thought that ran through Teddi's head regularly. Loudly. With heavy footsteps. She'd had a marriage, something she'd thought was solid. But she'd taken it for granted somehow. Did she really deserve a shot at a second relationship?

What if she ruined that one, too?

CHAPTER SEVEN

It was the Monday before Thanksgiving and Teddi needed a break. She and Preston had worked their asses off on Saturday on a wedding that had been one of the most difficult plannings she'd ever done. A bride who couldn't make up her mind. A mother-of-the-bride who thought she knew everything and that Teddi knew nothing. Twin sisters who had made final calls on more things than they'd had a right to. A groom who'd barely participated in one second of the planning. Not atypical, but not super common, thank God. Teddi and Preston had made sure their cleanup crew had things under control and then headed for the nearest bar.

Forty-eight hours later, and she still felt some residual stress. The shop had been busy—brides-to-be with upcoming holiday weddings were starting to panic. Teddi's day had been a long one, spent mostly on getting everybody to just breathe. A glance at her watch told her it was nearly seven.

Downtime. She needed it.

At her desk in her office, scrolling through Instagram, she saw an ad for the Classic Theater and Café. A chocolate raspberry torte special. A classic film. Teddi stared at it for a long while.

❖

Maybe I'm too early.

Teddi didn't stop to think about what she was doing. How ridiculous it might be. The Classic Theater was showing *You've Got Mail*. A classic romance. Right up Leah's alley, or so Teddi figured. If she stopped to think about how she was now going into the restroom to kill a little time before grabbing popcorn and a seat, knowing that Leah tended to be late and hoping that maybe she'd come in during that time, she'd have to admit to herself that Harlow was right. That she was, maybe—just maybe—into Leah Scott. For some reason, it seemed like something that was too big for her to swallow right now. Also, she hated when Harlow was right.

So she ignored it. And went into the ladies' room instead.

When she came out, she couldn't decide if the Universe was rewarding her or toying with her because there at the concessions counter, bag of popcorn in hand, was Leah. Casual Leah. No business suit. Just jeans and cute brown boots and one of those puffy down jackets, this one purple with a hood. Leah turned and surprise registered on her face when she saw Teddi. Then a smile.

"Hey," Leah said, her voice like warm honey. "What are you doing here?" Those green eyes were soft, and—dared Teddi think it?—happy. To see her? Maybe.

"Same thing you are, I assume," Teddi replied, hoping her response was playful rather than condescending. "To see a movie."

Leah made a show of looking around behind Teddi. "Are you by yourself?"

With a nod, Teddi told her, "Just about to grab some popcorn."

"Do you"—Leah shifted her weight, one foot, the other, back—"want to sit together? Totally okay if you don't." The last line was added in a rush after the first.

"Sure." Teddi ordered her popcorn. *Play it cool. Play it cool...*

They chose seats in the center, about two-thirds of the way to the front. It was a little closer than Teddi preferred, but she followed Leah anyway. This was kind of Leah's show, after all. This was something she did regularly and Teddi was more or less crashing it, so she didn't want to lay out demands about where to sit. They were exactly on time—as soon as their butts hit their chairs, the lights dimmed and the previews began.

❖

God, she smells good.

It was a thought about Teddi that Leah couldn't get out of her head. It was good thing she'd seen the movie twenty times. Otherwise, she might've missed important tidbits while she was busy trying not to be obvious about how deeply she was inhaling, taking in the vanilla and citrus, holding it, trying to identify it. Lime?

How weird was it to run into Teddi in the lobby? What were the chances? She tried to remember if Teddi had said she'd visited the Classic often during their last accidental meeting here. Leah had been surprised to see her. Very pleasantly surprised. Very, very pleasantly surprised. Teddi wore jeans and a marled beige sweater, the hem hanging past her hips and the sleeves surpassing her palms. Her ivory jacket had been unzipped, her dark hair loose. Leah'd wanted to bury her nose in it.

She'd have to settle for quietly inhaling Teddi's perfume instead.

Watching a movie with somebody new was always a dicey affair for Leah. If she was in her living room, that was one thing. Conversation—if kept to a minimum—was fine. But not in a theater. A vow to never sit next to JoJo at a movie ever again had been spoken more than ten years ago. JoJo had the attention span of a housefly, so she continually asked questions and kept a running commentary throughout the film. It was only Tilly's presence that day that had kept Leah from killing her. Teddi, however, turned out to be the perfect movie-watching companion. She didn't talk. She laughed in all the right places. She ate her popcorn quietly, didn't sound like a toddler crunching away, like the guy two rows behind them did. And when they came to the scene where Meg Ryan was leaving her bookstore for the last time and saw a vision of her late mother twirling around with her childhood self, Leah caught the shimmer of tears rolling down Teddi's cheek.

Sitting on her hands helped keep Leah from reaching over to wipe them away.

Was it weird that, even though they weren't touching and weren't on any sort of official date, Leah didn't want the movie to end?

Yeah. Definitely weird. Stop that.

Credits rolled, lights went up, and they were back to reality.

"Have you seen it before? I didn't even ask." Leah waited in the aisle for Teddi to exit their row.

"I have, but it was years ago. You?"

"Oh, only a few times." They strolled up toward the doors to the hallway. "Maybe thirty or forty."

Teddi's laugh burst out of her as if launched by a cannon. "Wow, only that many?"

"What can I say? Hopeless romantic, right here." Leah raised her hand, wiggled her fingers. "Hey, do you want to grab a coffee? Dessert?"

"I believe there's a chocolate raspberry torte with my name on it."

"Then I think we should find it."

"Lead the way."

The movie hadn't had more than fifteen or twenty viewers, it being a Monday and the week of Thanksgiving, but the café bustled a bit more. They placed their orders, found a table, and got comfortable.

Leah put her elbows on the table, clasped her hands, and held them near her cheek. "So, you haven't seen the movie in years. What did you think?"

Teddi pursed her lips, gave a nod. "I liked it."

"I'm sensing a *but*."

"Well…" She stopped as the waiter appeared with their desserts, Leah's coffee, and her tea. A few moments for them to doctor their drinks and take bites of their tortes, and they were making twin humming noises of utter delight.

"Okay, so go on," Leah prompted, taking a second bite.

"I take issue with the fact that Tom shut down Meg's business. Her livelihood, yes, but more importantly, something she'd put her heart and soul into."

"But that wasn't personal—it was business. He says so right in the script."

"Yeah, but it was absolutely personal to *her*. I have trouble with her not holding it against him, you know?"

Step carefully here. This wasn't a new viewpoint. Lots of people felt the same way about the film. But for Teddi, it *was*, well, personal. Very. And Leah knew it. "I get that. I do. But he was…" She wasn't sure the words that came next were ones she should say.

"Just doing his job?" Teddi said them for her.

Leah nodded. Braced. Sipped. Waited.

It felt like an hour went by as Teddi gazed off into the café, seemingly people watching. Finally, she let out a heavy breath. "Yeah. He was. I know." She took one more bite of her torte, then set her fork down, clearly done.

The mood had shifted. It was slight, subtle, but it had definitely shifted. A wall had gone up between them—no, that wasn't right. Wall was too strong a word. More like a curtain, a sheer one, something that veiled Teddi a bit from Leah's view. She sighed inwardly, bummed out that Teddi had withdrawn. They talked about a few more very surface things, but that was it, and Leah was more disappointed than she cared to admit.

On the sidewalk, they said their good-byes and walked in opposite directions toward their cars, Leah's mind a whirlwind of thoughts, predictions, wonders.

Reality: She'd enjoyed herself. Right up until Teddi had shut down on her, she'd had a better time than she'd had in months. It hadn't been a date, of course, but it had almost felt like one, which was strange to admit. Not a date. Maybe that was the reason her brain was on overdrive? Because it had felt like a date, but wasn't? And the other very big question: Why was Teddi even there? She didn't seem to be that big a fan of rom-coms. She'd already seen the film and didn't really like it. So why go? Was she bored and wanted to get out of her house? Or was she hoping to see somebody there...

Really? Think that highly of yourself, do you?

Leah shook away the thoughts as she drove. If tonight had proven anything, it was that the history she shared with Teddi was an obstacle that was likely never going to be hurdled.

"That's a damn shame," she said in the quiet of her car.

She meant it.

Chapter Eight

Leah sat in her car and blew out a breath. She could do this. She would do this. It was Thanksgiving. A holiday. She could grit her teeth and make it through a dinner that included Dylan's parents and not get into anything with them.

Dylan's parents made her decidedly uncomfortable. There was no way around it. They were nice enough, but they always seemed to hold that slight, not-so-subtle air of judgment. It hung around them like a mist. In their eyes, Kelly had been a terrible influence on Dylan. They didn't go to church (that was Dylan's choice; Kelly had nothing to do with it). They'd been "living in sin" for the past two years in Kelly's house. They weren't getting married in a church or by a priest. Kelly's parents were divorced and her sister was gay. So many strikes!

She didn't like the way they talked to Kelly. The way they looked at her, kind of sideways, like they were always judging what she was doing. Because they were. But Kelly had begged her more than once not to start anything. She'd made her swear it, told her she could take it. And much as Leah always wanted to stand up for her little sister—hell, that was her job—the silent, constant plea in Kelly's eyes always made her hold her tongue, swallow her anger, and keep her mouth shut.

The number of cars in the driveway—and the hands on her watch—told her she was the last one to arrive, as usual, and she took a breath and made her way inside.

"I'm so sorry," she said when she met Kelly's eyes and shed her long black coat. It was a line Kelly had probably heard from her sister thousands of times over the years. "Happy Thanksgiving, everybody. Oh my God, Kel, it smells *amazing* in here."

"You remember my perpetually late sister, Leah," Kelly said to Dylan's parents as Leah kissed the top of her head, then kissed Dylan's cheek and wrapped her mother in a hug from behind.

"Of course." Mrs. Maguire gave a tight smile.

"It's nice to see you again." Leah nodded to Dylan's parents. "How are you?"

"Can't complain," Mr. Maguire said, his voice so deep you could feel it in the pit of your stomach. "And you?"

"Ready for a glass of wine, that's how I am." Leah smiled at him. "Busy day working at home trying to get some stuff done." She held up the bottle she'd brought. "Mom?"

"I could use a refill," her mother said. "There's a bottle already opened in the kitchen."

Leah almost laughed out loud at the unspoken message that passed between her and her mother. The one that said *keep 'em coming.* "Me, too, please." She held out her glass.

Thanksgiving dinner went surprisingly well. Aside from requesting that they all say grace, which nobody had a problem with and Leah actually liked the idea of, they'd managed to avoid both politics and religion as topics of conversation. There had been little, if any, wariness around the table and Leah could see Kelly finally relax the smallest bit. She knew that, for her little sister, it was one thing to deal with the parent of one of her students who had drastically different views than her. She'd face them a few times and then they'd move on to the next of their child's teachers. But her future in-laws? People she hoped to be tied to for the rest of her life? People who'd be an enormous part of her children's lives? Yeah, that was a lot harder. So when a gathering that included them stayed tension free, Leah knew Kelly's gratitude was huge.

Today was not going to be one of those days, though.

"So, Leah, you're a lawyer, am I remembering that correctly?" Mr. Maguire forked a bite of pumpkin pie into his mouth.

"I am." Leah took a sip of her wine. *And here we go.*

"Real estate? Contract? Patent?"

"Divorce."

"Really?" Mrs. Maguire said, her perfectly tweezed brows flying up into her hairline.

"She's very good." Her mother reached over and squeezed Leah's forearm. "She's been at it for a while and has a stellar reputation." She looked across the table at the Maguires as if daring them to say more, and Leah loved her for that.

"I'm sure she is," Mrs. Maguire said. "But divorce? Doesn't it get to you after a while? All those sad and angry people willing to call it quits on their marriage rather than do the hard work?"

Leah's lips pressed together in a tight lineline, and when she glanced at her sister, Kelly pleaded with her eyes. Leah got the message.

"Actually, a lot of the folks I deal with are in agreement that they shouldn't be together, and the majority of them *have* done the hard work. It just wasn't meant to be. They are very often happier to have things done and over with." She held up a finger. "Not always, but often." She didn't look at their mother then, but Kelly bet she wanted to. "The end of a marriage isn't something I celebrate, if that's what you think. My job is to be as fair as I can in getting my client what he or she deserves from the dissolution."

The Maguires blinked. Mr. Maguire nodded slightly. Mrs. Maguire reached for her own wine.

"Seen any good movies lately, Leah?" Dylan's question may have seemed to come out of nowhere, but the wave of relief was palpable. Crisis averted.

"I saw *You've Got Mail* at the Classic a few days ago."

"Oh, we adore that theater," Mrs. Maguire gushed. "We go at least once or twice a month. And that cute little café attached? Those desserts are decadent."

"A good friend of mine is the pastry chef there," her mother said.

"Oh, Mrs. Antonio?" Kelly asked and Leah remembered the small woman who always brought homemade cookies on visits when she and Kelly were small.

Their mother nodded, then turned to Leah. "She said she saw you there. She was too busy to say hello but said you were there with some gorgeous brunette. Her words, not mine."

Kelly's eyebrows flew upward and Leah could feel her waiting for eye contact. Which Leah worked very hard to avoid. Their mother looked from Leah (concentrating very hard on her pie) to Kelly, then arched an eyebrow.

Leah picked up her wine glass and sipped, grimacing behind the rim. Oh, they'd be revisiting this…

❖

The Maguires were gone, thank God. It was amusing that Leah could see both Kelly and Dylan visibly relax once the door closed behind Dylan's parents. They were nice enough people, if you could set aside their obvious superiority complex, but they were a lot.

Dishwasher loaded and running. Dining room table cleaned, centerpiece back in its place. A plate of cookies that nobody wanted but still nibbled from on the coffee table in the living room. Refilled wineglasses.

Leah flopped onto an overstuffed chair as if she was boneless, a rag doll with no ability to stand. "I am so full. That was fantastic, Kelly."

"Mom did the hard stuff."

"I did not. I supervised." Her mother was in the upholstered rocker in the corner, one leg tucked underneath her, the other pushing it gently from the floor. She winked at Kelly, across the room on the couch, cuddled into Dylan.

"So, who's the *gorgeous brunette*?" Dylan made air quotes.

Kelly turned to him, "I love you so much right now."

"Wow, how long have you guys been waiting to interrogate me on that?" Leah asked.

"Since I mentioned it and you turned the color of a tomato and stopped talking." Her mom grinned at her.

"I have a sneaking suspicion I know who she is," Kelly said.

"You do?" her mom asked, sitting up a little straighter. "Are you going to tell me?"

"No, she's not," Leah said firmly.

"Of course she is," Kelly said, waving a dismissive hand at her sister. "It's my wedding planner."

"What?" Both her mother and Dylan said it together, and it would've been comical if Leah wasn't mortified.

"I know, right?" It was Kelly's turn to sit up as she explained the situation to her fiancé and mother while Leah sat there helplessly. All she could do was watch. And turn red. "They hit it off immediately. Our first meeting? I was barely there. My hair could've been on fire and neither of them would've noticed."

"Please." Leah gave the best sarcastic snort she could manage. "That's such an exaggeration."

"It's not, though. Your chemistry is off the charts."

"And you're dating her now?" her mom asked, sipping her wine.

"Oh, wait." Kelly's glee was so obvious. It was like they were kids again, Kelly with something to tattle about. Leah shook her head, wishing she could dive into her wineglass and swim away. "Teddi— that's my wedding planner—finally realized why Leah's name seemed familiar…" She let the sentence hang, presumably to see if her family could catch up on their own.

"No," Dylan said, just before her mom said the same thing.

"Yup. She represented Teddi's ex in their divorce."

"Wow." Her mother shook her head. "What are the chances?"

"Right? So then things got a little cool." Kelly glanced across at Leah and gave her a smile, one that said she was sort of sorry for sharing the story, but not really.

Little sisters, man. Leah sat quietly.

"But they were out together on Monday night, right?" Her mom looked from Leah to Kelly and back. "Isn't that what you said?"

Kelly looked toward Leah. "It is what I said. Is that who you were with, Leah? Was I right?"

What was she going to do, lie about it? With a sigh of resignation, she said, "Yes, I was with her on Monday. But"—she cut off the chuckles and knowing murmurs—"it wasn't a date. We didn't go together. We both happened to be there, so we sat together in the theater."

"And then went to the café together," her mom added. As a reminder, apparently.

"Yes." Leah's glass was empty, and she desperately wanted it to be full, but she stayed seated.

"And?" Her mom was way too invested in this already.

"And nothing. There's a history there that's like a spot that won't come out. You know?"

"You like her, though?" her mother asked. It was the first time it had been posed to her by somebody else, and while part of Leah wanted to stop, to really think about it, she didn't allow herself to.

"It doesn't matter, Mom. Are you listening? I represented her ex in her divorce. And while I won't discuss the details of the case, I can tell you that she ended up pretty unhappy with the way things went, and she blames me just as much as her ex." With a pointed look at her mother, she added, "You know how that is."

Leah watched as the proverbial wind left her mother's sails and she sat back in her chair again. "Yeah, I do." Kelly seemed to deflate a bit as well, and while Leah wasn't necessarily happy about them losing their glee, she was glad to put the subject to rest. Because the truth of the matter was, though she hated to admit it, she was just as disappointed as her family. She'd had Teddi on her mind since the café, even though it hadn't ended well. She could still see that faraway look that had floated across Teddi's face and settled behind her dark eyes. It had stayed with her for four days now.

The family moved on to other topics, gently letting Leah off the hook for now. Wasn't it interesting, though, how the phrase *for now* had popped into her head? Because she had zero doubt it was the case. Something deep inside her, in her head, maybe even in her heart, told her that was the case. That there would be more. She wasn't sure how or why, only that she was certain in general of one very specific thing: She wasn't done with Teddi Baker yet. Not by a long shot.

CHAPTER NINE

Christmas weddings were gorgeous.

There was no doubt about it in Teddi's mind. Combining the beauty of wedding gowns and bridesmaids' dresses and red flowers with standard, sparkling Christmas decorations like garland and tinsel and tiny white lights made for a stunning backdrop to any wedding. It was true. That being said, trying to plan a wedding around the biggest holiday of the year could be brutal.

Teddi had managed several, so it wasn't anything new to her, but it was extra strenuous. *I have my own holiday stuff to do, people!* ran through her head on a loop whenever she ended up with a bridezilla—a label she was not fond of, but one that often seemed alarmingly appropriate—who was losing her mind about tiny little details of her wedding. There was never any way to convince a bride-to-be that something she found super important—like whether the chairs at dinner had four slats or five or if her tablecloths were white or ivory—was something nobody else was really going to notice or remember. Teddi's job required a ton of nodding and smiling and conceding. But she was also a pro at *suggesting* something strongly enough to make it seem like it was the bride's idea all along. Those were her small victories.

It was December. She had the Sarto-Jennings wedding this weekend and the Carter-Bacon wedding the next. The week after that led into Christmas, and thank God she'd have a tiny bit of time to celebrate the holiday with her family and friends this year—last year, she'd had a New Year's Eve wedding to run. She was definitely ready for some downtime.

Meeting with Kelly Scott was on today's agenda, and Teddi tried not to dwell on that. More accurately, she tried not to dwell on whether or not Leah would be coming with her. She had for each past meeting, so there was no reason to expect otherwise, and she hoped it wouldn't be awkward, given the way their time at the café had gone a couple weeks ago.

Thank God for the ringing of her phone. Thank God her job was a fast-paced one. It kept her from slipping down into the dark recesses of her mind. Places she shouldn't go—no, places she *wouldn't allow* herself to go.

The day went by in a flash of phone calls and timelines and reassuring texts, as it always did when there was a wedding the coming weekend. While Teddi was on the phone with a caterer, Preston pushed his way through the door, also on his phone. The two of them were having nearly identical conversations. She could pick up from his side he was dealing with a florist and having an issue even as she dealt with a menu discrepancy.

Ten minutes later, they were both free of their calls. Preston slid out of his coat, looking ridiculously put together in his dark pants, red oxford, and Christmas tie with snowmen on it. His dark hair was freshly cut and styled, and he looked like a model, like he'd walked into Hopeless Romantic directly from an issue of *GQ*.

"Why can't they just listen to us when we suggest a vendor?" he asked as he popped a K-cup into the coffeemaker.

"That's the age-old wedding planning question, my friend."

"I hate Gerberman Flowers. Hate them. They're the worst."

"Should we Nope List them?" Teddi always did her best to remain open-minded and do what her client wanted, deal with whatever vendors he or she preferred, even if Teddi did not prefer them. It was rare that she openly steered a client away from a vendor. But over the years, that had become necessary with a few companies here and there, and she and Preston had come up with their Nope List. Vendors they would outright tell their client they refused to work with. And why.

"Yes. Please. In red Sharpie."

"Ouch."

Preston plopped himself into a chair next to Teddi behind the counter. "I hate being talked down to like I have no idea what I'm doing. No, I don't know everything, but don't be condescending. Don't assume I know nothing."

"Understood completely." She called up Gerberman on her computer and added them to the list. "There. They are officially noped."

"We ready for Saturday?" Preston sipped his coffee and they sat side by side, staring forward like mannequins. They desperately needed a break.

"We are." Teddi gave one nod. "I contacted every vendor again today, clarified the details, you're heading to the venue later, and I've sent about seventy-three hand-holding texts to the bride-to-be. So far."

"Ah, yes. The usual pre-wedding panic."

They both grinned. Hard-pressed to admit it in that moment of exhaustion, the truth was, she loved the job. The chaos lassoed into submission. The worries ironed into smoothness. The crazy schedule organized into a well-oiled machine. Teddi lived for this, and she knew Preston did, too.

An hour later, Preston was off to finalize everything with Saturday's venue, the top floor of a high-end hotel downtown. Teddi was just hanging up the phone and about to head to the back storage area to inventory her Christmas lights for Saturday when the front door opened.

"I'm here. The party can start now." Kelly Scott really was kind of adorable, and Teddi couldn't help but grin. She had a woman with her. A woman who was not Leah, but looked a lot like her.

"Thank God. I've been ready for the party to start since about ten o'clock this morning." Teddi crossed the shop floor and gave Kelly a hug—another thing she loved about her. Teddi often became friends with her clients, reached hug status pretty quickly. But some remained a bit aloof. Or Teddi did. And that was fine. Kelly Scott had fallen into the first category almost immediately. Totally hug-worthy. "And who do we have here? Another sister?"

The woman standing next to Kelly flushed prettily and smiled as she held out a hand to shake Teddi's while also giving her a not-so-subtle once-over. She was about the same height as Kelly, which was to say not very tall at all, and her hair had probably once been a brighter gold but now was more of an ash blond. Her face had that slightly weathered look of a woman who'd worked hard her whole life, likely in some kind of labor-intensive job, but that smile was inviting and friendly. "I'm her mother, and you need glasses, young lady." Her grip was firm, her hand cold from outside, but her eyes were warm and kind and the same hazel as Kelly's. "Patti Scott. It's nice to meet you. I've heard so much."

"Uh-oh." Teddi clenched her teeth and raised her eyebrows.

Kelly laughed. "Please. Like I'd have anything bad to say about you."

Teddi held out an arm to indicate the table, and they all moved in that direction. "Is Leah coming?" The question left her mouth all on its own, and she almost winced when she heard it.

Something passed between mother and daughter as they exchanged a look that Teddi noticed right away. "She's supposed to. You know her, though." Kelly's shrug was good-natured.

"Always late."

"Always late." Teddi and Patti said the two words at exactly the same time. Patti chuckled, and Teddi smiled weakly even as she felt like she was sitting in a thick stew of awkward as it simmered. Why was she so uncomfortable?

The three took seats and Teddi took out her tablet. "This meeting will be it until after the holidays," she began. "So I've got a couple things you should try to get done and a couple things for you to think about. Homework assignments, to use teacher-speak." Kelly grinned as she scooted her chair closer, and Teddi launched in. Losing herself in her work was always good. It could get her through almost anything, and she let her focus shift away from the facts that were bothering her right then: that Leah wasn't there and that her mother was.

Of course, the moment she started to relax, to relax into wedding planner mode and feel like herself again, the door pushed open, letting in the sharply cold air from outside and Leah Scott with it.

"Hi," Leah said as she hurried to the table, unbuttoning her long black coat as she did. "Sorry I'm late."

Don't stare. Don't stare. Don't stare.

It ran through Teddi's head on repeat. And it was hard to obey. What was it about the suits? Why was she suddenly so drawn to Leah in her work attire? She used to equate Leah's suits with the bad part of their history, but now? She equated them with attraction. Today's was a pantsuit, which Leah somehow managed to make look more feminine than a suit with a skirt. Navy with faint white pinstripes. A simple white blouse underneath. Nothing fancy. Nothing even remotely sexy. Except somehow, it *was* sexy. It was *exactly* sexy.

Leah's light hair was down rather than pulled back. Maybe that contributed to the sexiness? Teddi found herself mulling over that question as Leah pulled out a chair and sat, her green eyes catching Teddi's, holding them, smiling.

A clear of the throat. A reclaiming of her own gaze. A glance down at her tablet. Teddi pulled herself together.

For the next hour, she went over details with Kelly and her family. Things that needed to be done and when. She'd created a timeline for her, a checklist of sorts that she made for each bride-to-be. It listed things that needed to be decided on—venue, music, food, color scheme, design theme—and dates when Kelly needed to have each thing chosen, retained, paid for.

"So, how long have you been a wedding planner, Teddi?" Patti asked once they'd finished up and were all standing.

"More than ten years."

"Wow. Does it get stressful?" Patti slipped on her coat, seeming genuinely interested.

"It can. But over time, I've learned how to handle that type of thing. I'm a very organized person, and as long as you can stay organized, you can avoid much of the stress." She felt Leah's eyes on her but forced herself to stay focused on Patti.

Leaning in close, as if she was about to share a secret, Patti asked, "Any bridezillas?"

"So many," Teddi answered with a grin.

"But not my daughter, I hope."

"God, no. Your daughter hasn't even come close."

"It's early," Leah chimed in. "Give her time."

"Hey!" Kelly playfully slapped at her sister. "Shut up."

"What do you do for the holidays?" Patti asked. "Is your family in town?" Everybody had their coats on and buttoned. Ready to go. But it seemed like Patti wanted to stay, to keep talking. Leah shifted in what looked to be slight discomfort.

"Mom, let the woman work." Leah smiled—apologetically?—at Teddi.

"It's fine," Teddi said, and it was the truth. She liked the Scotts in her shop. *No, I like Leah in my shop.* Damn that inner voice of hers. "Yes, my family is in town. I'll spend Christmas with them. What about you guys?" Was she being polite? Or was part of her trying to keep them here a little bit longer? She didn't want to think about it.

"We spend Christmas together. We always have," Patti said, and the way her face lit up as she looked from one daughter to the other warmed Teddi's heart. "We do dinner on Christmas Eve and watch movies, and then my girls come back in the morning and we celebrate Christmas Day together as well. Then for New Year's Eve, everybody does their own thing."

"That sounds perfect," Teddi said. And nothing like her own Christmas with her family, which was a bit more formal.

"Well, we've kept you long enough," Leah said and made a gesture to get her mother and sister moving, using her arms as if she was corralling sheep toward the door. She looked back at Teddi, held her gaze for a beat longer than necessary, as she said, "Thanks for everything." Her voice held a hint of…was it sadness?

"Have a very merry Christmas, Leah." Teddi's voice came out softer than she'd intended.

"You, too."

And they were gone.

Teddi watched out the window longer than she had time to. It was supposed to snow that night. They'd had a few flakes here and there in the last couple weeks, stuff that hadn't stuck, but tonight, the forecast was for several inches. Teddi looked forward to it. Right now, everything was simply brown and cold. A blanket of white would make everything look fresh and new again. Teddi sighed.

God knew she could use a clean slate.

CHAPTER TEN

You cannot stay home alone on New Year's Eve. I won't allow it." Tilly's voice had taken on a firmer tone. They'd started out joking. Light. Zinging each other. But as soon as she'd understood that Leah was actually seriously considering spending New Year's Eve by herself, Take Charge Tilly had shown up.

"I'm sorry, you won't *allow* it?" Leah asked with playful sarcasm.

"I will not. I will drive my ass over there and drag you out of your house myself by your pretty blond hair. Don't think I won't."

"I would never think that." Leah couldn't help but smile because she knew, not a doubt in her mind, that Tilly would do exactly that. She'd show up at her door, march up to the bedroom, pick out an outfit, and stand there while Leah got dressed and ready. "I just wasn't really feeling celebratory."

"Pfft. Doesn't matter. It's New Year's Eve. There will be food. Champagne. Pretty people—I hope. You will *get* celebratory."

A sigh. "I guess maybe I could hand out some business car—"

"No!" The word was like a gunshot as Tilly interrupted. "This is not a networking thing, Leah. It's a holiday, for fuck's sake, and I swear to God if I catch you handing out business cards, I will take them from you and I will set them on fire. You're going to drink, meet some new people, and have a good time if it kills me. And you. Got it?"

"Well, that's enticing."

"And do not wear work clothes. Dress nice, but not like a lawyer. This is a *party*."

"Ugh. Fine." She wasn't going to win this. She knew it, and if she was being honest with herself, she'd kind of known it all along. Part of her had expected this call, waited for it, hoped for it even. Tilly was fantastic at dragging her out of the house, and she needed that or she'd stay inside with Lizzie way more often than was probably good for her mental health. But she faked some irritation anyway, just to make Tilly have to work a little bit.

"Good. I'll pick you up at nine."

Leah hung up the phone, turned from her spot on the couch to look at Lizzie, curled in a ball next to her, apparently in a good mood today. "I guess I'm going to a party."

Lizzie yawned widely, sharing her opinion on the subject.

"What should I wear?"

Big green eyes blinked.

"Ah, the slow blink. That says I'm hopeless. Fine. I get it. Thanks for the assistance, Ms. Bennet. You're fantastic for my ego." She kissed the cat's head anyway.

At nine, Leah stood in front of the full-length mirror in her bedroom and surveyed her look. Dark jeans. Black ankle boots with a heel—she hoped it didn't get icy, or breaking her neck was a distinct possibility. A white sweater, which could be a disaster if she ate anything with sauce, but she liked the way it hugged her body. A black silk scarf with small white dots. Her hair was down, and she'd used a large curling iron to enhance some of the waves just like Kelly had taught her. She'd even added a little eye shadow, as the idea of going to a party started to feel more like fun and less like a chore. Giving her reflection a nod of approval, she headed down the stairs just as the door opened and Tilly came in.

Her friend looked her up and down and gave a whistle. "Wow. Don't you clean up nice. I was pretty sure I was going to find you on the couch in your leggings."

"It was tempting. Believe me." Leah grabbed her coat off a hanger and slipped her arms in. "Where is this party?"

"At my friend Piper's place. She and her wife bought a new house a couple months ago and this is their first big party. Should be a nice mix—they know a lot of people."

"And who's there that you're interested in?" She shot Tilly a knowing look as she picked up her purse and keys and they headed out the door.

"Whatever do you mean?" Tilly's BMW was brand new and smelled like it.

"Mm-hmm. Tell me."

"There's a girl that Piper has mentioned more than once." Tilly started the car and pulled them out into traffic. "She's in social work, I think. Piper thinks we'd hit it off." She shot a glance at Leah. "Not that she's the only reason I'm going. Not at all."

"Got it," Leah said, nodding slowly. It was exactly the reason Tilly was going and also the reason she'd dragged Leah. In case the girl didn't show, or didn't float Tilly's boat, or any other number of reasons. "I'm your wing woman."

"Well…"

"It's okay, Til. I don't mind. It's a role I play well."

"You totes do."

Being Tilly's wing woman would be better than being home alone with her cat. At least, she hoped so.

The party was going strong by the time they arrived at nine thirty. Piper's house was nice. Not huge, not tiny, and in a nicer suburb of the city. White siding with black shutters. White lights twinkled, run tastefully around the front door and a small potted Christmas tree that stood on the side of the front stoop. The music coming from inside could just be heard from the steps. Something smooth and jazzy. Norah Jones, maybe? Leah strained to listen but wasn't sure.

The door was pulled open just as Tilly poked a finger toward the doorbell, and both she and Leah jumped.

"Hey, you made it! Come in, come in. It's freezing." The woman was a brunette, with big dark eyes that reminded Leah so much of Teddi's, she was afraid she'd stare. Quickly, she glanced into the house and shook the thought away. No, this was why she had agreed to a party: to keep her mind from drifting to thoughts that only made her antsy.

Tilly gave the woman a hug, then turned to Leah. "Piper Bradshaw, this is my very good friend Leah Scott."

Piper held out a hand and they shook. Her grip was firm but friendly, and she tugged Leah through the doorway and into her house. "I'm so glad you could come." They followed her through the foyer and into a large living room where maybe a dozen people had congregated, broken off into smaller groups. The music emanated from speakers mounted up in the corners of the room, and the television was on, muted, to the channel on which Ryan Seacrest would count down the ball drop in Times Square.

"What can I get you?" Piper asked as a blond woman came up to them and slid an arm around Tilly's waist.

"I didn't think you'd come," she said to Tilly, and her smile was bright, inviting. Leah wanted to be friends with her immediately.

"You wound me," Tilly said, feigning a pout. Turning, she grasped Leah's arm. "Lindsay, this is my good friend Leah. Leah, this is Piper's wife, Lindsay." More handshakes.

Leah squinted at her. "Have we met?" There was something so familiar about her...Then recognition dawned. "Oh! The wine bar. Vineyard. You work there?"

"We own it," Lindsay said with a look of pride. "Piper and I."

"Well, my sister and I loved it."

"I'm so glad," Lindsay said. "Listen, there's a ton of food, lots to drink. Some is out here, some in the kitchen."

"Yes, but is there wine?" Tilly asked, her voice teasing.

"Wine, you say?" Lindsay looked to Piper. "Do we have wine, my love?"

Piper tapped a finger against her lips, thinking. "Wine...wine... hmm..." Then she slapped playfully at Tilly, who leaned toward Leah.

Leah feigned seriousness. "So there's wine, then?"

Lindsay laughed and pointed around the staircase. "Tons. In the kitchen. We're totally informal here. Everybody's cool. Just help yourself and get comfortable. How does that sound?"

"That sounds fantastic. Thank you." Leah felt herself relax. Her shoulders dropped a bit, she exhaled and felt calm. She wondered if Lindsay had that effect on everybody. Regardless, she decided in that moment, she was glad she came.

"Wine?" Piper asked them with a wink.

"Yes, please," Tilly said. "Lead the way." They followed Piper toward the kitchen.

Leah admired the décor. She liked to think she was good at interior decorating, but then she'd see something that was really good and realize she was simply average. She didn't know if it was Piper or Lindsay, but somebody had a flair for design. The light oak hardwood floors gleamed, the runner that led down the hall along the stairs, thick and tasteful, all burgundies and deep blues. The walls were painted a subtle blue-gray, and the painting mounted over the skinny stand was abstract and eye-catching, using the same colors and adding more for interest. The table held three framed photos, and Leah made a mental note to stop on her way back and look at them. She followed Tilly's tall, thin form through the doorway that opened into a huge, open-concept kitchen-family room combination that was nothing less than completely inviting. She grinned as Tilly followed Piper to the right, and then stopped in her tracks. There, on the other side of the large granite-topped island, glass of red wine in one hand, the other at the side of her neck. Leah noticed her before she even registered any of the other people in the room.

Teddi Baker.

Seriously, what are the chances?

"Ladies, these are my friends. Tilly and Leah." Piper went around the room and pointed to each person, named them, but Leah didn't hear any of it. Teddi was holding her gaze so gently, yet so firmly. Leah couldn't look away.

"Hey." Tilly's voice yanked Leah out of her trance.

"Yeah?"

Tilly raised her eyebrows expectantly as she gestured to the wide array of wine bottles on the counter in a corner of the kitchen that served as a bar. Wine fridge underneath, glasses hanging from holders mounted above. Piper stood there smiling, waiting.

"Oh! Sorry. Um…" Leah faced the bar, scanned, pointed at the Merlot. "That would be great."

"You got it." Piper poured and handed the glass over. It took all Leah's willpower not to take a huge gulp.

"You okay?" Tilly asked softly as the doorbell rang and Piper excused herself to answer it.

"Yeah. Yeah, I'm fine. I just—"

"Hi." The voice that interrupted them was soft but effective. Leah swore to God her insides went mushy at the sound, and she turned to face Teddi, those dark, dark eyes.

"Hey." They stood there, and for the first time in her life, Leah understood what people meant when they said the rest of the room faded away. It was like there was nothing but Teddi. Her face. Her eyes. Her hair. The dimples that were peeking out just a bit. She wore tight jeans with a rip in the knee, a ribbed black turtleneck that hugged every curve of her body, knee-high black boots...

"Hi, um, I'm Leah's friend Tilly. Not that Leah was planning to tell you that, apparently. I don't think we've met." Tilly's voice seemed to boom through the air like a foghorn, and Leah blinked rapidly as Tilly held out her hand to Teddi.

"Teddi Baker. I'm planning Leah's sister's wedding." She put her hand in Tilly's. "It's nice to meet you."

Tilly, even though her eyebrows rose in what Leah could only assume was recognition, refrained from any inside jokes or smart-ass comments. Instead, she gave Leah a poignant look and excused herself to go talk to a woman across the room. Which left her alone with Teddi. Facing each other.

"So," Leah said. "Hi."

"Hi." Teddi smiled, probably at the repetition. "I am surprised to see you here. I mean, I wasn't expecting it. How do you know Piper and Lindsay?"

"I don't." Leah sipped her wine, took a moment to let the rich flavor of it coat her tongue before she swallowed. "I was told I was not allowed to spend New Year's Eve at home alone with my cat, and then was dragged from my house in protest."

"In protest, huh?" Teddi turned so she could lean her hip against the counter. After a beat, Teddi held her glass close to her lips and said, without looking at Leah, "Is it bad that I'm glad you were dragged out?"

A full-body flush. That's what happened to Leah at those words. Heat coursed through every inch of her. Heat. Arousal. Joy. She wondered just exactly how red her ears were now, and she had to search hard to find words but finally did. "No, not at all. In fact, I'm kind of glad now, too." She turned and mimicked Teddi's position so they were face-to-face. Why was standing like that, so close to Teddi, giving her all the feels? What was happening? Leah took a deep breath—quietly, so as not to give away her nervousness—and asked, "So, how do *you* know Piper and Lindsay?"

"Well, I've been a patron at their wine bar for a while now. One day, Lindsay and I got talking about wine and the venue and just really hit it off. I tend to recommend it to my brides-to-be as a great location for things like bachelorette parties or showers."

"I see."

"Have you ever been to Vineyard?"

"Yes, Kelly and I were just there a few weeks ago, but it sounds like I should've gone sooner because I've been missing out." Relaxed wasn't something she expected to feel standing with Teddi, but somehow, that was exactly how she felt. It was weird. Like all the nerves and worries and potential obstacles between them had simply disappeared for this moment.

"You have. Maybe we could go together sometime."

"Maybe we could." Okay, that was flirting. They were flirting, right? The words hung in the air for what felt like a long time before either of them spoke again.

"So," Teddi said, then sipped her wine as if organizing her thoughts before continuing. "What does Leah Scott do for fun? When she's not lawyering or being all lawyerly?"

Leah felt the grin bloom across her face at the question. "Well, you know how much I love rom-coms."

"I do. And we'll come back to that. What else do you do?"

Leah had to think about it, which probably wasn't good. "I don't really have a lot of free time..." She tried a different tack. "What about you? What does Teddi Baker do when she's not running flawless wedding ceremonies or calming down panic-stricken brides-to-be?"

"I cook."

"Really?" Leah's eyebrows shot up and she drew out the word even as she tried not to picture how sexy Teddi would look in front of a stove, whipping up something delicious.

"Mm-hmm. I like to experiment."

"What's your favorite thing to cook?"

Teddi pursed her lips, seemed to really think about it. "Hmm. I'm not sure I have a favorite thing to cook, but I do have a favorite meal. Breakfast."

"It is the most important meal of the day." Leah grinned. "And it's *my* favorite meal of the day."

"Mine, too."

They stood there, eye contact intense, and again, the rest of the room seemed to melt away until it was only the two of them.

"Why rom-coms?" Teddi asked suddenly.

"What do you have against rom-coms?" Leah countered.

"I don't have anything against them, but"—Teddi held up fingers, counting off as she said—"they're sappy, they're predictable, and they're unrealistic."

Leah counted off her response. "They're happy. They're happy. They're happy."

Narrowed dark eyes. A tongue poking the inside of a cheek. "Interesting."

"How so?" God, Leah was loving this. Was Teddi? Was this back-and-forth, this getting to know each other thing, turning Teddi on as much as it was her? She'd been so sure after that last time in the café that nothing would ever happen between them because of their history, but now? She *wasn't* so sure. Should she ask? Or just let things progress and see what happened? She decided on the latter and tried hard not to focus on Teddi's full lips as she spoke.

"When did your love of rom-coms begin?"

"Oh, early teens." Leah thought about it honestly. "I was probably...thirteen? Fourteen?"

"And what was happening in your life when you were thirteen or fourteen? Anything?"

Leah took a moment. She could blow this off. She could pretend. Make up something. Lie. But, strangely, she didn't want to lie to Teddi. She never wanted to lie to Teddi and had no idea why, where that thought had come from. She dove in. "My parents were divorcing. It was volatile." She cleared her throat, sipped her wine before continuing. "Lots of fighting. Lots of shouting. Hard to watch and hear and know. They didn't tell me anything, but I was old enough to understand something bad was happening, you know? So that was frustrating."

Teddi laid a warm hand on Leah's upper arm. "I'm so sorry. That must've been awful."

It wasn't a time in her life she liked to remember, but she did it for Teddi. "It was hard. I spent a lot of time kind of sheltering Kelly. She's eight years younger than me, so she was just a kid. I'd bring her into my room and play music really loud so we couldn't hear our parents shouting or saying terrible things to each other. And when it was just me, I'd escape into movies. The first rom-com I ever saw was *While You Were Sleeping*."

"With Sandra Bullock?" Teddi asked.

Leah nodded, pleased that she knew the movie. "It was so...I don't know. Uplifting? Heartwarming? And it made me want more."

"I actually really like that one."

"Yeah?"

"I mean, Sandra Bullock? Come on."

"There may be hope for you yet."

They laughed together and there was a comfortable beat of silence. Then Teddi asked, "And you watched more?"

Leah nodded, looked into her glass. "Looking back now, I think it was my therapy, you know? My friends were watching horror movies, and all I could think was that there was enough horror and heartbreak in my own life, so why would I want to watch it on a big screen?"

"I get that." Teddi reached behind them and grabbed a wine bottle, held it up. Leah held out her glass and Teddi poured.

As Leah watched the deep ruby of the wine fill her glass, only one thought was prevalent in her mind: *I'm so glad I came.*

❖

This was turning out to be the most unexpected New Year's Eve Teddi had ever had. Piper's invitation was really nice, but Teddi had wavered about coming right up until that afternoon. She'd originally planned to go to her parents' house. She'd done that the past two New Year's Eves, as she'd tried to navigate the holidays without Julia. It hadn't been easy, and being around a bunch of friends, most of whom were paired up, just wasn't something she could handle. But this year felt different. She was a little more solid in her life. Maybe not as confident as she once was, but it was slowly trickling back, and the idea of being in her early forties, single, and spending New Year's Eve with her parents was just too sad. She'd toyed with staying home alone, but she knew her brain well. It would run away with her, and all the newfound confidence would fly out the window as she browbeat herself into an I'm-going-to-be-alone-forever stupor. No, she needed to be around people, and she was very happy she'd made the choice to come.

Leah Scott had been icing on the cake.

Stunning. That was how Leah looked. And stunned was how Teddi had felt when Leah had come walking into Piper's kitchen. What were the chances?

They'd been standing there, she and Leah, just talking, just getting to know each other, for—she glanced at the clock on Piper's microwave—oh my God, over an hour? It felt like a ton of time had passed and also no time at all.

"Tell me about you," Leah said, interrupting Teddi's thoughts. "You have siblings?"

"Two brothers. Both older. Both married with kids. And my parents have been married for fifty-five years." She met Leah's eyes and was shocked to realize that Leah got it. She *got it*.

"Your divorce was extra hard, huh?"

"It was. It was so hard to be the only one in the family who couldn't seem to make her marriage work."

"You do know that's not the case at all, right?" Leah stood up straight after leaning against the counter, as if her posture would punctuate her statement. "It takes two to break up a marriage. Believe me, I know." Her half grin kept things from getting too heavy.

"I know that now, but when it first happened? Ugh." Teddi dropped her back and groaned. "I felt like a failure in my marriage and a failure in my family."

"Man, that sucks."

"It did. It really, really did." Teddi followed Leah's gaze across the room where her friend—Tilly, was it?—was standing very close to a petite woman and seemed to be having an intimate conversation. A niggling in her brain forced the question from her lips. "You and…" She gestured toward Tilly with her chin. "Are you…?"

Leah's eyes went wide. "Me and Tilly? No. Oh God, no. Tilly's my best friend from college."

"But no romantic history there?" Teddi didn't know why she was being so nosy, asking such personal questions, and she knew she was giving away a little more than she wanted to. But something in her needed to know.

"Not even a glimmer." Leah's grin said she was amused by Teddi's inquiries, and those green eyes held hers as she sipped her wine.

It was as if there were no other guests at the party. They talked only to each other, and in what seemed like ten minutes, Piper raised her voice and let everybody know they should move into the family room or living room where the TVs were.

It was almost midnight.

There were more guests at the party than Teddi had realized. As they flowed into the two rooms that had televisions, that became clear, and people ended up standing close together in order to see the ball drop.

She found herself pressed against Leah's smaller body, and she was more than okay with that. The top of Leah's head reached Teddi's nose, and when Leah looked up at her, those bright eyes sparkled, and Teddi knew Leah was feeling it, too.

What was *it*? What exactly was she feeling?

Oh, please. Stop pretending you don't know.

Okay, fine. She did know. She was devastatingly attracted to Leah Scott. She had been the second she'd walked into Teddi's shop. It was instantaneous. Teddi had never felt that before, not even with Julia. That instant, undeniable attraction to someone. It was almost tangible, like she could reach out and touch it. Taste it.

And now? With Leah standing so close, close enough to smell the coconut scent of her shampoo, close enough to see the flecks of gold and black in her green eyes, Teddi knew exactly where this was headed. Judging by the way Leah's eyes darkened, so did she.

"Ten! Nine! Eight!"

The whole room was counting down except for them. They stood together, gazes held, as if in some kind of trance.

"Five! Four! Three!"

Leah turned slightly so they were face-to-face. Teddi brought her hand up and brushed some of Leah's hair to the side, tucked it behind her ear.

"Two! One! Happy New Year!"

Teddi closed her eyes. Leaned down.

Her hand slid along Leah's face. Held it.

Lips met. Soft. Warm. Amazing.

Teddi wanted more. She knew it in an instant that this could not be the only time she kissed Leah. But this was not the time or the place to explore that warm, wonderful mouth, or to let her hands roam. She pulled back gently, opened her eyes, and met Leah's. And everything she saw in them echoed her own thoughts.

"Happy New Year," Teddi said, though her voice was lost in the revelry around them.

"I think it just might be," was Leah's reply.

❖

"Somebody's got some explaining to do." The words were out of Tilly's mouth the second she slammed her car door.

"So do you," Leah countered. "Was that the social worker?"

Tilly keyed the ignition, then held up a finger and waggled it. "Oh no. Don't change the subject. We're talking about you. And the hot wedding planner. And the kissing. Details. Now."

"I'm impressed you waited this long to ask." Leah grinned.

"It was not easy, believe me." Tilly pulled out onto the road and pointed the car in the direction of Leah's. "I mean, I knew who she was when you introduced us, but I thought you said nothing would happen because of the whole you representing her ex in their divorce thing."

"I don't know what to tell you. That's the impression I got."

"Well, you were *wrong*."

"Evidently."

The night could not have possibly gone in a more unexpected direction than it had, and Leah was trying to wrap her head around it even as she sat in Tilly's car, her lips still tingling from kissing Teddi, her brain still a jumble of caution, elation, and possibility.

"Now what?" Tilly asked.

And that was the question, wasn't it? Now what?

The party had died down pretty quickly after midnight, people needing to get home to their kids or their pets or simply to their beds, exhausted from a week of holiday celebration. She and Teddi had both been swept up in the leaving.

"So...I'll call you?" She hadn't meant to phrase it as a question, but it had come out that way. Luckily, Teddi had smiled because...She found Leah charming? Pathetic? Both? Leah wasn't sure.

"I told her I'd call her," she said now to Tilly, who turned and arched an eyebrow at her.

"Really? How romantic."

Leah dropped her head back against the seat and groaned. "I know! I am so not smooth."

"You're really not."

"Teach me. I'll pay you."

"Alas, my little friend, smoothness is not something that can be taught. You either have it, as I do, or you do not." Tilly waved a hand over Leah. "Case in point."

Leah turned her head, watched out the window as houses passed by.

"She's hot," Tilly said.

Leah grinned and turned her head the other way, caught the glance Tilly tossed her way, the raised brows, the wide eyes. "Right? So hot."

"Jesus God, yes. Those dimples?"

Leah sat up. "*Right? She should smile more because those dimples are life.*"

"I think that should be your new job."

"What?"

"Making that girl smile. The world needs to see those dimples. War will cease. Famine will end. It'll be a better place."

"I cannot disagree with you."

Half an hour later, Leah was home. Face scrubbed, teeth brushed, hunkered down in her bed with Lizzie purring next to her hip. She was exhausted but wide awake, replaying the night. Replaying the kiss.

It had been simple. Almost delicate. Not chaste, but certainly not overtly sexual. They'd been in a room full of people. They'd never kissed before.

But, man, that kiss did things to me.

How was that possible? There'd been no tongue, barely opened mouths. It had been tender. Gentle.

"And somehow, so fucking hot," Leah whispered into the darkness of her bedroom.

Before she could get lost in *that* thought, her phone pinged and the screen lit up from its spot on her nightstand. She picked it up. A text. From Teddi.

Tonight was unexpected.

Leah squinted at the words, then typed, *In a good way, I hope.*

The little gray dots bounced, and then the phone pinged again. *In a very good way.* Followed by several happy face emojis.

The smile that bloomed across Leah's face was out of her control. She felt it growing. That wonderful fluttering in her stomach? It had been missing for a long time, and now it was back. She'd missed it, realizing it only then. She typed a whole bunch of mush, then deleted it all. Nibbled at her bottom lip as she contemplated. Then she typed, simply, *Happy New Year, Teddi.*

Dropping her hand onto Lizzie's soft head and scratching her lightly, Leah kept smiling. Her stomach kept fluttering.

"Best. New Year's Eve. Ever."

CHAPTER ELEVEN

I'm just taking it slowly. Very, very slowly." Teddi sighed, feeling slightly winded for some reason after telling Preston all about her New Year's Eve.

It was January 2 and they were back in the shop. Snow was falling in big, fat flakes, and Preston was removing the window display so he could set up a new one. January tended not to be terribly busy for Hopeless Romantic as far as new business went, so they used it to refresh the displays, peruse new trends, and prepare for the onslaught of Valentine's Day nuptials that would flood them in six weeks.

Preston had been in the window bay, setting a table with burgundy place settings and eucalyptus greenery. He was dressed down today— or as dressed down as he ever was—in jeans and a navy blue oxford, the sleeves rolled up. He stepped out and parked his hands on his hips, surveying his handiwork. With a pivot on one foot, he looked in Teddi's direction where she sat behind the counter, answering email. "What happened to *She repped my ex in our divorce and I hate her?*"

"I never said I hated her."

Preston tipped his head, gave her a look.

What *had* happened? It was a valid question and one that Teddi had rolled around in her head for the past couple days, all the while dipping her toe in, starting with occasionally texting Leah.

"I guess…" She gathered her thoughts as she scrolled through a new line of bridesmaids' dresses and pretended to actually see them. Meeting Preston's eyes, she said honestly, "I guess I made a resolution to try to be more forgiving. And more open." She couldn't tell him that a stupid romantic comedy had made her think. That Tom Hanks and

Meg Ryan had her reevaluating where and how she placed her blame. Preston would roll his eyes and laugh her out of the shop.

"Yeah? That's awesome. I like it." Preston slit open a box and pulled out a new set of gold-rimmed wineglasses they'd ordered. "What do you think?" he asked, holding it up.

And this is how it starts.

The thought ran through Teddi's mind on and off throughout the day. Every time she sent a text to Leah—*Got some gold-rimmed wineglasses in. Thought they'd be classy, but look like they belong in a garage sale*—something inside her went softer. Warmer.

I'll give you fifty cents each, came Leah's reply over an hour later. Softer. Warmer.

And later that evening from Leah: *Chinese at my desk in the office. Hope your dinner is more exciting.*

Teddi texted back: *Chicken Milanese I made myself. Not exciting at all.* Then she sent a photo of her ridiculously good meal just because.

Leah sent back a drooling emoji. Teddi laughed out loud.

Softer. Warmer.

"Yes. This is how it starts," she said quietly to herself as she sat down in front of the television with her chicken and a glass of Sauvignon Blanc.

Once she'd finished eating, brought her dishes into the kitchen, and cleaned up, she flopped back onto the couch to relax. The brittle weather of the day had led into an icy night, and Teddi pulled a fleece blanket over her legs, wishing she had someone—or something—to cuddle with. She grabbed her phone.

Do you have a pet?

She didn't expect a response right away, but it came within a couple minutes.

I do. A cat. Elizabeth Bennet.

Teddi grinned wide. *Of course that's her name.*

I'm surprised you recognize it, given your unromantic nature. A wink emoji followed.

Teddi gasped, then chuckled. *How dare you? I took English lit in high school just like everybody else.*

Point taken.

Teddi let her phone rest against her chin for a moment. When had people become *this*? Words on a screen instead of actual humans with voices and inflection? The weird thing was, she kind of liked this. Almost preferred it. It felt safer that Leah couldn't see her right now. Couldn't hear her or look into her eyes. Teddi could keep her secrets for a while longer.

Is Elizabeth Bennet a cuddler? Then something occurred to Teddi and she typed a second text. *Still at work? I don't want to bother you.*

Several minutes went by before Leah's response came: *Lizzie cuddles on her own terms, which I kinda love. And yes, I am and please bother me or I may throw myself out a window.*

Please bother her. That's what she'd said.

And Teddi got warmer.

She kept her texts spaced out, slightly sporadic. She didn't want to be overbearing, and also, she didn't want to seem like she had nothing better to do, though the truth was she not only had nothing better to do, she had nothing else she wanted to do.

Are you thinking of getting a cat? Leah asked a little while later.

I'm just alone on my couch and wanted something to cuddle with. Teddi sent her response without actually thinking about it, then winced as she read it back. Waited for Leah. And waited. And waited. The dots bounced, disappeared, bounced again. Teddi waited some more, nibbling on her bottom lip and berating herself for being so transparent.

Finally, the text came: *I have lots of suggestions, but a cat is a very good choice.* And then came a wink emoji. A wink.

Teddi exhaled in relief. *One day, you'll have to tell me.*

Definitely.

They talked into the night, stopping so Leah could drive herself home. Teddi was in bed, curled up under the covers, television on, but no lights, absolutely not waiting for Leah's next text.

The Holiday is on, Teddi texted before she could think too much about what it meant. *Right up your alley.*

OMG, I love that one! What channel? Once they were both watching, Leah added, *Kate Winslet is just adorable in this. I want to hug her.*

I can agree with that.

You've seen this? I'm impressed.

Teddi grinned. *I have.*

They watched together, texting occasionally, commenting on a line here or a scene there. Much to her surprise, Teddi found herself having a fantastic time, despite the late hour and the yawns that were cranking her mouth open wide more and more frequently. When the credits rolled, she was both relieved and disappointed.

Time to sleep, Leah texted, and added a sleeping emoji with several z's. *Thanks for keeping me company tonight.*

It was my pleasure, Teddi typed back, and she'd never meant anything more sincerely.

Talk tomorrow?

Absolutely.

Have sweet dreams, Teddi. A kiss emoji followed. Leah's emoji game was strong, that was for sure.

You, too. Good night.

Teddi plugged her phone into its charger, clicked off the television, and snuggled down into her bed. Sleep was her thing. Always had been. She loved to sleep in. It was one of her favorite things in life. But tonight? She wanted to sleep fast. Because when it was tomorrow, she could talk to Leah again.

❖

Cheerful and looking forward to the day was not often how Leah woke up after a night when she'd been in her office working until after nine. But last night had been different, so very different, and she just lay there in her bed, grinning like a fool. How could simply texting with someone make her feel all mushy and joyful inside? There'd barely been any flirting. They just talked.

She remembered every text. Could almost hear Teddi's voice saying them out loud. That fluttering in her stomach had been near constant, until she was barely able to focus on her work. And while saying good night had been necessary, because of course it had, she hadn't wanted to. Leah could've chatted with Teddi all night long. Easily. Like a teenage girl talking to her first crush.

Phone in her hand, she began typing a morning greeting, but stopped herself and deleted it. They were taking things slowly, it seemed, by some unspoken agreement. Leah was okay with that but knew she'd need to see Teddi soon. Lay eyes on her. Be in the same room. Maybe she'd bring that up later today.

The loud scraping sound of a snowplow clearing her driveway made her put the phone down, got her up and moving. Lizzie hunkered down into the comforter, apparently not yet ready to face the day, and Leah couldn't blame her. It was *cold*. Leah gave her a scratch, and Lizzie shot her a warning look. "I love you, Your Highness." She dropped a kiss on the cat's head, then darted away before she got hit with a claw swipe.

In the bathroom, she noticed a small reddish spider up in the corner above the shower, where the wall met the ceiling. Normally, something like that would make her jump. Then she'd have to find a way to capture the spider but not touch it. Then carry it to the door and let it loose outside because she hated the idea of killing anything— except centipedes because they were creepy and scary fast and all had to die—but it was so cold, and she was in her pajamas and running late. So she stood there.

Finally, she stripped off her pajamas, keeping an eye on the spider the whole time, then stood there, hands on her hips.

"Okay, look. I'm in a good mood, and I would rather not squish you. But it's super cold out and I need to get to work, and I don't have time to try and herd you outside. So, let's lay some ground rules. You can stay there, in the corner, and I'll be just fine. But you are not to drop on me. And you are not to have any spider babies in my house. Understood? That would be definite grounds for squishing." She squinted. The spider didn't move, and she absently wondered if it was staring back at her. Once the water was running and she'd stepped in, she glanced up again. The spider hadn't moved.

Toweling herself off, she said, "You're a good spider. I'm going to name you Angelica and allow you to stay. As long as we have an understanding."

Dressed and ready to go, cat fed, Leah picked up her phone. The timing now seemed okay. She typed out a good morning and asked Teddi how she slept. Then she tucked the phone away, promising herself she wouldn't spend the day checking it incessantly for a response. *Stay breezy.* She donned her coat and headed out into the day, the cold January weather like a slap in the face.

❖

"Oh my God." Harlow laughed heartily, a big, toss-her-head-back-and-let-loose laugh that came from deep in her body. Teddi had filled her in on her New Year's Eve, sparing no details because, for some reason, she needed to talk about it. "This is the stuff rom-coms are made of, you know. The very stuff you despise, that makes you roll your eyes? You're living it right now."

"Shut up," Teddi said in a grumble, but a good-natured one, because Harlow was right and Teddi didn't care that she was living out a romance novel. There was nothing she'd rather do right then, and it was so confusing. How the hell had this happened?

They sat at the little round table in Hopeless Romantic, going over the February schedule, comparing notes on the upcoming weddings they'd both be working. "I don't understand it, Harlow."

"What don't you understand?" Harlow pushed aside the papers they were looking at, set her forearms on the table, and wrapped her hands around her warm mug of coffee. Teddi loved that about her—that she'd give you one hundred percent of her attention if you needed it. And Teddi needed it now.

Teddi took a deep breath and let it out slowly as she organized her thoughts, something she'd been trying to do since she'd opened her eyes that morning. "We texted last night for hours. Sporadic at first. I was careful not to seem overly anxious."

"Because…?"

Teddi blinked at her. "Pride?"

Harlow grinned. "Got it. Go on."

"But after a while, we stopped waiting between texts and just talked."

"Only by text, though. Not on the phone or FaceTiming or anything."

"Right. Just by text."

Harlow nodded, sipped, waited for Teddi to continue.

"And it felt…" Again, Teddi tried to organize what she was thinking, couldn't understand why it was so hard. "It felt right. Like it was exactly what we were supposed to be doing."

"*Okay.*" Harlow drew the word out, furrowed her brow. "And the problem is…?"

"How? How is it right? Given who she is. Given who I am. How is it possible that I'm still interested in this person? That I haven't been able to just write her off? I kissed her on New Year's Eve, for God's sake."

"Sweetie." Harlow's smile was slight, but Teddi knew her face well. She was hiding the fact that she wanted to grin widely. Closing a hand over Teddi's forearm, she made eye contact and held it. "Do you think you might be overthinking this whole thing? Just a tad?" Harlow's tone was careful, as if she was concerned about angering her.

"Am I?" It was an honest question. Teddi hadn't even considered she might be overthinking all this.

Harlow nodded, held her thumb and forefinger half an inch apart. "I think maybe a little, yeah."

"Huh." Teddi dropped her shoulders, slouched a bit in her seat.

"It *is* something you have a habit of doing."

She wasn't wrong about that and Teddi knew it. "Advice?"

"Relax. That's my advice. Chill out. Enjoy the ride."

"That simple, huh?"

"It really is. You seem to like this girl. She seems to like you."

Preston pushed through the door then, returning from a caterer visit. He stomped the snow off his boots. His black wool coat was sprinkled with snowflakes, the red scarf around his neck adding a pop of color to his dark outfit.

"Preston," Harlow said, "what's your advice for our friend here with regard to this new chick she likes?"

"For the love of God, woman, relax about it. Just have fun." He walked past them both and into the back room.

Harlow turned to her, brows raised in victory. She didn't actually say *See?* but she didn't have to. Teddi heard it anyway.

"Fine. Fine. I'll try to relax."

"Have you texted her today?"

"Not yet." Teddi felt the smile start to spread across her face. "But she sent me a good morning a little bit ago."

Harlow sat back in her chair, coffee in hand, and sipped, her eyes twinkling knowingly over the rim of the mug. "Text her back."

Teddi didn't have to be told twice.

CHAPTER TWELVE

Pizzeria Cannavale was small, and that was smart for business because it was always busy. Brick walls and small tables with white tablecloths gave it a cozy atmosphere. In the center was a horseshoe-shaped counter where people sat, watching the cooks making pizza, sliding it in and out of the wood-burning oven with spatulas the size of snow shovels. And the smell...tomato sauce, basil, Parmesan. Her mouth had been watering since she arrived a few minutes ago.

The table was perfect. Tucked in a corner, close enough to the counter to be able to see the pizzas being made, but far enough that she and Teddi would still be able to converse without having to strain to hear each other. She was toying with a long, skinny breadstick when she looked up and saw Teddi coming in the door.

Teddi took her breath away. Literally. She knew it should be impossible, but she didn't care. No air went in or out of Leah's lungs for what felt like a long time. She simply stared. Gawked, if she was being honest. It was snowing lightly, and Teddi's dark head and navy blue coat were sprinkled with dots of white. Those dark eyes scanned the small space and landed on Leah just as she raised her hand.

The eye contact sent Leah's insides to fluttering. Again. Was that going to be a regular thing now? Teddi crossed the room. Leah noticed a few heads turn and had to fight the urge to stand up and loudly announce, *Yes, this is my date, thank you very much, and the rest of you can suck it.* She stayed seated. And quiet.

"Oh my God, this has got to be what heaven smells like." Teddi draped her coat over the back of her chair and sat down. The black sweater was simple yet elegant, her hair pulled back, silver hoops in her ears. "Hi."

"Hey, you." Leah felt her smile grow, and an odd sense of what she could only describe as contentedness settled around her. She'd been nervous all day anticipating tonight, their first date. But now that Teddi was there, seated across the small table from her, she felt nothing but happy relaxation.

"This is awesome," Teddi said, looking around. "I've heard about this place, but I can't believe I've never been here."

"It can be hard to get a table, but I know the owner."

"Yeah? A client?"

"A classmate. In high school."

They were interrupted by the waitress, who took their wine order and told them the specials, then slipped away.

"We're getting pizza, right?" Teddi asked. "Please tell me we're getting pizza."

"Listen"—Leah leaned over the table, lowered her voice as if she had a secret—"all the food here is excellent, but I only come for the pizza."

"Oh, thank God."

"I don't know what Marisa does, if it's the dough or the sauce or the wood-burning oven, but her pizza is like magic. Or crack. Magical crack."

The waitress returned with their Zinfandel and asked after their order.

"What do you like on your pizza?" Leah asked.

"There's not much I don't like on my pizza."

"Pepperoni?" Teddi nodded. "Sliced tomatoes?" Another nod. "Green peppers?" Nod. "Perfect. That, please." The waitress grinned and left.

Teddi picked up her wine. "Shall we toast?"

"I think it's bad luck not to."

"Agreed. Okay, then…" Teddi pursed her lips, her thinking face stupidly cute, which Leah tried—and failed—not to notice. When Teddi settled on something, it was clear. Her face relaxed. Her eyes sparkled. Her lips turned up in a soft smile. "To magical crack pizzas and first dates."

"I will absolutely drink to that." They touched glasses with a light ping and sipped, Leah never taking her eyes from Teddi's face. "Tell me something."

"Okay. What would you like to know?" Forearms on the table, Teddi leaned in.

It had been on her mind since The Kiss. Yes, she thought about it with capitalization. The Kiss. Because it had solidified itself in her mind as something worth capitalizing. "What changed?" At Teddi's furrowed brow, she went on. "I mean, after that night in the café, it kind of felt like a period. You know? Full stop. Like it was clear we had an obstacle we weren't going to get past and nothing further would happen."

Teddi wet her lips, sipped her wine, gave a small nod. "I thought it was pretty clear, too."

"Cut to New Year's Eve and you kissing me out of nowhere." Sly. That's what Leah went for with her smile. Sly. Teasing. It worked because Teddi's cheeks pinkened.

"Yeah. Well. That was unexpected."

"No kidding."

"And it also wasn't."

Leah squinted at her. "Explain."

Watching thoughts and emotions play across Teddi's face was quickly becoming Leah's favorite pastime. She might do a good job at seeming stoic and serious, but Teddi's expressions were subtle and many if you only paid attention. Like now, as she obviously struggled to verbalize what she was thinking. Rapid blinking. Looking off into the distance. Slightly furrowed eyebrows. A slight nibble of the bottom lip. It was interesting and beautiful and Leah just watched.

"You can't laugh," Teddi finally said.

"I can't promise that."

Teddi shot a warning look that made Leah laugh.

"Okay. Fine. I won't laugh." As Teddi opened her mouth, Leah stopped her. "Wait. Can I chuckle? Snort? Grin?"

"No, no, and no."

Dramatic sigh. "Fine." A wink to keep it light.

Teddi looked down at the table, presumably to hide the grin Leah had coaxed from her. "It was the movie."

"The movie." Leah looked at her blankly.

"*You've Got Mail.* After that night, I kept thinking about it. Going back to it. How business and personal aren't always the same thing. That they can be separate."

Leah took a moment to absorb the words. "So, wait. Lemme get this straight." She held up a hand, paused for effect. "What you're saying is that I have Tom Hanks to thank for you kissing me at midnight on New Year's Eve?"

Teddi blinked at her. Once. Twice. "Yes. That's absolutely what I'm saying." A sip of wine. "You should probably send him a fruit basket or something."

Leah laughed. Really laughed. It bubbled up and pushed out and she noticed that it seemed to make Teddi's whole face light up. "I will do that. First thing in the morning. I'd better make a reminder." She pulled out her phone and made a show of typing info in.

The pizza arrived as they were laughing, and the waitress set it on a raised holder in the middle of the table, then dished out a slice for each of them. They lifted their slices and took a bite in tandem.

"Oh…ooh." Teddi held her hand in front of her mouth as she chewed. "Oh my God."

"Right?" Leah chewed her own bite, savoring the blend of flavors. The acidity of the sauce, the saltiness of the cheese, the slight spice of the pepperoni, the crunch of the peppers, and the brightness of the fresh tomato slices. "I can never tell what it is, but—"

"It's something, right? Is it the crust? Does the sauce have special secret seasonings? Like in *Mystic Pizza?*"

Leah couldn't hide her delight. "You've seen *Mystic Pizza?*"

Teddi merely smiled, a glimmer in her dark eyes. Leah's flutters, which had been butterfly-like, dialed up into bumblebee mode.

"Well. You get points for that."

"I do? What kind of points?" Teddi teased. "Rom-com points?"

"Exactly." They ate in silence for a moment. "So, what do you do to relax? I imagine your job can get kind of stressful. It can't be easy to manage the most important day in somebody's life. What do you do when it gets to be too much?"

"I go to the zoo." Teddi said it so matter-of-factly that Leah simply blinked at her for several seconds.

"Really?"

"Mm-hmm." A dab of a napkin. A sip of wine. Was it normal how much Leah loved just watching Teddi? Watching her do normal, unremarkable things like wipe her mouth with a napkin? "I go there and I just wander, observe the animals. Sometimes, I'll sit inside one of the buildings for half an hour or more, just...sitting."

"What's in the buildings?"

Teddi's dark eyes widened. "Have you never been to the zoo?"

"Not since I was a kid."

"Oh my God." Teddi set both hands flat on the table. "That is unacceptable. Our zoo is amazing. It's not huge, but it's lovely. I've always had mixed emotions about zoos—I don't love the idea of wild animals being in captivity—but our zoo is big on fundraising and sustainability and conservation. It works hard to help endangered species. And don't get me started on the aquarium part." As if realizing she was rambling, she blushed a bit and glanced down at her empty plate. "I did some research before I paid for a membership."

Her voice. Leah loved the sound of her voice. It was soft—she couldn't imagine Teddi raising it at all—and lilting.

"Hey, how are you ladies doing?" Their conversation was interrupted by Marisa Cannavale herself. She stood next to their table, white apron tied around her waist, thick dark hair in a ponytail, blue eyes sparkling, and even with flour dusting her hair and clothes and pizza sauce on her apron, Marisa was gorgeous. Leah stood up and hugged her old friend, who laughed and squeezed her back. "Careful, you're going to get flour all over you. How's the pizza?"

"It's amazing, as usual. Marisa, this is my friend Teddi Baker. Teddi, meet Marisa Cannavale, owner of this place and pizza maker extraordinaire."

Teddi reached out a hand and shook Marisa's. "I have never had a pizza this good. *Ever*. I swear to God. It's amazing." Leah could tell it was a totally honest statement.

"Well, that makes me incredibly happy." Marisa picked up the spatula and put another slice of pizza on each plate as she asked Leah, "Everything good? Your family?"

"Everybody's great. Kelly's getting married in September."

"What?" Marisa's eyes went wide. "Little tiny Kelly? Married? How did this happen? Isn't she still, like, ten years old?"

Leah grinned. "I know, right? In fact, Teddi here is Kelly's wedding planner. We were just discussing the zoo."

"And how Leah hasn't been there since she was a child."

Marisa gaped at her. "Seriously? Dude, go to the zoo. It's awesome."

"That's what I've been telling her," Teddi said, obviously happy to have an ally.

Marisa shifted her gaze to Teddi, then back to Leah, and Leah could see her mind working, testing out theories until she finally said to Teddi, "Totally with you on the zoo. The elephants are my favorite." Teddi's grin got bigger. "And please take good care of Kelly. She's the sweetest kiddo around."

"I promise," Teddi said with an unexpected level of seriousness, and Leah knew she meant it.

When Marisa turned back to Leah, those stunning eyes of hers almost seemed to hold knowledge, as if she'd figured it all out with just a quick scan. Leah felt herself blush as Marisa laid a hand on her shoulder. "I won't keep you. It was nice to meet you, Teddi. *Mangia.*" And she was off to another table.

"It's settled then. You're coming to the zoo with me." Teddi picked up her pizza, took a bite, and held Leah's gaze as she chewed as if daring her to argue about it.

"But it's winter."

"Wow. You are so much more than a pretty face. I had no idea."

Big grin. Huge.

"We'll just go to the inside parts and I'll show you my hangout." Teddi took another bite.

She seemed somehow more relaxed, Leah noticed, which was interesting. Her posture had lost the slight bit of rigidity it held, her shoulders dropping a bit. Even her face seemed to ease into an expression of comfort. Leah liked it and said so. "I like relaxed Teddi. Very much."

Cheeks coloring slightly, Teddi gave her a sheepish grin. "I'm glad to hear it. It can take a while for her to show up."

Leah took a bite of her pizza. She had a stupid grin on her face. She knew it. Could feel it. And she didn't care. There was nowhere on earth she'd rather be than right where she was.

Even though they polished off all but two slices of the pizza and nursed their wine in the hopes of stretching out the night, the date still had to end.

"I'm sorry we had to do this on a weeknight," Teddi said, voice laced with apology. "Saturdays are hard in my line of work."

"No worries. I completely understand." Leah wanted to add that she didn't care what day, she'd make the time to see Teddi, but she worried it might be too soon to go that far. Even for a lesbian. She opted for "I'm glad we were able to find a night that worked" instead.

"It's not every Saturday. I'm free sometimes."

"Good."

The waitress gave them each a box with one of the remaining slices. It took a brief argument, but Leah managed to snag the check. "I get the next one," Teddi said.

Next one? Doing a little victory dance in the middle of the restaurant crossed Leah's mind, but she somehow managed to keep control of herself.

The snow had stopped, but the cold air hit them like a slap in the face as they left the warmth of the restaurant and stepped out onto the sidewalk. Teddi hunched up her shoulders in her coat as they walked together toward the parking lot.

"Do you like winter?" Leah asked. "I'm asking because I figure if I keep my mouth moving, my jaw won't freeze shut."

Teddi laughed. "I actually don't mind it. Right now. But it's early. Ask me in March if there's still snow, and my answer will be different."

"Mine, too."

They reached the lot. "This is me," Teddi said, stopping next to a small white SUV six spaces from hers.

Leah stopped, too, looked off into the distance as she spoke. "I had a really great time tonight." Her gaze returned to Teddi, was captured by those dark, dark eyes.

"Me, too." Two simple words, but filled with so much.

They stood facing each other, inches apart, the night around them quiet and beautiful.

It was Leah's turn. She knew it. The flutters in her stomach had become waves, but she pushed her nerves aside, grabbed onto her courage with both hands, and leaned in, tilted her head up, touched her lips to Teddi's. Gently. Teddi's were soft. And warm, though how that was possible in thirty degrees, Leah wasn't sure. The only thing she knew was this kiss, and that she wanted more. Teddi must have felt the same way, as her hands came up, grasped the lapels of Leah's coat, and pulled her closer.

The kiss deepened. Lips parted.

Had the world fallen away last time? Because that's what happened as she leaned into Teddi, pinning Teddi deliciously between the car and Leah's body. There was nothing else. No other cars. No cold. No crunch of snow under the feet of other people in the lot. Only Leah, Teddi, and this kiss. Warmth and arousal and Teddi's tongue pressing into her mouth and *Oh my God, how have I never been kissed like this before?* It was sensual and erotic and so goddamned hot that Leah wouldn't have been at all surprised if her clothes ignited into flames. A jumble of hands and mouths and desperation of the sexiest kind, that's what they were, and when they finally wrenched apart, the clouds from their ragged breaths puffed up and floated into the night air, tattling on them. She stayed close to Teddi, noses nearly touching.

"Okay. Um." Teddi swallowed audibly, and the sight of her kiss-swollen lips in the glow of the parking lot light above them did naughty things to Leah's insides.

"Yeah. Agreed. Same."

How long they stood there was unclear. Leah thought it could've been five or ten minutes. Could've been five or ten years. She had no idea because all she could focus on was Teddi. But it was January and it was winter and the cold began to make itself known, as it always did.

"I should go," Teddi said, her voice barely a whisper.

"I know. Me, too." Leah lifted her hand, ran her thumb across Teddi's bottom lip, then pushed up on her toes and kissed her quickly. "If I kiss you any longer than that, they'll find us here in the morning, frozen solid."

Teddi's smile was worth all the money Leah had in the bank and more. "We can't have that."

"No. That's poor decision making."

A half shrug. "Might be worth it."

"Oh, would *totally* be worth it." Another beat passed as they smiled at each other. "Okay. Go. Please be safe."

"You, too. Text me when you get home so I know you're okay."

Why did that concern for her well-being wiggle into Leah's heart and make itself a home there? She stood there as Teddi backed out, then gave her a little wave and pulled onto the street. Leah watched her taillights disappear around a corner.

Pushing her hands deep into her pockets, she turned and headed toward her own car, the goofy grin she knew she wore feeling like it might be a permanent fixture.

She was totally okay with that.

CHAPTER THIRTEEN

These were the days of winter Leah loved the most. It hadn't snowed in nearly two days, giving the plows a chance to catch up and get things cleared, so driving was much less stressful. Lots of people out and about that Saturday, since the roads were wet and black and looked as clear and shiny as a plastic toy race track. The sky was a bright electric blue, and the sun made the snow sparkle like somebody had spent time sprinkling glitter everywhere. The whole world was bright and shiny, and Leah'd had to slide sunglasses on immediately or risk a headache from all the squinting. If winter was like this all the time, she'd be perfectly happy about it.

Amy's Bridal Shop was actually in a house, a pretty one. Leah didn't know anything about house styles—was it Victorian? Old English? Not a clue. But it was pretty, white siding and a big, open front porch with a gray wood floor and large pillars that still had Christmas lights and garland wrapped around them.

As she pushed through the front door, a little bell tinkled, and Leah kicked her feet gently against the threshold so as not to track any snow or salt onto the pretty area rug. To the left of the entryway was a large room—what would've been the living room had this been a family home rather than a commercial business—filled with mannequins in various styles of wedding gowns. A display of jewelry hung on one wall, and a large neon sign mounted above the fireplace read *Bride* in bright hot pink.

Her mother's high-pitched laugh cut through the air just as a woman came into the room, presumably in response to the bell. She had a big smile on her face and a bubbly energy that just rolled right off her.

"Well, hello there. Are you Leah?"

"I am. I can hear my mom back there." It made her grin, her mother's laugh. Filled her with warmth and, if she was being honest with herself, relief. There had been so many years, during and after her parents' divorce, when the sound was scarce.

"She and your sister are cracking each other up. I'm Amy." Her handshake was firm and quick. "Follow me."

Unprepared didn't seem to be a strong enough word for her response to the wave of emotion that hit the moment she entered the small, private room and saw Kelly standing there, her back to her. Up on a step. Large trifold full-length mirror in front of her. Gorgeous ivory wedding gown flowing down and around her as if she was some sort of goddess, a vision of pure angelic beauty. Her baby sister, now a grown woman, strong and smart and independent, and about to marry the love of her life. A lump formed in Leah's throat. A big one. She tried to swallow it down and brought her fingers to her lips in awe as her eyes welled up with so much love, it felt almost too big to handle.

Kelly met her gaze in the mirror and smiled tenderly. "Aw, Leah. Don't cry." But the tone of her voice was sweet and loving, not mocking or teasing. Kelly was touched, it was clear. She turned and looked over her shoulder.

Leah sniffed, wiped at the tear that had the audacity to spill over and course down her cheek. A dozen smart-ass comments flew through her brain before she sniffed again and whispered, "You look so beautiful."

"Doesn't she?" Their mother sat in a chair to the left, and Leah noticed that she, too, had tears in her eyes.

Leah shed her coat and took a seat in the empty chair next to her mom.

"You guys, this is only the second one," Kelly said. "You can't be crying over every single dress. What if I try on twenty-seven of them? You'll both dehydrate."

"Oh, no worries. I have plenty of water," Amy said with a wink. "And soda. And champagne."

"I knew I picked the right bridal shop," Kelly said with a laugh.

The mood sufficiently lightened, Amy brought out more dresses, and the fashion show continued for the next hour and a half.

By two that afternoon, the three of them were seated in Olive Garden, thank God.

"You were getting hangry," Kelly observed as Leah stuffed a bite of her second breadstick into her mouth.

"No kidding. I love you, baby sister, and initial emotion aside, I never want to watch you try on five dozen dresses again."

"It wasn't five dozen." Kelly waved a dismissive hand.

"Sorry. Four."

Their mother laughed from her seat across the booth, next to Kelly. With a bump of her shoulder, she said, "I'll watch you try on a million, honey."

"Thank you, Mommy."

Leah rolled her eyes in feigned irritation, but the truth was, she was ridiculously happy to be sitting there, just the three of them. The waitress arrived with their cocktails—after all, it was Saturday and they were celebrating something that, God willing, would never happen again. So drinks were in order. They placed their food orders and the waitress hurried away.

"I'd like to propose a toast," Leah said, holding up her vodka tonic. "To finding the perfect wedding dress in one day."

Kelly had a cosmo, their mother had Pinot Grigio, and the three glasses met over the center of the table.

Much was discussed over lunches of soups and salads and sandwiches. Work and houses and the holidays that had passed and wedding plans. When Kelly mentioned her next meeting at Hopeless Romantic, their mom held up a finger.

"Oh! That's right, I almost forgot. Guess who I ran into the other day in the grocery store."

Leah shrugged as she chewed. "I give up."

"Marisa Cannavale."

"Oh?" *Uh-oh.*

"She such a nice girl. We talked quite bit."

Leah nodded, knowing exactly what was coming.

"She said you were in her restaurant the other night with another woman."

More nodding. A large bite of breadstick.

Kelly watched but said nothing, a tiny but knowing grin turning up the corners of her mouth. She chewed her salad and waited.

"I asked what she looked like," their mother went on. "Sounded an awful lot like the wedding planner." The sparkle in her eye combined with the utter lack of surprise from Kelly told Leah loud and clear that her mother and sister had already talked about this. Probably at length.

Leah cleared her throat. "Okay, Nancy Drew. Yes, I had dinner with Teddi the other night."

"Was it a date?" Kelly asked and leaned slightly forward like she was waiting for secret information.

Leah hadn't felt like this in a long, long time. That mix of excitement over new possibility and the desire to keep it to herself for just a little while longer. She wanted to explode with how much she liked Teddi. But she was also thirty-nine years old. Old enough to know that one great date—and two amazing kisses—didn't necessarily guarantee a great love story, no matter how many romances she watched. Still. She could share a little, right?

"It was. Yes." She swore internally as she felt the heat crawl up her neck and knew her cheeks had colored.

"You're blushing," her mother observed, sealing Leah's suspicions.

"Yeah. Well." Warm vodka coated her throat.

Kelly studied her. Leah could feel her eyes without even looking at her. Her little sister knew her well, probably better than anybody, and Leah fought against the urge to squirm. Instead of asking more questions, Kelly simply said, "You keep us posted, yeah?"

That was weird, even though Leah was relieved, and she nodded. "I will." She wasn't ready to answer a million questions about her and Teddi. It was too soon and they were taking things slowly and she didn't want to jinx it.

Maybe Kelly sensed that.

❖

Stressful.

That was the only apt description Teddi had for her Tuesday.

The wedding planning business could be fraught with issues: unreliable vendors, clients who continually changed their minds, companies that went out of business, new trends, old trends. It was all to be expected. But when three or more of those things hit at once, even somebody as steady and calm as Teddi wanted to run away screaming.

Ten years was long enough to understand herself, to learn how her brain functioned. And this was a day when she needed to get away. Just for a short time—she wasn't abandoning her job or her clients or disappearing forever. She simply needed an hour or so away. It happened. She had places. Spots. Secret getaways where she could sit and chill and decompress until her brain calmed and she knew she could go back and face it all again without wanting to punch somebody in the throat.

Today was one of those days. And yet there was something different. Something she desired. A shift, a tweak, an experiment she wanted to try.

Before she could talk herself out of it, she picked up her phone and texted, *What are you doing for the next hour?*

Nibbling on the inside of her cheek seemed to be a good way to wait for a reply that she knew might not come immediately. There were any number of valid reasons why not, but she nibbled and waited anyway.

I can be free. Why?

Teddi had zero control over her smile. It bloomed all on its own. *Meet me at the entrance to the zoo?* More nibbling.

I'll head right over. See you there.

God, that was easy. Teddi felt her stress beginning to slide away already. Calling out to Preston that she was taking a break and would be back in ninety minutes, she grabbed her coat and pushed through the door out into the January afternoon. It took a few minutes to brush the morning's fresh snow off her car, but the drive to the zoo was quick and painless, the roads having been cleared nicely.

Winter and the middle of the week combined to make a rather empty zoo parking lot. Teddi was okay with that. She liked it that way. Not that she had any issues with kids running around, but it was nice not to have to crowd surf or dodge children who ran instead of walked. She got out of her car and saw Leah do the same several spaces away.

God, was it always going to be like this every time she saw Leah? Would there always be that tightening low in her body? That increase in her heart rate and breathing? That subtle tingle of excitement when her gaze rested on Leah's form? The simultaneous mix of lovely and freaky was something she wasn't sure what to do with.

"Hi," Leah said as Teddi approached. She looked…What was a good description? Words floated around in Teddi's head until she grabbed at a few. Elegant. In charge. Sophisticated. Beautiful. Dark pantsuit, boots with a slight heel, long black coat, black leather gloves.

"Hi. Thanks for meeting me. I hope I didn't pull you away from anything important." They fell into step together and walked toward the zoo entrance.

"Just some paperwork, and I will take any and all excuses to get away from that." Leah held the door open for Teddi as she added, "Not that I need an excuse to want to see you."

Teddi met her eyes, smiled, and turned away before that smile became too wide.

"That being said, one o'clock on a Tuesday afternoon *is* a rather odd time to show me the zoo…"

Gentle laughter bubbled up from deep within Teddi. "True."

"Hey, Ms. Baker," said the young woman behind the counter as they approached.

"Hi, Selena. How's school going?" Teddi took out her wallet, slid out her membership card. "Two of us, please."

"Last semester was great, but I'm dreading this one. They say the classes are really tough." Selena punched some computer keys, then handed the card back to Teddi. "Starts up again in a week."

"You're gonna do great," Teddi told her, then thanked her and gestured for Leah to follow her past the front desk and into the rest of the building. "Selena's a college kid who wants to be a marine biologist. She's worked here since she was sixteen. Good kid."

Leah nodded with understanding, then stopped in her tracks. "Wow. This is so different than what I remember."

Before them were two large doors. The one on the left led outside and to the mammal habitats. It wasn't a large zoo, but there was a lot to see. Tigers, elephants, rhinos, wolves, giraffes, lions, orangutans. To the right was the door to the indoor habitats. Reptiles, otters, penguins, seals, and Teddi's favorite place in the world.

"Come with me," she said, and held out a hand. Leah's was soft and warm, her grip firm, and Teddi didn't want to let go, a feeling that freaked her out just a little bit.

The lighting was dim through the doors on the right, blue. They walked along a dark hallway that suddenly opened into a huge area with glass all around. She turned to Leah, grinning. "Welcome to the aquarium."

Leah's green eyes were wide as she looked around, taking in the enormous tanks, the glass of the ceiling, and the underwater life that was suddenly everywhere.

"When I walk through those doors," Teddi said, gesturing behind them with the hand that was not still holding Leah's, "I feel an almost instant calm. I don't know if it's the blue light or the way the sound gets muffled or the peace of watching these beautiful creatures swim, or what, but I feel like my stress just melts away in here."

"I can see why." Leah craned her neck in every direction, let go of Teddi's hand and turned in slow circles, then walked up to the glass to get a closer look. Teddi sat on one of the benches like she always did, but this time, she watched Leah as much as she watched the sea life. Leah moved from wall to wall, tank to tank, obviously in awe. "The colors are…they're stunning. I always think of underwater things being gray and slimy, but this, this is just beautiful." After several minutes, she came and sat next to Teddi, laying a warm hand on her thigh. "What has you stressed?"

Those eyes.

Those gorgeous eyes of Leah's held such depth, such emotion. *You can read everything in those eyes.* It was a thought that came out of nowhere, echoed through Teddi's head, and somehow, she knew it to be true. And just like that, she had no choice but to be completely honest. She always wanted to be honest with Leah. And that thought terrified her.

"My job, while I love it, can drive me up the wall."

"I hear that."

"Today, I had a vendor make changes without approval, so I had to fight with them. I had a bride-to-be change her mind on her tablescapes—by the way, she gets married this Saturday. I found out one of my decoration vendors went belly-up yesterday, and I have three orders in with them. And I've got a caterer trying to raise his prices when he's already quoted my client."

"Yikes. That's a lot." Leah's hand was still on Teddi's thigh. Teddi hoped it stayed there. Forever. A small group of kids filtered into the space, increasing the noise level a bit, but there were only five of them, and their two chaperones kept them occupied by pointing out different sea creatures. Leah's hand stayed on Teddi's thigh.

"None of it is unusual, but when it all hits at once? Yeah."

A beat went by and then Leah said, "I can see why you come here." She glanced around with a happy expression on her face. "Even with other people here, it's so peaceful. I might have to borrow it from you from time to time."

Teddi leaned in to her. "I'll happily share it with you."

"You're kind."

And then they sat. Together. Thighs touching. Leah's hand still in place. Shoulders brushing. They sat in silence that wasn't at all awkward or uncomfortable. It was the opposite, in fact. Comforting. Content. *Right.* How could that be?

Teddi pushed the thought out of her head. She was here to relax, to feel calm, not to get her brain all revved up. Slow inhale through the nose. Long exhale out the mouth. She did it again.

"Are you meditating?" Leah leaned in and asked.

God, she smells good. Teddi swallowed. "Just doing my best to chill."

"It's definitely not hard to do here. You weren't kidding about that."

More questions, more observations ran through Teddi's head, and she squeezed her eyes shut for a moment, willed them away. Out. Gone. Slowly, she opened her eyes again. The stingray swam by, huge and imposing and sleek, and the little kids gasped, Leah's small intake of breath also audible. And just like that, everything was fine. Teddi's body relaxed—she took a deep breath, her head quieted—because this was right. Leah next to her, touching her, the two of them connected. It was perfect.

"How do you feel?" Leah's soft voice broke the silence, but not the spell. Not the feeling of contentedness Teddi had. She smiled.

"Much better. Need to get back?"

Regret was plain on Leah's face. "I'm afraid so."

Teddi nodded. "Me, too. Gotta face the problems and take care of them."

They stood together, put on their coats, and headed back the way they came. Comfortable silence reigned as they buttoned and bundled on the way out. It had started to snow again, and Teddi pulled the hood of her wool coat up to protect her hair. Leah walked close by her side, and Teddi enjoyed the feeling of her presence.

Leah's car was first. "Start it," Teddi said, "and we'll brush it off while it's warming up."

They worked together, and then Leah said, "Now you." They moved down the row and did the same thing with Teddi's car. By the time they finished, both cars were clear of snow and warm.

Leah opened Teddi's driver's side door and held it so Teddi could get in. Once she was settled, Leah leaned in and gave her a quick peck on the lips. "Thank you for inviting me here. It was something I didn't know I needed." She stood back up, told Teddi to drive safely, and shut the door.

Teddi sat there in her warm car and watched Leah walk back to hers. She didn't hunch against the snow or cold. Rather, she walked confidently, head held high, the gentle sway of her hips catching Teddi's eye and holding it. A ripple of surprise ran through her as she realized that if she could jump out of her car and coax Leah back into the aquarium to sit there with her for the rest of the day, she totally would.

A slow lean forward, and her forehead rested on the steering wheel.

"Oh, this is bad," she whispered into the quiet of the car. "This is so, so bad."

CHAPTER FOURTEEN

Stoicism. Leah was good at it. She had to be in her line of work. Most of the time, her job was done in an office with her client. It wasn't often that she had to meet with both her client and the person they were divorcing, but it did happen on occasion. This Friday morning had been one of those instances where the husband—not her client—called his soon-to-be-ex some horribly offensive names and said terrible things to her. To the point where his lawyer, who was a friend of Leah's, looked positively mortified and finally had to cut the meeting short, dragging the husband out by the hood of his coat.

Leah's client sat there for a moment. Quiet. No tears, but a look of sheer pain on her face. Leah stayed with her in silence—not wanting to remember the fights her own parents had had, but unable to control that—until the woman shook herself into movement again. Reassurance was what Leah had to offer, and she gave it, promised her there would be a fair division of the marital assets, no matter what the husband seemed to think. Her client nodded, tried to smile, understood that it was going to be okay. But underneath it all, Leah could see the pain. The hurt. The confusion over how she could've possibly loved somebody who would hurt her that badly. It was a thing Leah had seen many times, on her mother's face so long ago and on those of her clients almost every day, and she still had little to offer in the way of help. All she could do was be supportive and do her job. So she was, and she did, to the very best of her ability.

Back in her office and eating a salad at her desk, Leah gave herself some time to decompress. Meetings like that could take a lot out of her, and she'd learned over the years to take a few moments to just breathe. She stabbed a cherry tomato with her plastic fork and checked her phone.

The group text that included her, Tilly, and JoJo had new messages—they wanted to go out to dinner Saturday night. Kelly reminded her that she'd promised to go visit the florist with her next week. Her mother texted just to say hi. The fourth text was the one that made a smile creep onto her face.

Was thinking about you as I ate my lunch. Thought I'd say hi.

A few seconds went by. Then another text. *Hi!* With a smiley emoji. Teddi.

Leah typed back, *Hi! I'm eating my lunch, too. Hope yours is more exciting than my salad.*

She chewed a bite of lettuce, wished she had more dressing, when the response came: *Wish mine was pizza. I've been craving.*

A smile. More typing. *You got a wedding tomorrow?*

Yep.

What about Sunday?

A few beats went by, then, *I'm free on Sunday. I'll be beat from the wedding, but...* Teddi left the sentence hanging. The gray dots bounced. Then they went away. Returned. Bounced. Went away. Bounced. Leah was ready to scream when the words finally appeared: *I'd love to see you.*

Leah's face blossomed into happiness. She could feel it. Wet her lips. Typed before she lost her nerve. *Come to my place. We'll watch a movie. Order pizza. Just chill.*

A few seconds passed. A few more. Leah stabbed a cucumber slice. Chewed. Stabbed another tomato. And then it came: *Yes, please.*

Leah gave a whoop and shot her arm into the air in victory. The tomato flew across the office and rolled to the shoes of her secretary, who stood in the doorway, amusement on her face.

"Sorry, Greta," Leah said sheepishly and wrinkled her nose.

"Hey, if tomatoes are flying, good things are happening." Greta picked up the tomato and carried it to the trash, then handed Leah the file she'd asked for earlier.

Good things are happening.

They were. They really, really were.

❖

It was rare that Hopeless Romantic handled two weddings on the same day. Or it was rare *now*. Back when she'd had three locations, it was fairly common. But now that her business was smaller, she usually kept it to one wedding per Saturday. There were exceptions, though, like today. January 25 was a popular day this year for whatever reason, so she was handling one wedding, and Preston was heading up the other.

Things had run very smoothly. The ceremony had gone off without a hitch. Harlow had taken all the family photos and was now floating around after dinner, taking candids and scene shots. Teddi hovered in the kitchen, making sure the caterer had things under control, watching out the small window to keep an eye on things while she took a break.

"Here." Her friend Debbie was the head of Deets Catering, and they'd known each other, worked together, for several years now. Debbie shook her head, the beaded ends of her braids clicking together, as she arched an eyebrow and handed Teddi a plate. Chicken salad on a wheat roll. "I got Drake working on the leftover chicken and I haven't seen you eat a thing. As usual." She pushed the plate at Teddi. "Eat this. I don't want to have to carry your ass out of here because you fainted from hunger."

Teddi took the plate and a grateful bite of the sandwich as Debbie got back to work. Goddamn heaven on a roll. She hummed in delight. A hand in front of her mouth as she chewed, her eyes met Drake's across the kitchen. "You seriously *just* made this?" The chicken salad was tender and savory, and tiny bits of celery gave it some crunch. "It's fantastic." Drake gave her a shy smile and a nod of thanks.

She finished the sandwich in no time flat and shot Debbie a look of gratitude as she pushed through the door and back out into the venue. Friends who knew her that well—she was lucky to have them.

"Hey, there. Nice shindig you threw here." Harlow sidled up next to her and they stood and watched.

"Not my first rodeo." They stood side by side for a moment and watched an obviously drunk uncle dance like he thought he had moves. The bride rolled her eyes, but her smile stayed in place. "Bride's not about to let drunk Uncle Al mess up this day for her."

"I was just thinking that," Harlow said. As they watched, she asked, "How are things?"

"Things?"

Harlow turned to look at her, arched an eyebrow. "Really? We're playing this game, are we?"

A grin she had no control over. A drop of her chin to her chest. "Fine. You're right." The dance floor was lit in shifting shades of pink, purple, blue, and white light, and Teddi let her gaze roam out over it as she searched for words. "Things are...things are good. I think."

"You think?"

"Well, we're taking it slowly, and that seems to be something we sort of mutually agreed on without actually saying it."

"You still relaxing about it?"

Internally, Teddi snorted, but she stayed outwardly calm. "I am."

"And? How is that working?"

Slow nodding. A flash of Leah's smile. That warm, pleasant feeling in her gut. And lower. "It's working."

"You slept with her yet?"

Teddi shook her head. When Harlow made no comment, she turned to meet her gaze. Which was infuriatingly *knowing*. "What?" She didn't snap the word, but it was close, as she reconsidered the joys of having friends who knew her so well.

"Oh, nothing. Just the last time you waited was—"

"Don't say it."

"Julia."

"You said it." Teddi poked the inside of her cheek with her tongue.

"Don't get mad at me. I'm just pointing out facts." Harlow's voice softened. Well, as much as it could to still be heard over Lizzo's pumping beat. She reached out and rubbed her hand down Teddi's upper arm. "I've said it before, you obviously like her."

"I do." She had no qualms about saying that. It was true and there was nothing wrong with it. *What's not to like about Leah?*

"And you've been able to move past the whole divorce-attorney-of-your-ex thing?"

No hesitation with this nod. She really had been able to let that go, and she was proud of herself for it.

"Good. Then I say keep doing what you're doing." Harlow paused, and when Teddi met her eyes, she smiled tenderly. "Because you look great. You look happier than I've seen you look in a long time."

Teddi's blush was probably not plain to see in the dim lighting, but it was there. She felt the heat of it. The joy of it. The smile that blossomed across her face without her permission or control. Because Harlow was absolutely right. She reached for her friend's hand and squeezed it. "Thank you."

"Who knows?" Harlow said as she gazed out over those who still remained of the 250 wedding guests. "Maybe we'll be planning one of these for you down the road."

Teddi barked a laugh. One sarcastic *ha!* "No way. I'm never doing that again."

Harlow turned surprised eyes her way. "No?"

"No, ma'am. Once was enough, believe me."

Harlow nodded and returned her focus to the dancers. She lifted her camera and took a few shots but said nothing more.

"Why did I have the impression that you didn't cook?" Teddi asked. She was seated on Leah's kitchen counter, wineglass in hand, feet swinging gently, watching Leah stir.

"I really don't, but let's be honest. It's hard to mess up chili." She tapped the wooden spoon on the side of the pot, then put it in the black spoon rest her mother had given her and set the lid back on it. "A few more minutes," she reported, then turned so she faced the counter behind her, took two steps, and positioned herself between Teddi's legging-clad knees. "I like you on my counter."

"I like being on your counter."

Kissing. Kissing happened then. Lots of it. Leah loved kissing Teddi more than she even had the words to describe. Everything about it was incredible. Teddi's lips were the softest, and they melted into Leah's like they were meant to. Teddi's mouth was warm and she always tasted so good. Today, it was a mix of wine and just…Teddi. Leah moved her hands around Teddi's hips to the small of her back and slid her closer as Teddi's fingers dug into Leah's hair.

What was that rattling?

The sound was far away at first, though that was probably just Leah's awareness, which was elsewhere. But finally, it registered, and she reluctantly—very reluctantly—wrenched her mouth from Teddi's.

The top to the pot of chili. That was the source of the sound.

They blinked for a moment, breathing hard, cheeks flushed.

"I..." Leah jerked a thumb over her shoulder in the direction of the stove. "Chili."

Teddi nodded, and when she wet her bottom lip, Leah groaned and kissed her again. Hard. Which led to more kissing, which led to full-blown making out.

The rattling continued.

This time, Teddi pulled away—or as far away as she could get while sitting on the counter wrapped up in Leah's arms. "Your chili's gonna burn."

Leah nodded. "Okay." She pecked Teddi quick and turned to the stove.

"I'm going to use the little girls' room."

"Up the stairs and to the right. It's the one with the toilet in it."

"Funny." She felt Teddi's arms snake around her from behind and give her a squeeze. A kiss pressed to her head. "Be right back. Don't drink all my wine."

"I make no promises," Leah called as Teddi left the room. Then, quietly, "Jesus Christ, that woman's going to kill me soon." She shifted her hips, trying to adjust the damp spot in her panties she was suddenly *very* aware of, and knew she was grinning like a fool as she stood there stirring her nearly burned chili. Forcing herself to calm down, she inhaled deeply and held the breath. She was just exhaling when Teddi returned.

"There's a spider in your bathroom."

Leah snapped into focus. "You didn't kill her, did you?"

"Her?" Amusement. That was the best word to describe Teddi's expression right then.

"Yes, her. That's Angelica."

Teddi tilted her head. "The spider has a name?"

Leah turned the burner off, then reached into a cabinet for bowls. "Normally, I would scoop her up and let her go outside, but as you can see"—she gestured toward the window with a flourish, where snow could be seen falling steadily—"it's winter. She'll freeze. So we have an understanding."

"I see." Teddi refilled both their wineglasses. "And that understanding is?"

"She doesn't drop on me while I'm in the bathroom, crawl on me when I'm sleeping, or have a thousand babies in my house, and I won't squish her or toss her out in the snow."

"Well." Teddi's dark gaze sparkled. Yeah, that was definitely amusement. "That seems fair." She took a sip, then said, "It's a good thing she's up in the high corner or I'd have squished her myself."

Leah let out an exaggerated, horrified gasp. "You *monster.*"

They laughed together, dished out the chili, added cheese and sour cream, and grabbed corn bread.

"So," Leah said. "We have options."

"Hit me."

"We can eat at the table like civilized women. Or we can eat on the couch while watching TV like Neanderthals."

"Oh, Neanderthals, definitely. Let's be those."

"Neanderthals it is."

A few minutes later, they were sitting side by side on Leah's couch, their bowls, wine, and bread on the coffee table in front of them. Remote in hand, Leah said, "It's four o'clock. Any requests?"

"Surprise me."

"You sure? Because we will very likely end up on the Hallmark Channel, which should have a movie starting right about now, and I know how you feel about romance."

Teddi looked at her then and something flashed behind the darkness of her eyes, but Leah couldn't quite place it. Insult? Agreement? Challenge? Hurt? "I would *love* you to put the Hallmark Channel on." Leah squinted at her until Teddi laughed. "I mean it."

"Okay. You asked for it." Leah hit the right buttons, then set the remote down and dug into her chili as Teddi did the same. The movie was a Valentine's Day one from last year that Leah recognized and remembered liking very much.

"This is amazing," Teddi said of the chili. "Like, seriously good."

It made Leah happier than it should have, and she couldn't keep that stupid grin from reappearing. "Thank you. I'm glad you like it."

They ate in silence until Teddi pointed her spoon at the TV. "So, she's had her heart broken and needs to go home to the small town where her parents live so she can heal." At Leah's nod, she continued. "I bet you a million dollars she runs into her high school sweetheart."

"I suppose that's possible." It was exactly what was going to happen, but she didn't even care that Teddi had called it. *I mean, let's face it, it's not hard to call these plots.* She waited for Teddi's snide comment or subtle mocking, but it didn't come. Yet.

Gathering the empty dishes, she stood. "Be right back." She took everything into the kitchen, rinsed and deposited bowls and spoons into the dishwasher. When she returned to the living room, Teddi was on the couch under a black fleece blanket, and she'd left room behind her for Leah.

"Come cuddle under the blanket with me while we watch."

Because she wasn't an idiot, Leah slid right into the space. Teddi scootched her butt along the couch cushion and settled her back against Leah's front, their legs side by side, with the blanket over them. Wrapping her arms around Teddi's body, well, Leah didn't even have words to describe the feeling. It was so many things all at once. Delicious. Terrifying. Wonderful. Nerve-racking. Sexy. And absolutely perfect.

Lizzie suddenly appeared out of nowhere and jumped up onto the couch. "Hi, kitty," Teddi said and reached out a hand.

"Careful. That's Lizzie and she's moody." Then Leah watched in shock as Lizzie nuzzled Teddi's hand for a moment, allowed head scratches, then curled up on Teddi's lap and began to purr.

"Yes, I see that she's horribly moody." Teddi craned her neck so she could grin at Leah.

"Well. She doesn't like many people. Sometimes, she doesn't even like me. Seems you passed her test. Whatever it is."

"Good." They settled back into each other, Lizzie continuing to purr loudly as Teddi petted her softly and turned her attention back to the movie. "Called it," she said a few minutes later, pointing at the screen where the leading lady had just run into her old high school boyfriend. Then she picked up Leah's hand from her stomach and entwined their fingers, gaze still on the movie. "Okay, those two have chemistry. I admit it. I see the sparks. I see 'em."

Leah smiled and dropped a kiss on Teddi's head, inhaling the scent of lime and coconut. Without success, she tried to remember the last time she felt this comfortable.

And this comfortable with silence. Neither of them spoke a lot during the movie. A chuckle here and there or an offhand comment, but for the most part, they watched together in silence. Surprisingly,

Leah was totally okay with that because she had Teddi in her arms, the warmth of her body pressed against Leah. Lizzie hung out for a while, then hopped off the couch, probably to have some cat adventure Leah knew nothing about.

The movie went on telling its story in that romance formula way that Leah loved and that haters complained about. She kept waiting for the ribbing. The gentle teasing about how predictable it was. It never came, though, and when the movie reached the end, Leah was shocked to see a few tears trailing down Teddi's cheeks. She had so many things she wanted to say then—and yes, some would qualify as ribbing or teasing—but she said nothing. Instead, she gently wiped a tear away with her fingertips and tightened her hold on Teddi.

After another moment, Teddi sat up and turned to face Leah. "Okay. Fine. I loved it." And then she laughed. A beautiful, musical, sheepish laugh as she wiped her cheeks, sniffled, and Leah thought she'd never seen a more stunning woman in her life. With both hands, she reached for Teddi's face and pulled her in, kissing her with everything she had. She poured it all in. The passion. The desire. The hope. The joy. Everything Teddi made Leah feel went into that kiss, and she was sure Teddi felt them all as well because Teddi melted into her embrace so thoroughly that it became almost impossible for Leah to feel where she ended and where Teddi began.

The movie ended. A new one began. Probably. Leah had no idea and didn't care. The kissing. That was all she cared about. The kissing and the touching and the sounds. Good God, the sounds. Tiny whimpers. Ragged breathing. Leah was so turned on, she thought she might burst into flames.

After a long while, Teddi slowly pulled back until they were no longer kissing but still very close. Still entwined. Still breathing the same air. Her dark eyes seemed to search Leah's. Was she looking for something? Trying to make a decision? Did she want to ask a question? Leah tilted her head slightly but said nothing. Waited her out until Teddi finally shifted her gaze toward the window.

"It's snowing," she said quietly. "I should go."

"Or you could stay." The words were out before Leah could even think about them. Chewing on her bottom lip took the place of trying to pull the words back into her mouth.

"I could, but…" Teddi swallowed hard. Leah tried not to stare at her swollen lips, tried not to think about how sexy they looked, and that they were swollen because of her. "Not yet. Is that okay?"

Leah met her eyes then, and what she saw—uncertainty, worry, hesitation—made her want to cover Teddi with her body and keep her safe from the world, be her human bubble wrap. "Of course it's okay. Why wouldn't it be okay?"

"I mean…" Teddi sat up, swung her legs off the couch so she was sitting properly on it. "Some people don't want to wait."

Leah mimicked her moves, and they sat side by side. "Listen." She picked up Teddi's hand in hers and toyed with her fingers, felt the soft skin of them. "Do I want to make love with you? Oh my God, absolutely, there's nothing I want more. Do I look like a stupid woman?" Teddi grinned and things suddenly felt a little bit lighter. "But I want it to be right. For both of us."

"Me, too."

"I think we'll know when it is."

"Me, too."

"Okay. Good talk."

Teddi's smile grew until her whole face had relaxed and the seriousness clouding her eyes drifted away.

They sat there for a moment, playing with each other's hands, letting their shoulders brush, feeling the warmth of their closeness. Finally, Teddi sighed. "I really should go before the roads get bad."

Leah nodded. "Agreed. I don't want you getting caught in bad weather. I want you safe." She met Teddi's gaze. "Precious cargo."

Teddi leaned in and kissed her softly, then pushed herself to her feet.

They acted very much like a couple already, Leah mused. She held Teddi's coat for her as she slipped her arms in. Using her key fob, Teddi remotely started the car and Leah insisted on going out ahead and brushing the snow off it, despite Teddi's protests. By the time she finished, the windows were clear, the car was warm, and Leah grabbed a shovel and cleared the sidewalk from the house to the driveway so Teddi wouldn't have to trudge through it. Once Teddi was safely in the driver's seat, Leah bent to kiss her.

"Drive safely. Please text me when you're home."

"I will." Gloved hands on the steering wheel, Teddi stayed focused on them for a beat, then turned to look at Leah. "I had an amazing time today. Thank you."

"The pleasure was all mine, believe me."

"Next time, I cook for you."

"I look forward to it." Another quick kiss on the lips, one more plea to be careful, and Leah shut the door and stepped back. Teddi gave her a wave, then backed out and headed home.

Leah stood watching until the taillights were gone from sight. She continued to stand there for an extra few minutes. The snow fell softly in big, fat flakes, and the street was fairly quiet. Leah tilted her head back and stuck out her tongue like she had as a child, caught snowflakes, felt the happiness of such a simple joy. She felt light. Cheerful. Even the thought running through her head didn't scare her, and maybe it should have. Maybe she should've been terrified. Worried. Putting up walls. Instead, she just felt warm and happy and couldn't wait to see what was next.

I'm gonna fall so hard for that girl...

Chapter Fifteen

I can't believe I haven't seen you since Christmas, Theodora." It was a gentle statement but laced with subtle accusation designed to bring about guilt. And it worked. Every time. Teddi's mother was a pro at subtle accusation, and Teddi was a pro at letting herself drown in it, so they made a fantastic team.

"I've missed you, too, Mom." She hugged her mother tightly.

"Happy birthday. What are you now? Forty-five?"

"Ha. If only." She took the wrapped gift Teddi handed her. "Honey. I told you no gifts."

"And my mother taught me never to show up at somebody's house empty-handed."

"A smart woman, your mother. If you don't believe it, just ask her."

Teddi laughed, kissed her mother on the cheek, and headed into the large dining room where her father and two brothers sat around the table, which was set for a birthday celebration. The plates were paper, but festive, decorated with black and pink *Happy Birthday*s, streamers draped over the chandelier, a bunch of helium balloons in various colors floating in the corner. She could hear her two sisters-in-law milling around in the kitchen as she went around the room, kissing and hugging the guys. When her mother came in from the kitchen with a glass of white wine, Teddi took it gratefully, then took the same chair she'd sat in since she was old enough to sit at a table unassisted.

"You guys need help in there?" Teddi called toward the kitchen.

"Nope, all good," came the reply from Liza, her brother Doug's wife.

Warmth, love, comfort. Those were things you felt any time you walked into the Baker house. Any friends she had ever brought home always told her that. People loved to visit. They loved her parents. And what was there not to love? They were terrific people.

"What's new, Teddi Bear?" John was forty-seven, five years older than Teddi, and he'd given her the nickname when their parents had brought her home all swaddled in a blanket with bears on it. His kindergarten brain had seen the bears, listened when her parents suggested Teddi as the shortened version of her name, and just like that, she became his Teddi Bear. It drove her crazy when she was a teenager, but now, she kinda loved it.

"Not much," she told him. A plate of her mother's homemade chocolate chip cookies called to her and she reached for one. "Busy at work. Valentine's Day is next week."

"You hear that, John?" Ginny called out to her husband from the kitchen. "Valentine's Day is next week."

John, sitting across the table from Teddi, shook his head with a grin. Then on a whisper, he said, "Thanks for the reminder, Teddi." A wink.

Teddi gave him a thumbs-up just as the lights dimmed and Liza came in carrying a cake that blazed with candles. As they sang "Happy Birthday," Teddi watched her mother's face, the huge smile, the joy in her sparkling brown eyes. She was seventy-five now, and as much as Teddi wanted to always see her parents as young and vital, it wasn't possible anymore. Sure, they were both reasonably healthy, but their age was starting to show in the speed they moved, the extra caution they took on stairs or icy sidewalks, the television shows they watched. She loved them so much, and the little girl in her wanted to have them forever, while the adult in her knew that was impossible.

Singing finished, they cut the cake and the room became a hum of conversation.

"So," her mother said, grasping Teddi's forearm as she spoke. "How are you, love? You doing okay?" Sometimes, Teddi thought her mother was the only one who understood her pain, the pain of failure, the shame of sitting in a room with the whole of your very married family and feeling miserable.

"I am," Teddi said, and realized with a bit of surprise that she meant it.

"Yeah?" Her mother held her gaze, and Teddi was instantly nine years old again, having lied about stealing a Snickers bar from the store, squirming under that steady gaze until she cracked, burst into tears, and admitted that yes, she was a thief. Then she begged her mom not to call the police or let them take her to jail. This time, though? No squirming.

"Yeah. I'm actually..." A glance around the table to see that others were busy with their own conversations. Teddi lowered her voice. "I'm kind of seeing somebody."

Her mother's eyes went wide, and her whole face lit up. As she opened her mouth to speak, Teddi grabbed her hand and squeezed.

"Please, Mom. I'm not ready to share it yet. Okay?"

Crestfallen was the only word to describe her mother's expression then, but she recovered quickly. "Okay. But"—she held up a finger—"we need to grab lunch this week so I can hear all about her. Deal?"

"Deal." They took out their phones and set up a date for Friday. "It'll have to be a quick lunch. I've got a wedding the next day I need to prepare for."

The evening went on, filled with laughter, jokes, and love. It didn't last long, as it was a school night and everybody had to work the next day, but the whole time she sat there, Teddi pictured Leah sitting next to her. Squeezing her knee under the table. Talking about her cat with Ginny, who had three. Connecting with her dad over working in the business world and dealing with clients who thought they knew everything.

Bottom line: Leah would fit right in, and her family would adore her.

That realization warmed Teddi's heart and terrified her. In equal measure.

❖

Leah hadn't seen Teddi in over a week, and she had to admit, it was starting to grate on her. They'd both been ridiculously busy with their jobs, so it wasn't anything more than that keeping them apart, and they'd texted daily, which was great. But now it was nearly eight on a Thursday night, and Leah was still in her office working instead of cuddled on the couch—or something better—with the woman she was very quickly becoming crazy about.

The ping of her phone startled her in the quiet of the night, and Leah flinched as she reached for it. Speak of the devil...

Still at work? Teddi.

Unfortunately, yes. How are you?

The bouncing dots. Then: *I sent you something. Did you get it?*

Leah furrowed her brow. *You did? I haven't seen anything.* What was she talking about?

Left it with your secretary.

That was weird. It was very unlike her secretary not to let her know she had a delivery, despite the fact that Leah had closed her office door to get some quiet. In this job, timing was super important, so every delivery was handled immediately. Even personal ones. *Hang on,* she typed. *Gonna check.*

Muscles protested as she stood, letting her know she'd been sitting way too long. Leah allowed herself a moment to stretch her legs and reach her arms over her head. Wow, everything felt so tight.

Shrugging her shoulders up and down as she moved, she crossed her office and opened the door to see if there'd been anything left on her secretary's desk—and stopped in her tracks.

"Oh my God." She blinked several times, then literally pressed her fingers into her eyes because she didn't trust what she was seeing.

"Hi," Teddi said, enormous smile on her face, a small thermal bag on her lap and a plastic grocery bag by her feet, as she sat primly and properly in one of the chairs in the waiting area.

Leah was hit with so much at once. Absolute joy, disbelief, low coping skills because of how tired she was. Her eyes filled with tears as she returned the greeting. "Hi, baby." Her voice cracked.

"Oh no." Teddi stood quickly, set down her bag, crossed to Leah. "This is supposed to be good. Not make you cry." She laughed softly and wrapped Leah in her arms.

Thanking her stars above that she was able to not openly sob, Leah held on to Teddi, let herself sink into the feel of her warm body, take in the scent of her perfume—something woodsy and deep today—absorb the fact that she'd traveled to Leah's office at night in the dark, in the snow and cold, to bring her... "What's in that bag?" she asked, pointing at the couch.

"Oh." Teddi let her go, grabbed the bag, unzipped it. "I brought you some stew."

"Seriously?"

"Well, you said you were going to be working late, and I know you have a habit of either not eating a decent meal for dinner or, better yet, not eating at all, so I decided to bring you some of the stew I made for myself." She made a worried face. "Do you even like stew?"

"It's eight at night and I'm still at work. I haven't eaten since..." Leah stopped and squinched up her face to think. "Since I can't remember when. It's cold and snowy outside. What's not to love about stew? Especially if you made it and then sent a hot chick to deliver it to me."

Teddi's face brightened. "Good." A few minutes later, in Leah's office, she had dished out thick beef stew—which was still hot, thanks to her thermal bag—into a bowl she'd brought. From a smaller plastic bag, she pulled a foil-wrapped package that contained two thick slices of what appeared to be homemade bread. Also still warm.

Leah sat at the small table in her office and just stared. Awed. And a little bit in love, though she kept that to herself. "This..." She shook her head slowly as she picked up a spoon. "This is amazing, Teddi. Thank you so much."

Teddi smiled, shifting on her feet as if she'd suddenly become slightly uncomfortable.

"You okay?" Leah asked. A spoonful of stew and lots of humming followed. "This is friggin' delicious."

Teddi was slowly wandering the office, hands clasped behind her back, looking at the various photos and framed certificates and such placed around the room.

"Teddi?"

"Hmm?" Teddi turned that gorgeous face to her, eyebrows raised in question.

"I asked if you were okay. You're kind of quiet." Leah watched her carefully, watched as she seemed to school her expression.

"I'm fine. It's just a little weird to be in this building." Teddi didn't look at her, just continued to peruse.

For a moment, Leah was puzzled, but then it hit her. "Oh! Oh, right. I didn't think about that." And she hadn't. "You were never here, though, right?"

A shake of the head. "No, but I became very acquainted with the address from all the paperwork. Plugging it into my GPS was surreal in a way."

Leah wasn't sure what to say or how to act or what to think, so she stayed quiet. Ate her stew. Watched Teddi's orbit around the room.

"Is this your dad?" Teddi asked, holding up a frame.

"Yeah. From graduation."

"You don't talk about him much." Teddi turned her head, met her gaze.

"True. He lives downstate with his new wife and her kids. I don't see him very often."

"No? How come?" The photo back in its place, Teddi sat down across from Leah.

Leah dipped her bread, bit, chewed slowly. There never seemed to be a quick and easy edit to the story of her dad, but she liked to do bullet points, so to speak. Maybe because of her job. *This, this, this, and here we are.* Teddi leaned her forearms on the table, her interest obvious, her attention steady. "He and my mom split when I was young and Kelly was tiny. It was super messy. My mom had never really worked outside the home because my parents married young. I think she had a cashier job at a grocery store when she was in school, but once they married, she was a housewife. It was all she ever wanted to be, a mom who stayed home and took care of her family. So when my dad decided he wanted out of the marriage and left, he took the income with him. Sure, there was child support—which he complained about incessantly, always a great way to make your kids feel wanted—but no alimony. He had a great lawyer, and my mom did not. He left my mom, my sister, and me with very little. We ended up having to move, change schools, go on public assistance for a while. My mom had never had a job and suddenly had to find one. She was a wreck for a while, and I did my best to hold it all together while my dad was gallivanting and *sowing his wild oats* because he'd never had a chance to." She made air quotes as she rolled her eyes.

"Oh, Leah, that's awful." Teddi's expression had changed, a divot forming above her nose as her eyes studied Leah. "I'm so sorry."

"It was rough. But it also helped me plan my future." *How to say this, how to approach it?* Leah chewed on the inside of her cheek for a moment. "I always wanted to be a lawyer, but seeing what my mother went through made me sure. I wanted to help people that were in her position. I wanted to make sure that divorces were…" She hesitated, but pushed on. "Financially fair." She clenched her jaw and waited. For an outburst? The storming out of the office? She wasn't sure.

Teddi sat quietly, scraped at a spot on the table with her thumbnail. Finally, she said, her voice quiet, "I get that." A subtle nod. "I get it."

Leah chose her words carefully. "It's not about punishment or taking sides—though, believe me, I've seen enough horrible people to *want* to take sides—but it's about fairness. Plain and simple."

More quiet from Teddi, who gazed off into the middle distance. Leah slowly ate the rest of the stew as she waited.

"Sometimes…" Teddi's voice was barely above a whisper, and Leah got the strangest feeling that listening and understanding her were very important in that moment, so she set down her spoon, wiped her mouth, and simply focused on the gorgeous woman across from her. "Sometimes, you just need time, I guess. Or a person to walk into your life at just the right moment? I don't know." Back to the spot on the table. "I was pretty sure I'd never be able to get past my divorce. It wrecked me. I didn't want to meet someone new. I didn't want to date. It was fine. I was fine. Bitter at times with everything a little dimmer than it was, but fine. And then you walked in, and things suddenly started to light up a little bit. And then I realized who you were, and I was pretty sure I'd never be able to get past the role you played in my disaster."

Leah swallowed, not at all sure which direction this was going. Heart hammering in her ears, she folded her hands together and white-knuckled them.

"Look, I don't know if you were meant to show up when you did or if I was meant to have this crazy attraction to you or how the hell it was all meant to go. What I do know is that my attraction, my feelings for you have grown and eclipsed everything else. You were doing your job. That's all. Julia wasn't happy and needed to get out. That's all. I created a successful business and she helped me do it. That's all." Those dark eyes were wet now as Teddi settled her gaze on Leah's. "It's time for me to let go and move forward, and I *so* want to. I'm *so* ready to. With you." As soon as she closed her mouth, her eyes went wide, as if she couldn't believe what she'd just said. As if the words had escaped on their own, and she'd been powerless to stop them, and now she was completely freaked out.

They sat in silence for a beat, the only sound in the room the ticking of the clock on Leah's wall and the distant, barely audible clacking of a keyboard that told them somebody else was also working late. How did Leah feel? Surprised? No, that was too gentle a word. Stunned was more like it. She reached a hand across the table, captured Teddi's, which was cool, slightly clammy, and Leah felt a tremble run through it.

"I can honestly say when I opened the door and saw you sitting there, I was surprised and thrilled and so glad to see you, but never in a million years did I expect things to go down this path."

Teddi wet her lips but said nothing, and Leah could tell just by looking at her face, just by feeling that tremor still running through her, that she was bracing, and Leah wanted only to let her off the hook. Wipe that worried expression away.

"There is nothing more I want than to walk that path with you. I've never felt like I clicked with somebody the way I click with you. Despite our differences. Despite the fact that you make fun of my rom-coms." That got a smile. She waited until those deep brown eyes were locked on hers before she said the next thing. The big thing. "Let's find out where this goes. Wanna?"

Leah searched for words to describe the way Teddi's face lit up, the enormous grin that blossomed on it, the sparkle that appeared in eyes so dark, the color that flushed that smooth skin, but nothing seemed expressive enough. Instead, she stood up just in time to catch Teddi in her arms, and it didn't matter that Leah was shorter, smaller. It didn't matter at all because she held on tight. She held this woman, this beautiful, kind, trusting woman in her arms and vowed right then and there that she would never, ever do anything to hurt her. Ever.

"God, I didn't really plan to come here and spill my guts like that," Teddi said, still in Leah's arms, as she covered her eyes with one hand. "I'm not a mushy person, and that was *way* mushy."

"I like mushy," Leah said. "Mushy is good. I'll take mushy any day."

"Well, don't get used to it. I'm a hardass, you know."

"If you say so."

And then came the kissing. And it was different somehow. Deeper. More important. They hadn't exactly made promises to each other, but Leah knew they'd come close. She'd been with Teddi long enough to know that she didn't go around pouring her heart out to any woman on the street. This was big. This meant something. *She said she has feelings for me.* This was leading them in a very specific direction...

Stop. Stop it right now.

Not wanting to get ahead of herself—or jinx anything—she focused on Teddi's mouth instead. The warmth rapidly turning to heat. The softness that was also firm. The way Teddi's hands held her face, again with the soft but firm. Leah gripped Teddi's waist, her fingers clutching the silky fabric of her top.

There really was nothing in the world like kissing Teddi. Leah became sure of it right then, in the moment Teddi pressed her tongue into Leah's mouth and she was sure her entire body had melted. Gone boneless. That Teddi's hands on her face were the only things keeping her standing as electric arousal shot through her veins, through her very being. Lost. That's what she was. Lost, in a good way. Lost in that kiss, in that heat, in that woman.

My God, when we get there, we're going to set the bed on fire.

Soon. It was going to have to be soon. Leah wouldn't survive otherwise. But it couldn't be now. Not here in her office. Not now when she had a big case to prepare. Reluctantly—so reluctantly!—she gently broke the kiss but stayed close, stayed holding tightly to Teddi's body. It didn't seem possible for Teddi's eyes to get any darker, but they were nearly black as she looked down at Leah, her face completely flushed pink, her chest rising and falling fast.

"If it was any other night..." Leah began.

"I know. Me, too."

"Sunday? Maybe?"

"Sunday definitely. Come to my place?"

"Deal."

More kissing, sporadic kissing, as they gathered Teddi's things and Leah helped her into her coat, walked her into the admin area. One more kiss—this one lingering—and Teddi was gone.

Later that night, when Leah was finally in bed and replaying the evening—which she'd done about a thousand times so far since Teddi'd left—she remembered that last conversation. How they'd spoken in a sort of shorthand about Sunday, both knowing exactly what the other meant. Leah tried to think of any time in her life when she'd been around somebody who got her that easily. Who understood her thoughts. Who would likely get to a point where they finished her sentences.

Never.

That's the last time she remembered that happening. It was never.

She rolled onto her side and felt Lizzie's tiny paw smack at her foot before Lizzie settled in the crook of Leah's knees and began to purr. Her eyes grew heavy.

That night, she dreamed of make-out sessions, sex-tousled dark hair, and beef stew.

CHAPTER SIXTEEN

Saturday lunch with the girls was always different—i.e., better—than lunch during the workweek, simply because there was more time and relaxation. Nobody had to hurry back to work. They could drink if they wanted. Everything was casual and comfortable. Bonus: Today, JoJo didn't have to get home to her kids because they were spending the weekend with her mother.

The Blackbird was a neighborhood bar and restaurant, something you might pass up as you drove by, but was actually full because people who lived nearby knew how good the food was. Leah had found it by accident one day and suggested it for a lunch, and now it was in their regular rotation.

"How are things with Little Miss Social Work?" JoJo asked Tilly as their meals arrived. Tilly blinked rapidly and looked down at her plate, which made JoJo gasp. "Are you blushing?" She turned to Leah. "Did you see that? Am I imagining it?"

"You are not. That was definite blushing. Judges?" Leah looked around the restaurant at the other patrons, who were paying her zero attention. "Yes. Yes. The judges say definite blushing was seen."

"Fuck both of you," Tilly said, but a half grin was forming on her face.

"Oh no, sounds like that's reserved for the tiny girl." JoJo was having way too much fun, and Leah couldn't help but laugh.

Tilly made a *way* exaggerated horrified face. "How dare you?"

"Please. You were merciless when I first started dating Rick."

Leah watched her friends go back and forth in sheer happiness.

The zingers always hit home, but were never mean. And never less than any of them deserved or had given to another at some point.

"I like her," Tilly said, and her voice was quiet enough that JoJo and Leah exchanged wide-eyed looks. "She gets me."

"Really? So she's a psychological genius in addition to the social work?" JoJo sipped her dirty martini and grinned over the rim.

"Funny." Tilly took a slug of her beer. "I don't know how to explain it. Jen just…we fit. You know?"

"Oh my God," Leah said and sent another shocked glance JoJo's way. JoJo looked the way she felt.

"What?" Tilly said, looking from one to the other in confusion. "What?"

"Her name is Jen." Leah leaned forward. "You rarely give us a name. Of anybody you've dated."

"What? That's not true." Tilly made a face. Scoffed.

"*Rarely*," JoJo said.

Tilly blinked at them, and Leah could almost see her going through her brain, through the people she'd dated in the past, trying to figure out if her friends were right.

They were and Leah knew it. She reached across the table and grasped Tilly's arm, gentled her voice. "No more teasing. We're just so glad things are going well for you. And *Jen*." She emphasized the name.

"No more teasing for the moment," JoJo clarified as she popped a French fry into her mouth. "*For the moment*."

For half an hour, they talked about Jen, and Leah was so happy for Tilly that she tingled. Tilly dated. Both men and women. And while there had been one or two that had lasted longer than a few months, Tilly had never been so obviously happy. It was nice.

"What about you?" Tilly asked as she and JoJo both turned to her. "How are things since the big New Year's Eve kiss?"

Leah tried to hide her grin and looked down at what remained of her salad.

"Oh my God, *both* of you? *Both* of you are blushing today?" JoJo's volume went up enough for a few patrons to glance at them, and Leah swiped at her with her napkin as JoJo laughed. "Your turn. Dish."

"Okay, but be nice to me. I'm freaked out enough."

"We're always nice," JoJo said.

Leah shot her a look. "I mean it. No teasing, or this conversation is canceled."

JoJo looked at Tilly, who shrugged, then sighed. "Fine. No teasing. God, you two take all my fun."

"Thank you." Leah sipped her beer, took a deep breath, and dove in. She filled them in on everything from New Year's Eve forward. The pizza date. The aquarium. The movie watching at home. She ended with two nights ago when Teddi had come to her office with dinner in a bowl and her heart in her hands.

"We've been taking it really slow, just being relaxed. Taking our time. But that—I didn't expect that. And it was…" She shook her head. "It was amazing."

"Sex?" JoJo asked. The waitress arrived with her second martini, raised her eyebrows, then left.

"Not yet, but…" Leah hesitated.

"But what?" Tilly wiped her mouth with her napkin and slid her fork and knife onto her plate, a clear sign she was finished.

"But…probably tomorrow."

"Oh?" JoJo leaned forward, her eyes almost comically bright.

"It's killing you not to pounce, isn't it?" Leah arched an eyebrow.

"You have no idea." JoJo visibly clenched her teeth, and Leah laughed.

"Sundays are good days for her because she usually has a wedding on Saturday, and if it's an evening one, which it often is, she works late." She paused, sipped. "She asked me over tomorrow."

"For sex." JoJo stated it, didn't ask.

"Well, she didn't *say* that, Jo."

One raised shoulder. "It's implied, though."

Leah wanted to argue, but JoJo wasn't wrong. After the discussion in her office, the invitation did kind of imply more. Didn't it? Or was she way overreaching? Seeing things that weren't there.

"You look worried." Tilly's brow was furrowed, expression serious.

"Nervous," Leah corrected, then grimaced at the admission.

"Oh, man," JoJo said, eyes a little wide. "You *really* like this one, don't you? That's why you're doing the whole slow burn thing."

Leah had been trying not to think about exactly that, but she'd failed spectacularly. Because it was there. It was definitely there. And it scared the hell out of her. Instead of replying, she simply looked from JoJo to Tilly and back again.

"Oh, sweetie, it's fine," JoJo said and reached across the table, making Leah wonder what expression her face was making that her friend was suddenly all mushy and gentle. "It's all going to be fine."

JoJo's voice was soothing, her expression positive. Tilly was... well, Tilly—stoic and hard to read, but with a ghost of a smile. JoJo was right about one thing, though: Leah liked Teddi. A lot. And maybe it *was* all going to be fine and she was way overthinking it all. All she knew for sure was that she couldn't wait for tomorrow. She already had those anticipatory flutters in her stomach, and she had another twenty-four hours to go, at least.

Was Teddi having the same thoughts?

❖

Every now and then, a wedding would make itself known as a Murphy's Law Wedding: Everything that could possibly go wrong would. Saturday's wedding wasn't quite that bad but had more crises than an episode of *Grey's Anatomy*, and Teddi felt like a firefighter, running around putting out fires all over the place, dragging a heavy hose behind her.

The day had been sunny and crisp, but the wedding was an evening one, and by late afternoon, the wind had picked up, clouds moved in, and snow began to fall, whipping around and causing drifts that made driving a little dicey. In the bridal room, the bride stepped into her dress, fastened it up, and the bodice was just loose enough that she was worried her girls would give an unexpected appearance the second she moved. A meltdown came next, complete with bridesmaids doing their best to calm her so as not to ruin the makeup that had taken over an hour to apply—something Teddi never understood, even as a woman who could appreciate a smooth foundation and a lifesaving under-eye concealer. Luckily, a distant cousin was a seamstress and, once located and brought to the bridal room, was able to work safety pin magic and secure the boobs from possible escape. A groomsman had been overserved and had the entire staff looking for the lost wedding bands until they finally found them in his inside jacket pocket. The minister was late. The DJ forgot a very important cable and then mispronounced the groom's name, even after being coached.

But now Teddi stood off to the side and watched the daddy-daughter dance in relief. As she finally felt herself calm down, her shoulders drop, she watched her client, this young woman she'd met with for nearly a year, helping her organize, take care of scheduling, make difficult decisions, as she swayed in her father's arms, both of them teary with enormous smiles. Across the dance floor stood the groom, also watching, also smiling.

The scene must've nudged something in Teddi, loosened a couple of the screws she'd used to fasten a lid on the emotions surrounding what she'd done on Thursday night. When she'd left Leah's office, she'd felt like she was floating, like her shoes were little jetpacks, zipping her along without her having to make any effort.

That lasted until she'd gotten home.

Then she'd panicked. And the questions had hit.

What the hell was I thinking?

How stupid am I?

On what planet was that a good idea?

And back to *What the hell was I thinking?*

She was a smart girl and none of this confused her. She knew exactly why that panic had set in: vulnerability. Since the end of her marriage, she'd taken that, packed it up in a lockbox, and put it away on a high, high shelf, vowing never to open it.

Ha.

The panic and the questions plagued her all day on Friday, even as she texted back and forth with Leah, spinning around in her head like the numbered balls in a bingo cage, until she thought she'd scream. And then something strange happened.

She saw Leah's face in her mind.

Not just her face in general, but her face when she'd opened the door of her office and seen Teddi sitting there. The way it had gone from exhausted and flat to lit up and smiling. She saw Leah's face as Teddi had sat there and poured out her heart like a sap. Leah hadn't looked at her like she was a sap, though. She'd looked at her with excitement, and—

if Teddi hadn't mistaken what she'd seen—an element of admiration, as if Leah understood completely that Teddi didn't normally do that, didn't normally slice herself open and let somebody see inside.

Once that had happened, once she'd had a clear reminder of how Leah looked at her, all the panic, the nerves, the internal freak-outs had simply dissipated like dew on the grass on a summer morning.

And now, as she stood there watching two newly married twentysomethings dancing and laughing and totally in love with each other, she was able to take a deep breath and just enjoy it.

To the right, Teddi could see Harlow precariously balancing on a chair, snapping photos, using the DJ's red, blue, green, and yellow lighting to create some gorgeous ambiance and mood shots. She knew this from experience. Harlow was the best she'd ever seen, and she went to extremes to get the best shots. After Harlow got what she wanted, she headed over and stood next to Teddi.

"Too bad there are no trees in here for you to climb," Teddi teased, thinking back on an outdoor wedding two years ago that had featured Harlow in a giant oak, way too many feet off the ground.

"Hey, did you see that shot? Totally worth nearly breaking my neck."

"Your husband didn't think so."

"Yeah, well, in my defense, you weren't supposed to tell him."

They stood side by side, watching as things wound down and guests began to trickle out. Another hour and it would be safe to start breaking down the venue.

"How are things?" Harlow finally asked, and Teddi knew exactly what she meant.

"This seems to be when we talk about that subject, doesn't it? When we're waiting for a wedding to die down."

Harlow smiled her agreement. "It's a good time to talk to you. All the pressure is off, no more stress—you're just chilling."

"I see your point. And things are going well. She's coming to my place tomorrow." Teddi did her best to remain steady, keep her usual resting bitch face the same as always, but something must have given her away because she could actually feel Harlow's eyes on her. She waited as long as she could before it began to drive her crazy. "What?"

Harlow shook her head, bit down on her lips, and failed miserably at hiding a grin. "Nothing. Nothing at all." To prove her point, she lifted her camera and took a couple random shots of the dance floor. Lips still rolled in, smile still not very stifled.

To her own surprise, Teddi grinned back. Even softly laughed. And then her whole body flushed with heat and anticipation.

Leah was coming over tomorrow.

CHAPTER SEVENTEEN

Turning in a slow circle in the middle of her living room, Teddi gave things a final once-over. She'd vacuumed the area rug and even used the long, skinny nozzle to get into the cracks and corners of the room. She'd dusted everything, her very least favorite chore in the entire world, and one she really should think about doing more often given the amount of crud on her dust cloth. She unfolded the fluffy purple blanket and refolded it.

The doorbell rang.

Inhale deeply through the nose. Out through the mouth. A takeaway from the three yoga classes she'd taken last year, but it definitely worked and helped her feel more centered.

Here we go.

"Hi." Leah stood on the front steps looking super cute in her casual winter attire. Snow had fallen last night, but today was clear, sunny, and very cold. Leah's ski jacket was a bright blue, a white knit hat on her head that Teddi wondered if Kelly had made. Low boots on her feet, her white mittens cradling a bottle of wine. Those green eyes were bright, sparkling, and her excitement to be there was apparent. Teddi felt her entire body relax at the sight.

"Come in. It's freezing." Teddi stepped aside as Leah entered the foyer, stopping to give Teddi a quick peck on the lips.

"Hi again."

Pounding heart, heated cheeks, nerves and joy racing each other for dibs in her head. That was Teddi in a nutshell. "Hi," she said back. "Here, let me take your stuff." They went through the whole shedding of outer garments that was a regular routine of winter in the northeast. "You know, I don't mind winter, but I hate wearing sixteen layers in order to go outside."

"Like, why can't winter just be warmer, right?" Leah's eyes crinkled at the corners whenever she smiled, and Teddi realized in that moment how much she loved those laugh lines.

"Exactly. I don't think that's asking a lot. Do you?"

"Not at all. Should be an easy fix. You just need to get your request to the right people."

Teddi hung Leah's coat in the closet, hat and gloves tucked into a sleeve just like her mom had always done. "Well, I happen to know a great lawyer, so who knows?"

"My God, it smells good in here." Leah lifted her nose, still red at the tip from the cold, and followed it in her socked feet to the kitchen. She wore faded jeans worn through at the knees and a simple green crewneck sweater that made her eyes pop. "What is that? Heaven? Is this what heaven smells like?"

"If heaven smells like roasted chicken with rosemary, then yes."

"I hope this goes." Leah handed over the bottle of wine. "I like to drink wine, and I know the names of what I like, but I am completely uneducated in what goes with what."

"Pairing."

"Yes. That." Leah pointed at her and their gazes held as the kitchen clocked ticked softly. "I'm so happy to see you."

"I'm really glad you're here." Teddi stepped into Leah's space because she simply couldn't not be next to her any longer. Leah's arms slipped up and around Teddi's neck just as their mouths met. The kiss was sensual, but the heat index ratcheted up so quickly, Teddi was surprised they didn't burn each other. Oh yeah, they were so going to have sex tonight. Teddi knew it, could feel it in her bones—and other places low in her body. If they could wait that long. When Teddi finally broke the kiss, it was only because she really needed to check on the chicken.

"Corkscrew?" Leah asked, and Teddi indicated a drawer as she donned oven mitts and tried not to stare at Leah's swollen lips.

They moved around each other in the kitchen like they'd done so for years, which blew Teddi's mind a little bit. She remembered trying to maneuver around the kitchen when she was with Julia, how they'd bump into each other constantly, how Julia was always exactly in Teddi's way. Not so with Leah. They sidled by each other, turned sideways here and there, never once bumped or had to stutter-step.

Once the wine was poured and the chicken was sliced and plated, the two of them sat at Teddi's square bistro-style table to eat. She had placed the table settings across from each other but noticed Leah had slid hers over one chair so they were closer together. No argument there, as they sat and Leah's knee pressed against hers.

"I'm so glad you're here," Teddi said for the second time as she raised her glass.

"I'm so glad *you're* here," Leah said and touched her glass to Teddi's.

"Well, since this is my house and I live here..."

"You'd be here anyway."

"Pretty much, yeah."

Gazes held. Happy expressions stayed. Leah leaned over, pressed her lips to Teddi's, then sat back before the kiss could take on a life of its own. "I want to say I'm not surprised by this table setting, but my God, woman. It's just me. You didn't have to go to all the trouble. This is gorgeous."

Teddi looked at the table. Charcoal place mats, black chargers under her deep red plates. Black linen napkins and hammered silver utensils. Wineglasses with red accents. A gray slate vase in the center, with a lovely combination of dahlias and zinnia in red and white. It was a beautiful setting, if she said so herself. "Oh, this was no trouble."

Leah's expression screamed skeptical.

"I'm serious. This is just regular for me."

"Oh, so I'm not special, I'm just regular?"

"You are *so* not regular to me. Trust me." It was another moment that held them, that cranked the sexual tension in the room up yet another notch, along with Teddi's arousal. She wondered if Leah was feeling it, too, but was afraid to ask.

"Well. I like knowing that. You are also very irregular to me." Light brows furrowed adorably. "Wait..."

"Ah, I see how it is."

"Let me rephrase."

"Overruled."

"Are you trying to lawyer-talk a lawyer?" Leah pointed her fork at Teddi.

"I am because I watch a lot of *Law & Order*, so I probably know as much about the law as you do. Is it working?"

"It's amusing, I'll give you that."

"Amusing is good. I'll take amusing."

More held gazes, and when Leah's finally slid away, it went south first, to the peek of cleavage Teddi knew her white V-neck sweater revealed. Another notch up on the tension scale. Teddi wondered how long it would be before she simply burst into flames right there in her chair.

Perhaps wondering the same thing, Leah picked up her fork and knife and cut into her chicken.

Okay. We're eating. This is good. Teddi followed suit.

Dinner went quickly and was delicious, if Teddi said so herself. Leah solidified that with continual hums of joy and delight as she chewed, along with constant compliments about how good everything was. And while neither of them spontaneously combusted, the level of sexual tension stayed high enough to keep Teddi perpetually wet.

They cleaned up together, again, as if they'd been doing so for years, sidling expertly past each other, working in a rhythm that felt more natural than things had ever felt with Julia. Kind of freaky, if Teddi was honest.

"I thought maybe we'd just relax and watch a movie or something," Teddi said as she wiped her hands, then folded the dish towel over the handle of the oven.

"Cuddle on the couch?" Leah asked, and the hope in her eyes made Teddi laugh.

"I'd like that."

They settled the other way this time, with Teddi in the back, Leah's smaller form between Teddi's knees, leaning back into her. Alarmed and amazed was the weird mix Teddi felt at their perfect fit. She could probably sit there forever, just like that, Leah's warmth in her arms, Leah's hair close enough to her nose that Teddi could smell the scent of strawberries and a hint of vanilla…

"What should we watch?" Leah's soft voice yanked Teddi back to the topic at hand.

Handing Leah the remote, she said, "You choose."

"Oh, dangerous. You know where I'll go."

"I do. It's okay, I'm braced."

The channel surfing began, and it was instantly obvious that Leah was a channel surfing pro. She zipped through channels and made decisions in less time than it took Teddi to register what was on.

"Um, are you trying to send me into a seizure?" she joked.

"Listen, you've got to keep up. I can't help it if your brain is way slower than mine." Leah barked a small cry and then laughed when Teddi squeezed her knees together, giving her a little smoosh. The surfing stopped as Leah said, "Oh," and drew the word out softly. "Have you ever seen this?"

"What is it?" Teddi vaguely recognized one of the women onscreen.

"*Imagine Me & You*. It's a romantic comedy with two girls."

"I hardly knew there was such a thing."

"Yeah, that's the problem. This one is really good, though. What do you say?"

"You're the expert here. I trust you." That last sentence felt almost loaded, like it had dual meanings, and Teddi realized that it did. She trusted Leah to find something for them to watch. Of course she did. But also, she trusted Leah. Period. A hard swallow followed that mental statement.

Leah hadn't been kidding about the movie. An hour and a half later, Teddi was completely invested in Rachel and Luce, and when they stood on top of cars to shout their commitment, Teddi's eyes filled with happy tears.

"Excuse me, but are you crying?" Leah had craned her neck around so she could see Teddi's face. "You? The romance hater? You're crying over a romance?"

"Shut up," Teddi said, wiping the traitorous tear that had spilled over and left a wet line down her cheek.

Leah turned slightly, and her expression softened. "Oh, honey. I'm sorry. I was just teasing. Honestly, I'm really so happy that it touched you."

"Well, it did." Teddi probably sounded like a child, but Leah only smiled bigger.

"You are so cute, you know that?"

"I am?"

"Yeah, but you're also…" Leah shifted her position so she sat up enough to turn all the way around and face Teddi. Leaning closer, she whispered, "You're also super hot."

"Is that so?" Teddi barely got the words out before Leah's mouth was on hers, and Teddi absently thought how makeout sessions on couches were apparently their thing now. A thing they did very, very, *very* well.

She sank into the kiss. Teddi had heard that phrase before, sinking into a kiss, but had never really understood it. Until then. Until that moment on that couch with that woman. Like a bolt of lightning hit her and completely lit up the meaning, made it inarguably clear. *This right here? This is how you sink into a kiss. This.*

Leah pushed herself up so she was nearly lying on top of Teddi, who didn't mind because it gave her better access to Leah's mouth. A playful battle ensued, tongues moving, exploring, plundering. Leah's body was warm, and when Teddi slid her hands up under the back of Leah's shirt, hit skin, they both sucked in air, stopped for a moment. Leah gazed down into Teddi's eyes, and there was so much there. So much that was beautiful and sexy. So much that scared the bejesus out of Teddi. With her fingertips, she touched Leah's lips, traced them, top first, then the bottom, marveled at how full they'd become after they'd kissed, how pink and luscious.

"Maybe we should take this to the bedroom," Teddi said softly, then hid her own surprise at the words that had come out of her mouth all on their own.

"Maybe we should." Leah's eyes had gone dark, heavy-lidded, her cheeks rosy.

Yeah, this is happening.

Teddi was so there for it.

❖

Leah wasn't even a little bit surprised by the pristine nature of Teddi's bedroom. It was ivory with slate-blue accents and black furniture. The comforter and the myriad of pillows on the bed were all ivory, with the exception of three of the pillows in blue. The floor was hardwood, with a thick ivory area rug in the center. A chair in the corner was ivory with a slate-blue afghan folded neatly over the back. Everything seemed new. Fresh. Clean.

Leah wanted nothing more than to mess it all up.

Also not surprising, since that was one of the first thoughts she'd had about Teddi when she'd realized the depth of her attraction. *I want to grab on to that put-together, neat and tidy exterior and mess it the hell up, leave her all disheveled and breathless.* The thought hadn't changed. Seeing Teddi's room only made it intensify.

Teddi led her across the room to the bed, stopped at the edge, and took Leah's face in both hands. Teddi seemed to be looking for something in Leah's eyes, searching for…what? Permission? Leah didn't make her wait. She pushed up on her toes and met Teddi's warm mouth with hers.

There was something different now. Leah had felt it on the couch and she was pretty sure Teddi had as well. That moment when she'd stopped, gazed into Leah's eyes, run her fingers across Leah's lips— there had been something in her face, in her eyes, that Leah'd never seen. Not so much a defeat as a relaxing. A surrender.

Now that they were in Teddi's room, literally standing next to her bed, the intensity, the sexual tension between them was almost too much to bear. Leah could feel it in every inch of her body. Her heartbeat pounded everywhere. Her chest, her head, her fingers, her center. With curiosity, she laid her palm against Teddi's chest and felt hers as well. Steady, but definitely pounding.

"I think we're both nervous. I know I am," Leah confessed. "Are you?"

Teddi tucked some of Leah's hair behind her ear, let her fingertips dance down the side of Leah's neck. "I'm nervous, but I'm not scared."

"Me neither." A lie, on both their parts. Leah could feel it. In fact, it helped ease her mind a bit knowing Teddi was afraid as well. It was okay to be afraid. After tonight, nothing would be the same. Leah knew it. She felt it from the tips of her toes to the top of her scalp. *Nothing* would be the same. And she was all in. She was so all in. "We can go slow."

"Okay." Teddi's word did not match the kiss she then crushed to Leah's mouth. Not slow. Not slow at all. Not gentle. Not even a little gentle. Hard. Demanding. And so incredibly sexy, Leah was sure her heart was going to explode right out of her chest. That would certainly mess up the room.

Teddi turned them so Leah's back was to the bed and gave her a tiny nudge so she fell onto it. Teddi followed right after, pushing Leah's thighs apart with her knee and settling her weight carefully onto her.

"Am I hurting you?" Teddi whispered.

"God, no," Leah said, and to show how much Teddi was not hurting her, she pulled her down more firmly, shifted her own body so Teddi's hips fit snugly between her legs. "I have just decided I love feeling you on me like this."

"Yeah?"

"Absolutely."

"Good." Teddi kissed her again.

Maybe it was because they were so good at it, so good at the kissing, but as much as Leah wanted to move things forward, wanted to feel more than Teddi's mouth, she simply lost herself in the kiss. Was it feasible to say you could have a perfect match for kissing? Because that was her and Teddi. Their mouths slid together sensually. Their tongues teased. They knew when to tilt their heads and which way, and they did so seamlessly. Everything about this kiss was ultra hot, and Leah couldn't get enough. She kissed Teddi with everything she had, only wanting to be deeper into her, literally and figuratively.

That's when that desire for more finally won out.

Leah wasted no time or energy pulling Teddi's sweater off. "This sweater has been teasing me all night." Teddi's grin said she was perfectly aware of that fact. Efficiently over Teddi's head and onto the floor in no time flat went the sweater, and then there was Teddi. Topless, in a white lace bra that fit perfectly with the rest of her room, because of course it did. Which was why Leah reached around back, unclasped it, and tugged it off.

Now this is the definition of sexy.

The thought screamed through Leah's brain as Teddi hovered over her on all fours. Dark eyes that had gone impossibly darker took her in, held her gaze. Small breasts, right there for Leah to touch, which she did, with both hands. She kneaded each one slowly in her hands, almost cried out at the softness, felt Teddi's nipples harden in her palms. She zeroed in on them, rolled them gently with her thumbs and forefingers, then a little more firmly when she heard Teddi's breath catch. A very subtle rhythm began, Teddi's hips lightly pushing into Leah's center, pushing the ridge of her jeans into her most sensitive spot, until Leah groaned.

"These need to come off," Teddi said, running a finger under Leah's waistband.

"They really, really do."

The rest of the clothes came off fast, almost comically so, and Leah smiled as she whipped off the last of her outfit. When they were both naked and kneeling on the bed, facing each other, time seemed to stop. Teddi was beautiful. It wasn't like Leah expected anything less, but Teddi's naked form, kneeling there, waiting for Leah to touch her, actually, literally, took Leah's breath away. Felt as though she'd stopped breathing, didn't inhale for what seemed like a long time. She simply looked. No—stared. She stared at the body in front of her that was nothing less than gloriously female. All smoothness and curves and softness…

And then Teddi was on her.

Suddenly. Surprisingly. Leah felt her own arousal surge to off-the-charts status and Teddi's tongue plunged into Leah's mouth and her body ignited. Leah reached for her, for her breasts, tried to slide a hand between her legs, but Teddi caught both her wrists and pinned them above her head in a devastatingly sexy display of dominance. Teddi's face was mere inches from hers. They breathed the same air in ragged breaths. Teddi simply looked at her, held her gaze in the most delicious eye contact Leah had ever experienced.

And then Teddi said the sexiest line Leah had ever heard in her life, whispered, "You're not in charge right now."

If Leah was ever going to burst into flame, it would've been then. She heard herself gasp, had just enough time to before Teddi crushed their mouths together, pushed her hips into Leah's aching center, and everything blurred after that for Leah.

Teddi was everywhere. Leah lost track of what were hands and what was a mouth. Tongue and fingers and teeth and hips…they all melded into one giant web of sensation. Leah had never been at anybody's mercy in bed, but then? On that night? Teddi could've done anything she wanted. Leah had no willpower, no strength, barely any brain function. She was one large organism of pleasure. It was all she felt. Teeth teased her nipples to almost-pain, hands kneading her breast, a mouth sucking in as much of her flesh as it could. Fingernails scratched down her sides, hard enough for Leah to hiss air in through her teeth but not enough for her to protest, because it honestly ratcheted her arousal even higher. And when Teddi quietly ordered her to keep her hands were they were, still above her head, and Teddi's mouth closed over her, over the very core of her and sucked hard, Leah was sure the top of her head would simply blow off. All that blurred sensation, all the pleasure melted together suddenly focused, met in one spot, and Leah felt every single thing Teddi did to her down there. The shift from combined sensation to very specific pleasure was unexpected, and Leah wondered if she'd survive it. But if she didn't? What a way to go.

Teddi teased her for a while. *Was* it a while? Or was it mere seconds? Leah honestly didn't know, but her body was moving on its own, undulating, writhing. She obeyed orders and kept her arms above her head but found pillows to grab, to hold on to for dear life, until Teddi finally zeroed in on the exact place Leah needed her, as if she'd known where it was all along and had been taking the scenic route.

Leah unraveled.

Shouts. Cries. Screams. None of those had ever been parts of an orgasm for Leah. On the contrary, she was fairly quiet in bed. But that night, sounds were ripped from her throat that she hardly recognized as her own voice. One hand gripping the back of Teddi's head, the other holding a pillow over her own face so she didn't wake the entire neighborhood, Leah came hard. Hips raised up off the bed, taking Teddi with them, every single muscle in Leah's body tightened, and colors exploded behind her eyelids like fireworks.

Time became nonexistent. Leah finally opened her eyes with no idea how long she'd been recovering, and there was Teddi. Gentle smile. Dark, inviting eyes. Tousled waves of deep chestnut hair. And the dimples. God, those dimples. Looking down at her like that. Just waiting patiently until Leah found herself again. It was the most beautiful sight Leah had ever seen, and she reached a hand up, laid her palm against Teddi's cheek as if she wanted to hold the moment, literally, in her hand.

"Hi," Teddi said, then kissed her softly on the mouth.

"Hi yourself," Leah whispered. "Also, oh my God, that was incredible."

"Yeah?" Something passed quickly across Teddi's face. Worry? Uncertainty? Was that even possible from a woman as confident and put-together as Teddi Baker?

"As soon as I can feel my limbs again, I intend to show you exactly how incredible."

"So you're saying if I'm patient, you'll make it worth my while?"

"Worth your while and then some."

"Oh, I like the sound of that." Teddi lowered her mouth to Leah's, and that kiss suddenly recharged Leah's everything. Flex, push, press, and Teddi was on her back, looking up at Leah with those big, expressive eyes.

Leah made it totally worth her while. Totally.

CHAPTER EIGHTEEN

Teddi was pretty sure Leah hadn't intended to stay the night. After all, it was Monday morning, and not being her own boss like Teddi, Leah had to get to work at a certain time. But it had snowed overnight, and it was cold, and they'd been not only toasty warm all hunkered down in Teddi's bedding, but it had been close to two in the morning before they'd given in to the need for sleep. Teddi could've gone all night long—Leah's body was that captivating, as were the sounds she made, her responsiveness to Teddi's touch—but instead, she'd set her alarm for six thirty and wrapped Leah up in her arms.

Cuddling while sleeping wasn't something she was used to. Julia had never been a snuggler. No reason other than it just wasn't her thing. She didn't need, crave, physical touch like Teddi sometimes did, and Teddi had learned to get along without it. Unless they were having sex, she and Julia had rarely had any physical contact. Leah was different. The polar opposite, in fact. She slept wrapped around Teddi like a spider monkey. Arms around Teddi like vines. Leg tucked between Teddi's. Head either on Teddi's shoulder or up against her back. The biggest surprise? Teddi didn't hate it. In fact, she kind of loved it. She'd woken up twice and simply grinned in the dark at the feel of the woman so securely wrapped up in her, she wondered if Leah actually had more than two arms and two legs.

Way too soon was when the alarm went off, but just-waking-up Leah was even more adorable than wrapped-around-you-like-ivy Leah. Green eyes blinked. Muscles stretched. A huge grin formed as a good morning was croaked. And while Teddi would've loved to keep Leah in bed with her for several more hours, she also knew Leah needed to get up for work. Leah decided to shower in Teddi's bathroom, then run home to change, so after a quick kiss and a long hug, Leah hit the shower and Teddi slid her arms into her fleece bathrobe and went to the kitchen to make coffee.

It would not have been hard to lose herself in replays of last night. It sounded silly, she knew, but she'd never had sex that good. Ever. In her life. It was as if she and Leah knew all about each other's bodies. Where to touch, how much pressure, when to stop teasing and allow release. Teddi's sexual energy had seemed endless; she wanted to touch Leah, make her come, watch and listen as she did, forever. And when Leah had turned the tables, Teddi felt like she was being worshiped, like Leah couldn't believe her good fortune. That's how Leah made her feel. And when Leah'd pushed her fingers into Teddi... She closed her eyes briefly and lost herself in the feeling again. As the coffee brewed, she stood silently, watching the snow fall outside the window, and relived every moment of the previous night, the throbbing between her legs becoming insistent, until the coffeepot beeped to announce the end of its brewing cycle and yanked her attention back to the present.

Coffee poured and doctored, she carried both cups back to the bedroom and felt the haphazard knot she'd used to belt her robe slipping, one of the drawbacks of fleece. By the time she got to the bathroom, her robe hung open.

Leah was dressed in a pair of yoga pants and an old sweatshirt she'd borrowed from Teddi so she didn't have to put yesterday's clothes back on. Her hair was wet and combed back from her face, and she was plugging in a blow-dryer. When she glanced up into the mirror and saw Teddi's reflection, her eyes went wide.

"Oh, my, is this a naked coffee delivery? Is naked coffee delivery a regular thing? Because I'd like to put in a request. For, like, every morning. Some afternoons, too. And evenings. Definitely evenings. Who do I have to talk to?"

Teddi could feel her own blush, the heat moving up her neck in a wave to settle in her cheeks.

Leah turned to face her. "God, you're beautiful." Reverence filled Leah's quiet voice as she reached out and ran tender fingertips over Teddi's nipple, which stood at attention instantly.

A hard swallow. "I'd love nothing more than to drag you back to bed," Teddi said softly. "But I might never let you out of it again, and that wouldn't do much for your status at work."

Leah blew out a breath, kicked one hip to the side like a sulky teenager. "I know you're right, but this"—she repeated the motion of her fingers—"would be so worth it."

Teddi stepped closer, kissed her quickly, then stepped back and held out a mug. "Consolation prize."

Leah scoffed in a ridiculously cute way and took the coffee. "Fine." As Teddi retied her belt, Leah pouted. "Well, that's just sad."

Teddi placed a quick kiss on Leah's head and put some distance between them. She sat on the bed and watched Leah finish getting ready. How something as mundane as blow-drying hair ended up looking astonishingly sexy, Teddi had no idea, but Leah made it so. Blond hair flying, surreptitious—and not-so-surreptitious—glances at her in the mirror, the heat from the dryer as well as the glances…it all combined to wake up Teddi. More accurately, to wake up her body.

Yeah, she needed to get dressed and stop staring.

Instead, she stood up and walked into the bathroom, wrapped her arms around Leah from behind, moved her nearly dry hair to the side, and closed her mouth over the sensitive skin of Leah's neck. The blow-dryer clattered to the counter as Leah turned in her arms and kissed her hard. And then Teddi's robe was on the floor and she was up against the bathroom wall and Leah's hands were everywhere and what day was it again? Teddi couldn't think. Only feel. So she did.

Leah was late for work.

❖

"And I barely made it out of her place this morning." Leah was blushing. And smiling like a goofball. She could feel both things and could also tell by the way Tilly was looking at her across the table at lunch.

"That first time." Tilly's voice had an oddly dreamy quality to it, one Leah didn't think she'd heard from her friend before. "It can be…" Not only did her voice trail off for a minute, but her eyes seemed to glaze over, and she stared off into the small café as if searching for the right words in the lunch rush air.

"Hot? Awful? Sexy? The worst ever? Mind-blowing?"

"Intense." Tilly met her gaze, and what Leah saw in her eyes surprised her. Wonder. Uncertainty. Fear.

"Intense in a good way?"

Several beats of silence went by before Tilly responded. "Yes, mostly. Yes."

Leah narrowed her eyes and waited. Tilly wanted to say something. Leah could see it, but there was no forcing it. She waited.

Tilly picked up her sparkling water and took a sip, then another. She pushed her salmon salad around on her plate before finally facing Leah across the table. "I slept with Jen on Saturday night."

Leah grinned. "So we both had great weekends." She lifted her glass of Diet Coke and waited for Tilly to cheer her. She didn't. She simply held Leah's gaze and blinked. "Tils?"

"I slept with her for the first time."

Leah blinked. This was big. Holy shit, this was so big. "Wait. For the first time?"

Tilly nodded.

"So all the joking last week about you saving your fucks for her?"

"JoJo said that, not me."

Leah held up a finger. "Let me get this straight. You've been seeing Jen since New Year's Eve, and you only just had sex with her two days ago. In February. You've waited nearly six weeks to sleep with her." Six weeks was obviously not a long time to wait to have sex, but it was an eternity for Tilly, who usually sealed the deal by the third date. At the very latest.

More nodding, and Tilly looked miserable. But adorably so.

"Oh, Tils." Leah's entire face was lit up with joy and she knew it. She'd never seen Tilly this out of her element, and it warmed her heart as she reached across the table and grasped Tilly's arm. "You really, really like this girl, don't you? Oh my God, are you crying?"

"What? No! Of course, I'm not crying." The sniffle and the quick swipe at her face spotlighted the fib. "Shut up."

Leah sat back and just looked, just smiled at one of her dearest friends. "I am so happy for you, Matilda Beth." Tilly shot her a look, the off-limits name giving her something else to focus on so she could pull herself together. Leah's intention, totally.

The waiter came and asked if they wanted boxes, since neither had finished her lunch.

"No," said Tilly.

"Yes," said Leah. Then, "Give me hers, too. All in one box. I'm taking your salmon. You are salmon irresponsible."

That got a chuckle from Tilly, and they smiled at each other across the table as the waiter cleared their plates. "I'm happy you're happy," Leah said.

"Same. You're happy? Right? I sort of hijacked your story. Sorry about that."

"Please. No worries at all. I'm so glad you told me. Or, rather, I'm so happy that I pried it out of you. And yes, I am happy. Really happy. So happy that I'm afraid of jinxing it by telling too many people how happy I am."

"Oh my God, right?" Tilly sat up straight and leaned forward, forearms on the table. "I feel like that, too. Like, if I talk too much about things being good, some force in the universe will decide I don't deserve it, reach down, and snatch it away."

"We're ridiculous."

"We really are."

They sat in quiet wonder as the waiter dropped off the box and the check. Neither moved once he'd left. Several moments passed.

"I'm scared, Leah," Tilly whispered. And in that moment, Leah realized she completely understood because holy cow, she was scared, too.

"I know. I get it. I think it's good that we are?"

"Yeah?"

"I mean, if we're afraid of losing these girls, afraid of screwing things up, we'll step more carefully. Right?"

Tilly tipped her head from one side to the other. "Seems logical. Are you…" She hesitated but found her thought and continued, "Are you afraid of giving yourself? Of opening up all the way to somebody else?"

Leah didn't want to answer truthfully, didn't want to tell Tilly that hell, no, she'd been waiting for that for what seemed like her entire life, and she was more than ready. She knew Tilly was a tough nut to crack, that she rarely opened herself up to anybody, friends *or* lovers.

Hell, it had taken her and JoJo longer than she cared to remember to get through Tilly's thick, sarcastic outer shell. Tilly's fear made complete sense to Leah. So in order to not embarrass her, Leah fibbed just a little. "I am a bit, yeah."

"God, it terrifies me." Then she wet her lips, and one corner of her mouth turned up just the tiniest bit. "But I also really, *really* want to."

"I haven't seen you look like this in…ever. I can't wait to get to know this girl of yours. You need to start bringing her around, you know. Your friends deserve to know her, and she deserves to know your friends."

Shockingly, Tilly nodded in agreement. "I think so, too. And the same with you. We want to get to know your wedding planner. Who knows? Maybe one day she'll be planning your wedding."

"I mean, it's a little early for that," Leah said, feeling both excitement and fear at the idea. Because yeah, of course, she'd absolutely thought about what a wedding with Teddi might be like. *Way* too soon to think about that. *So early!* But it hung out there in the back of her mind anyway.

"Yeah, but who knows?"

"Who knows?" Leah's smile had a mind of its own and plastered itself across her face. Widely. God, Teddi made her happy.

"We should double-date."

A gasp of delight. "We totally should."

"We'll have to invite JoJo and Rick, though. So…triple date?"

"That actually sounds kind of awesome." Yet another unlikely statement from Tilly.

Leah began to wonder just how much of a magician this Jen must be to have captivated Tilly so completely. But then her mind tossed her a collage of images of Teddi from the night before and that morning. Teddi cuddling with her on the couch while they watched a movie. Teddi holding her in the dark, her fingertips brushing Leah's shoulder lightly. Teddi offering her yoga pants and delivering her coffee, fixed exactly the way Leah liked it without Teddi having asked. Teddi naked, pressed against the bathroom wall with Leah's fingers buried deep inside her.

"Hello? Earth to Leah."

Rapid blinks and a clear of her throat and Leah was back at the table.

"You were having flashbacks, huh?"

"I totally was." Leah laughed. "I feel like I'm sixteen."

"Can we make a pact?" Tilly's eyes grew serious.

"What kind of a pact?"

"One that says we look out for each other and don't let the other do something stupid? Not to fuck up what we have and not to allow ourselves to be fucked. Deal?" Tilly held a hand across the table.

"No fucking up allowed. Either way. Deal."

They shook. Tilly moved her napkin from her lap to the table as she said, "Valentine's Day is Friday."

Leah was well aware. "It is. Gonna take Jen out?"

"Definitely. I've got reservations at Rinaldo's." One of the swankiest restaurants in the city.

"Oh, *nice.* I hear the food there is spectacular. I want to hear all about it. Everything you did, but more importantly, everything you *ate.*"

"Will do," Tilly said on a chuckle as they stood in tandem and gathered their things. "What about you two?"

"Well, sadly, Valentine's Day is a big wedding day, so Teddi has to work two weddings. She'll be wiped. Which doesn't mean I'll let the day go by without acknowledging it. I have plans. They were plans in theory until…"

"Until you had the sex."

"Yes." Leah snort-laughed.

"And now they are actual, honest-to-God plans that will happen. And I want to hear all about them." Tilly held the door as they left the restaurant. About to part and go to their separate cars, they stopped. "We're doing just fine. Right?"

"Yeah, we are."

Tilly looked off toward the street, cars whooshing by through the slush made from earlier snow that had morphed in the sunshine. "And it's okay if we're a little freaked out. Right?"

"Absolutely okay." Leah gave a determined nod and found that reassuring Tilly helped her to feel more solid in her own situation. "It's absolutely okay. It's probably healthy, actually. We're good."

And then Tilly grabbed her in a hug. Super unusual move for

Tilly—she was not a terribly physical person. She wasn't a hugger. Said it made her feel awkward. Shoving aside her shock, Leah wrapped her arms around her friend and squeezed. It was like they were a team now, in this together.

"We got this," Leah said. "And we deserve it."

"We do, right?" Tilly smiled at her, then gave her a playful push on her shoulder, which was a much more typical display of Tilly expressing her love for a friend. With that, they went their separate ways.

Leah walked to her car and, for the first time, really understood what it meant to have a spring in your step. How was it possible that things had changed so much after one simple night? Okay, one simple, sexy, super hot night, but one night just the same. How?

A man passed her in the parking lot. Leah smiled at him. Said hello. Told him to have a wonderful day. He furrowed his brow at her, grunted a response, kept walking. She didn't care. She was happy, and nothing was going to take that from her.

Nothing.

CHAPTER NINETEEN

Valentine's Day was a holiday for lovers. People in love. People celebrating love. It was also a day of insanity for wedding planners everywhere. Couples loved to get married on Valentine's Day, and it didn't matter if it was a Saturday or a Tuesday. They wanted to get married on that exact day.

Teddi had long ago given up on trying to talk couples out of it. She could caution them about the budget, explain that venues and vendors alike would jack costs up on Valentine's Day simply because they could, that prices would be much more affordable on February 13 or February 15, but it rarely worked. A Valentine's Day wedding was a fairy tale come true to them. What she *couldn't* point out was that if they had their wedding on Valentine's Day and things didn't work out down the line, that day would be forever tainted for them because of it. All that being said, it was, of course, a big day of business for her, so she had learned several years ago to shut her mouth and do her job, and it had served her well as far as the books were concerned.

She could also admit that the decorations for a Valentine's Day wedding were some of the most beautiful, coming in second only to Christmas weddings. All the red and silver and hearts. Teddi did her best to keep things tasteful and elegant, even as she met the requirements of her brides-to-be, even as she made sure they got what they envisioned. She had a good eye and she knew it. Talking her clients into toning down what they had in mind was a skill she had honed well, and she'd had more than one bride get her photos back and thank her profusely for making her wedding look so gorgeous. She had a folder full of emails, a drawer full of thank-you cards, and nearly a thousand positive Yelp reviews to prove it.

All that being said, Valentine's Day was freaking exhausting. She'd had a wedding at two and then she'd switched off with Preston so she could head up another at six. And she had a wedding the next day, because some people didn't mind getting married *near* Valentine's Day. It was now approaching eleven p.m., and the last few guests were gathering their belongings. One of the groomsmen was putting the gifts into his car, and the caterer was just about packed up. Thank God. Teddi was practically dead on her feet.

Not quite an hour later, she pulled into her parking space, got her purse and messenger bag out, and headed toward her front door, digging for her keys as she walked.

She heard a car door slam to her right, and when she looked up, she stopped in her tracks.

Leah stood there in the parking lot next to her car, a bouquet of red roses in her hand. If ever there was a sight for sore eyes, it was Leah in that moment, and Teddi took her in. Jeans, low boots, ski jacket over a navy blue sweater.

"Oh my God, hi," Teddi said, and if she'd wanted to stop herself, she wouldn't have been able to. She detoured right into Leah's open arms.

"Hi," Leah said quietly against Teddi's hair. "Happy Valentine's Day. You made it with seven minutes to spare."

"Then let's not waste them." Teddi kissed her, and honest to God, nothing felt more perfect. Her lips were soft and warm and she tasted like peppermint and Teddi couldn't get enough. It was only when they parted, slightly breathless, that Teddi noticed the bags in the back seat of Leah's car. "What have you got?"

"Well, I wasn't sure if you'd be hungry when you got back, but I have stuff for a light midnight snack if you are. If not, I also brought the makings for French toast in the morning." Leah rolled her lips in then, as if just realizing the assumption she was making about staying the night.

"What if I want French toast for my light midnight snack?"

It was like somebody turned on a light switch inside Leah, the way her face lit up. "You can have anything you want."

"What if I want more than French toast?"

"Negotiations are allowed and encouraged." Leah kissed her quickly on the mouth, then reached into her car and grabbed the bags.

"Excellent. Follow me."

Half an hour later, the roses were in a big glass vase and French toast was sizzling in the frying pan. Teddi had a glass of Pinot Noir and was sitting on the counter, not helping at all—Leah's orders—and swinging her feet gently as she watched the chef at work.

"You're really sexy when you cook."

"Yeah? Well, don't get used to it. This is one of four things I know how to make." Leah flipped two slices of egg-coated bread and smiled up at Teddi.

"What are the other three?" Teddi sipped. The warmth of the wine felt better than she could even describe. She was exhausted, but Leah's presence kept her alert. It especially kept her *body* alert.

"Let's see." Leah held up the spatula to punctuate each item. "Omelets. Frittatas. Popcorn."

A snort. "Popcorn isn't a meal."

"I didn't say I can make four meals. I said I can make four *things*."

"So breakfast and a movie snack. That's your entire repertoire."

"Hey, it's kept me alive so far."

"Wait. You forgot chili."

"Oh my God, that's right. *Five* things. My stock just went up." Leah said it so proudly, with such a goofy grin on her face, that Teddi couldn't help but laugh.

"I'm really glad you're here." The words were out before she knew she was going to say them, and Leah met her gaze, her green eyes softening around the edges.

"Me, too." Leah plated the slices and handed them to Teddi, then dunked two more and dropped them into the hot pan. "I wasn't sure if I should. I didn't know your exact schedule and didn't know if you'd even be up for company by the time you got back. But I've been so stupidly busy this week and..." She hesitated before she looked at Teddi and finished. "I missed you. Like, a lot. And it's Valentine's Day."

"Well, it was," Teddi teased, pointing to the clock that read 12:27 a.m. "But you squeezed it in, and that's impressive."

Teddi hadn't had anyone in her space since she'd moved in, not like this. She'd dated once or twice, but nobody had harnessed her attention. Not like Leah had. And nobody had been here. "Can I tell you something?" The butterflies in her stomach turned to something solid enough to bang against her insides. Wasps? Hornets?

Leah plated her own French toast. "Always." They sat at the small table to eat, Leah's eyes on Teddi, waiting patiently.

"I said that I like having you here."

"You did. I'm glad. I like being here."

"Well, there's a little more to it." Teddi exhaled through her nose, and she tried to find words to match her feelings. "One of Julia's complaints about me was that I was never vulnerable with her." Yeah, this was embarrassing, but she couldn't turn back now. "She said if a conversation contained any kind of emotion, I would avoid it. She wasn't wrong."

"Okay." Leah watched her, chewed and listened, didn't interrupt. The kindness in her eyes made Teddi feel safe. Safe enough to continue, which Teddi wasn't ready to analyze just yet.

"Don't get me wrong, it took some therapy before I realized that she was right, but I got there. So"—she cleared her throat as she stabbed a piece of French toast—"I haven't had anybody here, in my space, since I moved in two years ago."

Leah's eyebrows went up, but she said nothing.

"But I like having you in it. I like it a lot. More than I expected." There. That was vulnerable, wasn't it? Admitting something like that? There was more to it. More, like she didn't normally like *any* people in her space, but Leah had somehow become an exception. More, like she had astonished herself by not being the least bit annoyed to see Leah waiting in her parking lot. Rather, she'd felt like her entire being had lightened somehow at the sight of her. More, like having Leah here, eating French toast with her in the wee hours, felt absolutely right.

It terrified her.

And she was okay with that.

"Well," Leah said finally, apparently waiting to see if Teddi was finished talking, "I can honestly say that I really like being here. With you."

Something hung in the air between them. Teddi could feel it, like a vapor or a mist hovering above the table, but not in an ominous way. In an odd, life-is-good kind of way that Teddi hadn't felt in years. *Years.*

"I think we should go to bed," Teddi whispered, and she watched as Leah's eyes darkened. She stood up and collected the dishes. "Leave them." Teddi held out a hand. Leah took it and they turned off the lights as they went.

Teddi'd had every intention of taking the lead, but Leah wasn't having it, and Teddi was on her back on the bed before she'd even realized it.

Things were different this time. Slower. Still intense. Still with the crazy chemistry they had. But different. Teddi felt it in her head and, more alarmingly, in her heart. Leah took her time. Kissing. Touching. Tasting. Teddi felt like her body was a musical instrument and Leah was playing her, expertly, her fingers and her mouth taking Teddi to symphonic heights she didn't even know existed. When Leah finally allowed release, finally nudged her over that edge and into oblivion, Teddi's world exploded in colors and sensations and emotions so big, so intense, they brought tears to her eyes even as her muscles strained in climax. Her hips dropped back to the bed as a small sob left her throat. Leah was instantly up and facing her, their bodies pressed together.

"Oh my God, did I hurt you?" Her voice was soft and laced with concern. She brushed Teddi's hair off her face and noticed the wet on her cheeks. "Oh, Teddi. I'm really sorry. I must have gotten carried away—"

Teddi place her fingers over Leah's lips and shook her head. "No. You didn't get carried away. You didn't hurt me. I just got a little lost in my feels." She chuckled, hoping to lighten things up, not wanting to delve into what it meant, not ready to analyze it. Leah seemed to get it, if the way she beamed down at Teddi was any indication. She wrapped her arms around Leah, pulled her down for a sizzling kiss, then flipped them so their positions were reversed. A moment to enjoy the surge of arousal on Leah's face, and Teddi got busy exploring the gorgeous body beneath her. Nothing changed. She felt exactly the same way the entire time she made love to Leah.

Things were different now.

CHAPTER TWENTY

After one last blast of winter—snowstorms in March were, sadly, not uncommon in upstate New York—spring was finally making an effort. While Leah hated the brown mud-slush combination that was part of the uniform of the end of winter, she loved the impending spring. It was early April and things were changing. Winter was fading. New growth began to appear—the color green was returning, buds were forming on trees, and daffodils and crocuses peeked up from the earth slowly, as if checking to see if the coast was clear.

Leah inhaled deeply, taking in the scent of new life. "God, I love spring," she said quietly to no one as she pulled open the door to Hopeless Romantic and stepped inside.

"Hey, Preston," she said.

He looked up from the counter, recently grown goatee so perfectly shaped it was as though it had been drawn on his face with a template. "Hi, Leah. How's life?"

"Life is fantastic. She back there?" She indicated the door behind the counter.

"She is."

Teddi was at her desk, her squinting focus on the computer monitor.

Was there ever going to be a time when Leah looked at Teddi and did *not* have the breath stolen right out of her lungs? Because there hadn't been one yet. There had never been anyone in Leah's life who had affected her the same way. Whenever she laid eyes on Teddi after being away from her for a while, a list of things happened. Her heart rate kicked up. She felt a fluttering low in her belly. Her entire being seemed to relax. It was as if she got a shot of some sort of downer, something gentle, something that said *It's okay, all is right in the world now. Just chill.*

"If I need to call the eye doctor myself and make you an appointment, I will." Leah said it quietly so as not to startle Teddi, but then wrapped her arms around her from behind. They'd had this discussion every time Teddi squinted at her computer. Or book. Or phone. "Besides, you'd look super sexy in glasses."

A big sigh brought Teddi's shoulders down slightly in Leah's embrace. "I hate to admit it, but I think you're probably right." She tilted her head back and Leah pecked her lips with a gentle kiss. "Hi. To what do I owe this lovely surprise?"

"Hello there, you gorgeous creature." Leah stood and began to massage Teddi's shoulders. "I just finished up a lunch meeting around the corner and thought I'd pop in to see my girlfriend for a few minutes to get me through the rest of my day."

"What would happen if you couldn't see me?" Teddi poked a couple keys and squinted at the screen again.

"I mean, I would probably wither up and blow away like a dried-up leaf. Wouldn't that be awful?"

"I'd certainly miss you. Your massages, mostly." Leah squeezed extra hard, causing Teddi to cringe with a laugh and lean away. "Ow. Ow. I'm kidding."

Leah grinned and leaned close to Teddi's ear. "You'd miss a lot more than my massages," she whispered, then punctuated the statement with a gentle suck on Teddi's earlobe. She felt the aroused shiver run through Teddi's body under her hands and secretly cheered. The physical effect she had on Teddi was apparent, and it bolstered Leah, gave her a shot of confidence that she loved. It also helped that Teddi had the same effect on her. It was kind of crazy. Just being in close proximity to Teddi would flip Leah's switch. She felt like a teenage boy.

"Hey, I'm trying to work here." But Teddi's words were soft.

"What time should I pick you up tonight?"

"Reservations are at what? Seven?" At Leah's nod, Teddi said, "Why don't you come by around six and we'll have a glass of wine and then go?"

"Perfect. Nervous?" They were double-dating with Tilly and Jen tonight. It would only be the second time Teddi had met Tilly, and while she hadn't come right out and said it, Leah was getting better at reading her, and she could tell there was some trepidation around tonight.

Teddi's nibble of her bottom lip corroborated Leah's assumption. "A little?" Teddi looked up at her, face open, reluctantly vulnerable.

"Is it weird if I love...that?" *Whew! That was a close one.* Leah swallowed, held Teddi's gaze, hoped she hadn't noticed the slip, as neither of them had said the L-word yet, and for reasons unknown to her—or maybe just well hidden—Leah didn't want to be the first. But it was there. She knew it. She felt it. Head over heels crazy in love, that's what she was. But they were still in Taking It Slow mode, and the last thing Leah wanted was to scare Teddi away by emoting all over the place like a hot mess.

"Well, since you're weird in general, no."

Leah gave Teddi's hair a playful tug. "Funny. Okay. I gotta run. Just wanted to pop by and give you this." Still holding a chunk of Teddi's hair, she pulled her head back with it and kissed her. Not a peck. Nothing chaste about it. She ravished Teddi's mouth, practically claimed ownership. When she pulled back, Teddi's dark eyes had gone impossibly darker, her breathing ragged, her cheeks flushed. It was a sight Leah would never get tired of. "See you at six."

Teddi nodded, and Leah took great pride in knowing that was all Teddi could do in the moment.

She waved to Preston, who was sitting at the table with two women, and pushed out the front door of the shop with a grin plastered on her face so wide she could feel it. Oh yes, it was a gorgeous spring day.

❖

Plated was a trendy, super-popular new restaurant in town, and Teddi knew reservations could be hard to come by. Apparently, though, Leah's friend Tilly knew somebody and got them a coveted seven p.m. reservation for four at a corner table. Out of the way enough to be able to converse easily, but with a view of the restaurant so you could still see the comings and goings.

Her nerves had settled, and that was due in no small part to having Leah by her side, warm hand on the small of her back as they walked through the dining room to their table and sat. Tilly and her date had not arrived yet, and Teddi was okay with that, taking the chance to look around. Lighting was dim, as in any fancy restaurant. Ambiance. Teddi loved it until it came time to actually see her food. The thought brought a smile to her face as she scanned the space. White tablecloths draped over round tables, small votives flickering in the center of each one. Waitstaff in black pants and white shirts, black aprons tied around their waists. A bar ran along her right, super sleek and modern, a gray granite bar top with black leather stools lined up. The shelves of bottles behind it were lit as if from within, a soft blue glow that was almost ethereal.

"What do you think?" Leah asked, her voice quiet as if she thought she'd disturb something or someone. She looked gorgeous in a little black dress that accented her curves and allowed her light hair and green eyes to stand out. *When can I take that off her?* was the first thing that ran through Teddi's mind when she'd opened her front door. She'd almost said it out loud, almost deepened their hello kiss, but she knew if she did, they'd be late for dinner. Very late. If they made it at all. So she'd smiled, told Leah she looked amazing, and stepped out onto the front stoop as quickly as she could.

"It's really nice. I like how sleek the bar is." Behind it, the bartender was shaking a martini. "I think I want one of those."

"A bartender?"

"I was thinking a martini, but now that you mention it, my own personal bartender wouldn't be a bad thing."

"Agreed." Their waiter came by and asked if they'd like to order drinks while they waited for the rest of their party. "As a matter of fact, we would," Leah said. "Two dirty martinis, please."

"Extra dirty for me," Teddi said, then enjoyed the way Leah turned slowly to look at her. The waiter left to get their drinks.

"You like things extra dirty, do you?" Leah waggled her eyebrows in what was likely an attempt to be sexy but only made Teddi laugh.

"You look like somebody's creepy uncle when you do that. And I like my *martinis* extra dirty, yes."

Leah's response was interrupted by the arrival of their double-dates. Tilly was somebody who stood out in a crowd, Teddi noticed right away. Tall, lean, androgynous with a shock of white-blond hair that swooped in a way Teddi thought only cartoon hair could do. It was fascinating. Her large blue eyes seemed not to miss a thing. Her skin was smooth, her lips glossy, and she wore a black pantsuit that accentuated her androgyny. Teddi was drawn to her and also found her slightly intimidating. Jen, on the other hand, was the complete opposite. Petite to the point of being almost tiny, cute burgundy dress, brown hair in a ponytail, expressive brown eyes, and the friendliest smile Teddi had ever seen. She wanted to be BFFs with her immediately.

Introductions were made, handshakes occurred. Tilly ordered drinks for her and Jen when the martinis were delivered, and the double-date dinner began.

Conversation was easy, and Teddi was pleasantly surprised. Tilly was witty. Jen was charming. And Leah was as happy as could be. The bond between her and Tilly was strong and apparent, and it made Teddi grin.

"You guys met at law school, yes?" she asked when their dinners had arrived.

"Yup," Leah said. "Me, Tilly, and JoJo ended up in a suite together. We didn't know each other at all."

"And the rest is history. We've been friends ever since." Tilly winked at Leah and picked up her wine. "JoJo would've been here tonight, but her son has a...something." She raised her eyebrows at Leah.

"I think his play is tonight." Turning to Teddi, she said, "He's playing a tree, if I'm not mistaken."

"Wow. That's a tough role." Teddi grinned over the rim of her water glass. Turning to Tilly, she asked, "You're a lawyer, too?"

"I am. But not a divorce lawyer. I'm in contract law. I honestly don't know how Leah does it, dealing with angry, heartbroken people all day."

Leah glanced at Teddi, likely searching to see if she took offense at the remark, but Teddi was surprisingly okay with it. After all, it was simply fact, right? She imagined the majority of the people Leah dealt with were one of those two things: angry or heartbroken. Teddi herself had certainly been both.

"It can be hard," Leah said. "The worst is when they use their children for leverage. That makes my stomach hurt."

"That *is* awful, isn't it?" Jen said. The three of them went around, two lawyers and a social worker, touching on all the tragedy they'd seen in their jobs over the years. Then Jen turned to Teddi and grinned.

"You are the only one at this table whose job must be, like, full of happy people. Right?"

"The majority of the time, yes." Teddi dabbed at her mouth with her napkin. "Once in a while, I'll get somebody who is determined to be miserable with every choice she makes or any suggestion I make."

"Like a bridezilla?"

"I've had a few."

Jen looked bewildered. "But they're planning their wedding. What's to be miserable about?"

"I've been doing this for a while, and what I've figured out is this: Generally, if somebody is miserable or freaked out over wedding plans, it's simply the way their nerves are manifesting."

"So they're just nervous." Tilly tilted her head to one side.

"Exactly. Different people react different ways to that kind of pressure. And trust me, planning a wedding *is* a lot of pressure."

"Which is why they have you," Leah said, the pride on her face unmistakable. It made Teddi feel warm inside.

"I do my best to take as much of that pressure off as I can."

"But then you end up taking it on," Jen said, observant.

With a nod, Teddi agreed. "Wedding planning isn't for everybody. You have to be super organized—"

"She is," Leah piped in.

"Good under pressure—"

"She is."

Teddi squeezed Leah's knee affectionately under the table. "And you've got to be assertive. You deal with several different vendors at once, and you can't let them bully you or get lazy. You've got to stay on top of them."

"And do you have certain vendors that you work with all the time?" Jen leaned her elbow on the table and propped her chin in her hand, apparently riveted.

"I do, now that I've been in this business for a decade. But problems can arise when the bride-to-be has her own vendors she wants to use. Most of the time, it's fine. It's her wedding, after all. I don't get to choose for her. But if she's got her heart set on a florist or a caterer or a videographer that I know for a fact is going to be a problem, I try to find a diplomatic way to steer her in a different direction." Teddi sipped her water. "Doesn't always work."

"This is *fascinating*," Jen said, her enthusiasm sounding genuine. Teddi laughed as the waiter arrived and they all ordered coffee.

"I need to hit the little girls' room," Leah said, rubbing a hand over Teddi's thigh.

Tilly stood. "I'll join you."

"Oh, good, we can talk about them now," Jen said loudly as the two walked away. Then she laughed and turned back to Teddi. "I love your job! It's sounds like so much fun. Would you plan your own wedding?"

"I'm actually divorced, but no, we got married at the courthouse."

Jen's eyes went comically wide. "Oh my God, that seems like such a..." She shook her head like she couldn't find the right words. "A travesty. A wedding planner getting married at a courthouse?"

"Right?" *Don't think about it.* Teddi nodded and smiled.

"What about the next time?"

"What next time?"

"The next time you get married. You're young and gorgeous. You and Leah seem very into each other. I realize I'm overstepping a bit, and maybe you guys haven't even touched on that at all, but would you plan your next wedding?"

"Oh no. No, I'm not doing *that* again. Once was enough. Why do you think I'm dating a divorce attorney?" Jen laughed at the joke and Teddi joined her.

"Well. That's too bad. I think it would be fun to have insider knowledge on the best plan."

Tilly and Leah returned at the same time the coffee arrived, and the conversation shifted to movies. Teddi was inexplicably relieved.

"Jen, are you a horror movie buff like Tilly?" Leah asked. "Do you enjoy stupid teenagers being dismembered one by one by a crazy killer in a mask?"

"*No*," Jen said comically, drawing the word way out and then grimacing. "I hate them. They terrify me."

"But if you're scared, you cling to me." Tilly shrugged and sipped her coffee.

"Aha," Teddi said, pointing at Tilly. "There's a method to the madness."

"Always," Tilly said. A charming wink.

"What kinds of movies do you like, Jen?" Teddi asked.

"Rom-coms."

Tilly groaned and rolled her eyes at the same time Leah did a little fist pump.

"Favorites," Leah said. "Go."

"Let's see...*Notting Hill*. *You've Got Mail*, definitely. *Crazy Rich Asians*."

"I loved that one," Leah said.

Teddi watched the back-and-forth. The way Leah leaned on the table toward Jen, eyes wide, face open. How she knew every film Jen named, and they talked a little bit about each. The subject animated her and it was so much fun to watch. Teddi knew she was smiling endlessly, but she couldn't help it.

"You like rom-coms, Ted?" It was Tilly pulling her attention.

"I'm working on it," Leah said before Teddi could answer.

"You mean you're forcing her to watch them with you?" Tilly teased.

"So she gets all mushy and lovey-dovey and *clings to me*?" Leah made air quotes around the words Tilly had used just a few minutes ago. "Yes, I am." She bumped Teddi with a shoulder, letting her know this was play.

"She's slowly converting me." Teddi grinned at Leah.

And then they were off, talking about the rom-coms that Teddi had seen, discussing plot points and actresses. Tilly made a show of sighing and rolling her eyes, but Teddi noticed that she watched Jen as she animatedly used her hands when she spoke, and the love in Tilly's eyes was so crystal clear to Teddi that it almost made her tear up. Did she look at Leah that way? Did Leah look at her that way?

"Okay, then, I say our next double-date is movie night." Jen sat up straighter, as if her idea had bolstered her posture. "We have to watch a rom-com together, and we have to watch a horror movie together. But," she said, holding up a finger and cutting off Tilly before she could say anything, her mouth open but no sound coming out, "Tilly is not allowed to choose the horror movie, and Leah is not allowed to choose the rom-com."

Leah and Tilly looked at each other, and their pouts made Teddi chuckle. "I like that idea," she said. "How about I choose the horror movie and Jen chooses the rom-com?"

"I think that sounds fabulous. Let's do it." Jen reached a closed fist across the table. Teddi bumped it.

"I think our girlfriends just hijacked our next date," Tilly said, brow furrowed comically. "How did we let that happen?"

"I don't know," Leah said. "But they sure are pretty, aren't they?" She looked at Teddi with exaggeratedly dreamy eyes and Tilly did the same to Jen, which made the entire table erupt in laughter.

Teddi watched Leah as the foursome settled the bill and gathered their things. She very much liked this version of her, how comfortable she was around Tilly, how relaxed, how open and welcoming to Jen. Teddi had been nervous, it was true, but she knew now that she'd had no reason to be. This had easily been one of the most fun gatherings she'd ever been a part of.

She'd arrived worried and nervous, and she was going to leave with two new friends. You couldn't really beat that.

Chapter Twenty-one

I had such a good time tonight," Teddi said as Leah took her coat and hung it in the hall closet.

"Yeah? Good. I told you you'd like Tilly." The nerves Leah'd had earlier were now gone. Deep down, she'd known Teddi and Tilly would get along well—and she chuckled now at the similarity of the names of her best friend and her girlfriend—but she'd still had some worry around it. Because what if they didn't get along? What if they'd hated each other for some weird reason? What would she do if her girlfriend and her best friend couldn't stand each other?

"I do," Teddi agreed, "very much. And Jen is just a sweetheart." Teddi tugged Leah to the living room and down onto the couch. "Did you like her?"

"I did. Very much. I've met her once before, but only briefly." She pointed at Teddi. "At the New Year's Eve party, remember?"

Teddi squinted up at the ceiling, and Leah was hit with such a surge of warmth and affection, it stole her breath for a moment. "I remember the party, but not Jen. I do remember that I met Tilly then, but very briefly. Tonight, I got a better synopsis of her."

"A synopsis?" Leah shifted so she was leaning against Teddi. Lizzie appeared from some secret hiding place and hopped up onto the couch next to her, stretching out along Leah's thigh.

"Yeah, don't you do that? You get, like, an overview of somebody when you spend time with them for the first time. You know? A synopsis."

"Why don't you just say overview?"

"Because I like the word *synopsis*."

Their gazes held, smiles wide. *Good God, this woman.* Another surge of affection. "And what's her synopsis?"

Teddi toed off her booties and snuggled down into the couch cushions, wrapping her arms around Leah. "Tilly is intimidating at first, which I imagine suits her well, but once you get to know her, you realize that she's kind and generous—I caught you two fighting over the bill with your eyes." Leah barked a laugh and Teddi went on, "She's got a wicked sense of humor, a dark wit, and she's head over heels in love with Jen."

"Wow, that's alarmingly accurate." And it was. Teddi had seen all the best qualities in Tilly, had harvested them all from one single dinner. Leah was impressed, she had to admit. "You think they're in love?"

"I do," Teddi said without missing a beat. "The way they look at each other. It's super cute."

Leah had to agree. Tilly was different, somehow, since dating Jen. Softer. More patient. "I've never seen Tilly quite so comfortable with somebody. It's nice."

"But?" Teddi said it softly, her dark eyes searching Leah's face. "I can see it on your face. There's a but."

"It's scary how well you know me already." Teddi kissed the top of Leah's head as Leah continued, "You're right. Don't get me wrong. I'm thrilled for Tilly. Thrilled. She deserves to be happy."

"But?"

"I'm worried. Somewhere, down deep inside, I have this sliver of fear for her because Tilly may be intimidating and a badass, but she's super tender-hearted, and if things with Jen don't work, if Jen breaks that tender heart, she will crash. Hard. I just don't want to see that happen."

Teddi's arms tightened around her, and weirdly, it was exactly what Leah needed to feel. "You're a terrific friend, you know that?"

A shrug. "I mean, I try to be."

"Well, Tilly is lucky to have you."

Leah craned her neck so she could look up at Teddi, meet that dark gaze. "Thank you," she said softly. Teddi leaned down and kissed her with tenderness. "So," Leah said when they parted, "what's *my* synopsis?"

"I was waiting for that," Teddi said, her shoulders shaking as she laughed. A deep breath, seemingly to center herself or something, and she began, "Your synopsis is this: You're unfailingly kind. You put others before yourself and you always have. You are fiercely protective of those you love, and you're also willing to protect those you don't know but who need protecting. Thus, your job. You project a confidence that you often don't feel, but nobody knows that. You don't let it show because you're the caretaker, and people can't have a self-conscious caretaker. Also, you have zero idea how attractive and sexy you are. It's part of your charm."

With every word, Leah felt herself melting a little bit more in the arms of this gorgeous creature. "Wow," she whispered, then swallowed the lump of emotion that had formed in her throat. "I don't know what to say. I'm kind of speechless."

Teddi lifted one shoulder. "You don't have to say anything. How about kissing me instead?"

"That I can do." Leah shifted her position, much to the dismay of Lizzie, who meowed her irritation and hopped up onto the back of the couch, so that she was higher than Teddi. Leah looked deep into Teddi's eyes before swinging one leg over so she was straddling her lap.

"Oh, this is nice."

"You like it? There's more to come." Leah moved slowly, brought her lips to Teddi's but didn't kiss her, just stayed there, no more than a millimeter or two between them, hovered for a moment and listened to Teddi's breathing increase, heard her swallow, before finally pressing her mouth to Teddi's.

There was nothing else in life that Leah enjoyed more than kissing Teddi. That was not to say that sex with her wasn't mind-blowingly amazing, because it was. But kissing her? The intimacy and the trust and the softness and the heat? How it could be gentle and sweet or passionately primal on any given day, even shift from one to the other in a matter of seconds? The way she and Teddi just seemed to *fit*? Yeah, making out with Teddi was definitely at the top of Leah's list of life's greatest pleasures. She could do it forever.

"How do you feel about taking this to the bedroom?" Teddi hissed at the last word as Leah sucked on a spot on Teddi's neck she'd learned to be particularly sensitive. That sound Teddi made did things to Leah, kicked her level of arousal up a notch or twelve.

Leah said nothing. Simply stood, hand out, and led Teddi toward the bedroom. Teddi's words about her, her synopsis, still hung out in Leah's head, and she wanted to show Teddi that she felt the same way about her.

Slowly. Tenderly. That's how Leah made love to Teddi that night. Taking her time was not easy—how could she be expected to go slow with a figure of such sensual nakedness beneath her? But she did her best to worship her the way she deserved to be worshipped. Fingertips on smooth skin. Kisses all over Teddi's body. Leah trailed down Teddi's body with her tongue. From her chin along her throat over her chest and between her breasts. Over her stomach, a circling of her belly button, then off to the side, tasting the insides of her thighs and avoiding the center of the heat, the center of it all. Leah lingered there, running her tongue over all that beautiful skin, smooth and silky, inching closer and closer to the apex until Teddi finally begged her with a whimpered "Please," and Leah plunged in.

Teddi's moan was guttural, came from deep in her throat, raw and gravelly, and it sent Leah's own arousal through the roof. Still, she forced herself to take her time, not to drive Teddi right to the edge yet, and she swirled her tongue. Explored each fold of hot, wet skin. Dipped inside her, then back out, then in again, until Teddi had a pillow clenched in one hand and a fistful of Leah's hair in the other, her hips moving seemingly out of her control.

"Please." The word came again, this time a little louder, at a lower register than Teddi's regular voice. "Please, Leah. I can't take it. Please."

Something filled Leah then. Something warm. Comfortable. New. She stopped moving and waited until Teddi craned her neck and looked down her body to lock eyes with Leah.

It held.

"I love you." Leah said it softly, quietly, but Teddi heard it. She could tell by the light behind her eyes, by the slight rising of her eyebrows, even in the darkness of the bedroom. Leah didn't wait for a response. She didn't say it because she wanted to hear it back. She said it because she simply couldn't *not* say it.

Without warning, Leah pushed her fingers inside Teddi and continued with her mouth, adding extra pressure, taking Teddi higher and higher and watching her take flight. Teddi's hips rose off the bed as she came, Leah holding on to them so as not to lose the perfect spot, sounds wrenched from Teddi that were beautiful and erotic and sexy as hell, and Leah held on.

She held on. And she knew in that moment that she wanted to always hold on to this woman.

Tears filled her eyes and she smiled against Teddi's center as her hips returned to the bed.

❖

The clock read 1:14 when the need for sleep took over the situation. Leah's head was tucked under Teddi's chin, Teddi's arm around her, fingertips dancing lightly over her shoulder. She couldn't remember the last time she'd come three times in one night, but she had, and she was sore and exhausted and stupidly happy to prove it. She was just starting to drift off when Teddi's voice brought her back.

"Leah?"

"Hmm?"

"I love you, too. You know that, right?"

Leah felt her own face light up. "I do now."

"Good." They were quiet again and Leah started to drift until, "Leah?"

"Hmm?"

"I have to pee."

The sound Leah made was a mix of chuckle and groan, and she rolled aside to let Teddi out of bed. Then she pulled the covers up around her and slid over to Teddi's side so she could smell her.

"The spider's gone," Teddi said as she slid back under the covers and they resumed cuddling positions.

"Angelica."

"Excuse me. The spider you creepily named Angelica is gone. Did you kill her?"

"What? Of course not. She's just moved on to somewhere else."

"You mean somewhere else in this house." A shiver ran through Teddi's body.

"Mm-hmm." Leah's eyes were closed and she snuggled in closer.

"If she crawls on me while I'm sleeping, I swear to God—"

"If she crawls on you while you're sleeping, you won't know. Because you'll be sleeping. See?"

Teddi squeezed her hard, causing Leah to groan on a laugh. A kiss was pressed to her forehead. "Good night, weirdo."

"Good night, scaredy-cat."

This. This was exactly what Leah had been waiting for. To have a silly argument with somebody who would then laugh it off and cuddle with her anyway. This was what she'd wanted to be for so long, and now? Now she was. Leah let sleep claim her as that thought stayed in her mind as she drifted off.

She was the other half of a couple.

CHAPTER TWENTY-TWO

May was a crazy busy work month for Teddi. Not only did a lot of people choose to get married in May because of the beauty of spring—assuming the weather was on their side—but it was also the month before June. Her biggest month of the year. So May had its own slate of weddings, plus Teddi had tons of prep work for next month's nuptials.

For the most part, she loved the pace. She lived for last-minute organization and the enormous sense of pride and accomplishment that came when a wedding went off without a hitch. But it was a lot, and that meant she didn't get to see Leah as often as she'd like.

That was going to change today, though, because she had a meeting set up with Kelly. Her wedding was at the four-months-away mark, so there were some things they needed to discuss, some solid dates they needed to set for finalizations, things like that. In addition to Kelly's mom tagging along, Leah was going to be there. Teddi's heart warmed just at the thought of it. Between the crazy demands of both their jobs, she hadn't seen Leah in nearly a week, and that was far too long as far as Teddi was concerned. Teddi would normally have Preston handle this kind of meeting during this time of the year. But she wanted to see Leah. Badly.

The day flew by, as it always did when Teddi was booked solid.

"The Shaw wedding is all set and ready to go," Preston told her, referring to one of two weddings they had this weekend. "I finalized both the caterer and the DJ for Bennington, and Harlow was able to squeeze them into her schedule, so we're good there as well."

"You, my friend, are a godsend," Teddi said as she kissed him on the cheek on her way past him. The Bennington wedding had been a disaster from day one with a bride-to-be who couldn't make a decision to save her life and a mother-of-the-bride and three bridesmaids who *could* make decisions, just none of them were the same. "I need to call Harlow and thank her." She headed back into her office.

"Are you surviving May so far?" Harlow asked a few minutes later when Teddi had her on the phone.

"Barely."

"You love it." Harlow knew her so well, and it made Teddi smile.

"I do. It's true."

They chatted quickly about a few business things before Harlow said, "Things with Leah going well?"

At the mention of her girlfriend's name, Teddi felt herself slow down. Everything went calm. Her heart rate, her breathing, even her shoulder muscles seemed to relax when she thought about Leah. "They really are. I have a meeting in a few with her sister and mom, and Leah's tagging along just to see me. Our jobs have been nuts, so we have to squeeze in time when we can."

Harlow let out a dreamy sigh. "Ah, I remember those days with Rashim. Thought about him all day, couldn't wait for any amount of time with him, even if it was only a few minutes. That's the best."

"I'm not really sure how I got here," Teddi said, and it was the truth, something that had been in the back of her mind, but she hadn't made verbal until now. "I mean, Julia wrecked me. I never in a million years thought I'd be here again."

"Where? In love?"

"Yeah." A wave of pure joy ran through Teddi then, warm and blissful. "In love."

"You deserve it, babe. And it happens when we're not looking. The old saying is absolutely true."

"I guess so."

A few more back-and-forths and they hung up.

As fast as her busy days went, it seemed like it took eons for four o'clock to arrive. It finally did, of course, and Teddi set Kelly and her mom up at the round table, got them coffee, grabbed her tablet. By the time she'd done those things, the bell on the door dinged and Leah walked in.

Not only did Leah walk in, she walked right across the floor to

Teddi, grabbed her face in both hands, and kissed her soundly. In front of God and everybody. Teddi blushed, felt the heat in her cheeks, but not because she was embarrassed. Because she was giddy.

"Well, hello there," she said softly as Leah ended the kiss but still held Teddi's face.

"Hi, baby," Leah said back. "I've missed you."

"Same. So much same."

They stayed that way until Kelly not so discreetly cleared her throat. "Okay, you two lovebirds. This is lovely and everything, but *I* am the bride-to-be, and that means *I* am supposed to be getting all the attention here."

Leah smiled that gorgeous smile of hers as Teddi laughed. "You're so right," Teddi said as she pulled out a chair and took a seat. "My bad. Please forgive me."

"Well, I mean it's not really your fault my sister manhandled you before she even said hello."

"This is true," Teddi said, tossing a wink in Leah's direction.

"I was going to ask how things were going with you two," Patti said, and her eyes crinkled at the edges with her grin. "But I guess I don't have to."

"Things are great, Mom." Leah took off her coat and draped it over the remaining chair before she sat. Tossed a look at Teddi, those green eyes sparkling and filled with love. Yeah, things were beyond great. Teddi tried to tone down her own glee and focus on Kelly and her upcoming wedding.

Within an hour, they had solidified the menu, picked the details for the tablescapes, and narrowed down gifts for the bridal party and groomsmen. Kelly was that combination of stressed and excited that all brides-to-be hit at around this mark. She couldn't wait to get married, that was obvious. It was also clear that she was feeling a bit overwhelmed. When she looked up at Teddi, the worry clear in her eyes, Teddi reached across the table and grasped her forearm.

"Hey. Relax. We got this. Okay?" Teddi gentled her expression, tilted her head slightly, and looked Kelly directly in the eye. "I know you're stressed. But I promise you, it's going to be the best day of your life. All right? Trust me. I've got you."

"Okay." The relief was clear on Kelly's face and she let out a loud breath. "It's just..."

"A lot," Leah piped in, wrapping an arm around her sister. "It's a lot." She met Teddi's gaze. "But you're in good hands."

Teddi quickly stood and excused herself to grab the printout of the bridesmaids gifts off the printer in the back. As she walked away, she heard the conversation.

"I hope it goes this smoothly when *you* get married," Patti said, and when Teddi glanced over her shoulder, Patti's gaze was on Leah. She looked proud and happy.

"Oh my God, right? Me, too." Leah chuckled along with her, then caught Teddi's eye across the room and winked at her.

Teddi was caught short. They hadn't discussed anything remotely having to do with legalizing what they had. They hadn't touched on how Teddi felt about marriage in general—it was a sham. And they certainly hadn't yet gotten into her feelings about getting married again—no, thank you. Things were good. Hell, they were great, weren't they? They didn't need to change a thing, and they certainly didn't need a piece of paper to say they loved each other. They were together. They were exclusive. They were perfect just the way they were. Maybe Leah was just humoring her mom, because she couldn't possibly be thinking about a wedding.

Could she?

❖

"Holy cow, I feel like I haven't seen the two of you together in ages." Tilly hugged Leah, then leaned around the table and hugged JoJo as well.

"*Holy cow?*" JoJo said, her eyebrows raised in major question. "Not *holy shit* or *Jesus Christ* or *what the fuck*? You're going with *holy cow?*"

Tilly rolled her eyes, but there was the ghost of a smile on her face. "Listen, Jen has asked me to clean up my language a tiny bit, so I'm doing my best." She sat, blew out a breath. "But it's fucking hard, you know?"

"And the world has righted itself," JoJo said with a nod.

"Where is the lovely Jen, anyway?" Leah asked. "You know we like her better than you now."

"Oh, I'm aware, bitches." Tilly picked up her menu to peruse. "I invited her, but she insisted that this was my thing with my girls and she didn't want to encroach on that."

"And now I like her even more," JoJo said. "If you ever break up, we're keeping her and getting rid of you."

"I would, too. That's definitely the smartest option." Tilly closed her menu as the waiter arrived and took their lunch orders.

"So, what's new with you guys?" Leah asked as they handed over their menus. It had been several weeks since they'd been able to make a lunch or brunch or dinner work for all three of them, so there was much catching up to do in a fairly short period of time.

JoJo talked about her boys and the impending end of the school year. "They've become little monsters." She called them that often, but the love in her eyes when she said it cleared up any confusion over how she really felt. "They're climbing the walls."

"Like they do every June, right?" Tilly sipped her water.

"Like goddamn clockwork, yes. They're driving me crazy."

"Maybe you should just kill 'em. You know? Save yourself the trouble next year." Leah shrugged nonchalantly, then shot a half grin JoJo's way.

"Don't think for one second that hasn't crossed my mind," JoJo replied. The waiter arrived with their food, and her tone softened, became wistful, as she continued, "Actually, what I'd really like is for them to stop growing. I mean, how did I get here? Weren't they tiny babies, like, last month?"

"Sure seems like it," Tilly said, digging into her tuna salad.

"Anyway. Tell me something happy." JoJo popped a French fry into her mouth and turned to Leah. "How goes the wedding planning? I got my Save the Date magnet last week. Is Kelly nervous yet?"

"She's getting there." Leah felt herself warm at thoughts of the wedding. "It's so surreal to watch all of this, you know? Like you just said about your boys, I feel like Kelly's still a kid. Like, she can't be getting married yet. She's too young."

"Except she's not." Tilly.

"Except she's not." Leah took a bite of her grilled cheese sandwich, let the sharpness of the Gruyère dance on her tongue. "She's going to be somebody's *wife*. In three months."

"And then she's going to be somebody's *mom*," JoJo said, pointing her fork.

Leah shook her head. "Oh my God. I can't even."

"*You're* such a mom. You know that?" JoJo said it with love, and she wasn't far off.

It was such a weird emotional journey Leah had been on. She was certainly not Kelly's mom, but because of their eight-year age difference, she'd often felt more like a parent than a big sister. Kelly's impending wedding was causing opposing reactions in her. Pride and melancholy. Joy and a bit of sadness. The closer the day got, the more intense Leah's feelings became.

"It's just bittersweet." Leah's smile came from her heart. "I'm stupidly happy for her. It's just really weird to see her so grown up. Wait until your boys get married."

"What do you mean?" Tilly asked. "Those boys are never getting married. Nobody will ever be good enough for their mother."

"You got that right." JoJo sat up straighter. "So, what does Kelly have left to do?"

Leah scrunched up her nose as she thought, trying to remember what they'd talked about at the most recent meeting with Teddi last month. "Let's see. She's still up in the air a bit on the flowers. She needs to decide on shoes. She keeps going back and forth between heels and slight heels."

"Oh my God, tell her to go with the slight heels. Or even better, flats." JoJo's expression was adamant. "She's going to be on her feet all day long. She can thank me later."

"I'll pass that along." Leah finished the last bite of her sandwich and dabbed her face with a napkin as Tilly reached over and snagged a fry off her plate. "Salad remorse?" Their usual exchange.

"Every damn time." Tilly shook her head as she munched the fry.

"Is all the planning making you think about what you'd like for your wedding when the time comes?" JoJo asked. "Whenever I see a bridal show on TV or *Say Yes to the Dress* is on, I start to think about what I'd do if Rick and I ever decided to renew our vows."

Leah felt her own sheepish grin bloom. "I do. I admit it. I think I'd do a spring wedding."

"Yeah? Rick and I got married in June, but so does everybody else in the universe, so I think I'd pick a different season if I could do it again."

"I like what spring symbolizes, you know?" Leah felt herself becoming a bit wistful as she imagined her own wedding. "New beginnings. Freshness. Rebirth."

JoJo agreed, then glanced at Tilly. "You're awfully quiet over there. No opinion?"

Tilly shook her head. "Nope."

"Seriously?" JoJo cocked her head.

"What's wrong?" Leah asked. She knew Tilly too well, and JoJo was right. Tilly without an opinion was unheard of. Tilly shifted in her seat, looking super uncomfortable. Leah furrowed her brow. "Seriously, Tils, what is it?"

Tilly sat up, shook her head casually. "Not a big deal, really. Just, remember when we were at dinner last month? And you and I went to the bathroom and left Jen and Teddi together?"

"Yeah…" Leah drew the word out, having zero idea where Tilly was going.

"Jen was asking Teddi questions about her job, how she liked planning weddings, and did she have ideas for the next time she got married."

"Okay…"

"Teddi told Jen that she wouldn't get married again. That she'd done that and wasn't going to again and good thing she was dating a divorce attorney." Tilly gave a chuckle, but then chewed on her bottom lip.

"Huh." It was all Leah could think to say.

"I mean, they laughed about it, Jen said, so I'm sure it was just lighthearted. That Teddi was just joking around." Tilly looked to JoJo, seemingly for help.

"Of course she was joking," JoJo said, jumping into the mix. "I mean, what kind of a wedding planner doesn't want to get married?"

"Right?" Tilly nodded with great enthusiasm, then waved a hand dismissively.

Leah wasn't sure what to think. It was very possible that Tilly was right. That Teddi had been joking around, being light and fun with somebody she'd just met. Yeah, that was probably it. That had to be it. Because the alternative wasn't something Leah wanted to think about. No, she didn't want to get married *now*. Or even soon. But she did want to get married. It was important to her, that commitment. And the idea that she'd fallen hard for someone who didn't share that view was almost too much to handle. Because she'd know, right? She'd know if Teddi didn't want to get remarried. Wouldn't she?

"I'm sure Teddi was just playing," she said, waving it off. "She's fun and has a great sense of humor."

Tilly and JoJo both agreed, and Leah tried not to notice the relief on their faces as they all laughed. Oh, that Teddi. So funny, right? Such a jokester. But it was relief Leah didn't feel. She was going to have to talk to Teddi about this at some point, wasn't she? She had no idea how, though. She'd have to think on that for a bit. Find the right time, the right approach. Because it was important. It was the future, and the future meant so much to Leah.

And then a thought struck.

What if Teddi's view of the future was completely different from hers? How did she not know this already? What if they simply did not want the same things?

What the hell would Leah do then?

CHAPTER TWENTY-THREE

I had no idea you could grill. Or that you'd look so sexy doing it."
Teddi put a plate on the side shelf and wrapped her arms around
Leah from behind, setting her chin on Leah's shoulder. "Your stock just
went up again."

"Yeah? I'll have to add that to my online dating profile." That got
her an extra tight squeeze and a pinch to her side. "Ow!"

"That's what you get. No more dating profiles. You're mine now."
A kiss on the cheek punctuated the statement and Leah smiled. "God,
it's hot out here."

"The burgers are almost done. Go inside. Be in the a/c. I'm right
behind you." Leah watched Teddi head inside, laughing softly as she
blew a kiss in Leah's direction.

Happy.

That's what Leah was. Happier than she'd ever been. Thrilled
beyond measure over how lucky she was to have a woman like Teddi.
Leah was thoroughly in love. Totally, completely, deeply submerged
in Teddi. This relationship was what she'd always wanted, what she'd
waited *so long* to find.

July had shown up on a blaze of heat. It was still early in the
summer for that kind of crazy humidity, and Leah felt a trickle of sweat
roll down the center of her back as she slid the burgers off the grill and
onto the plate Teddi had brought her.

The air-conditioning hit her like an icy slap when she walked into
the house. She'd made the mistake of letting Teddi set it to her liking.
"I didn't realize my thermostat had a setting marked *arctic*," she called
out, sliding the door shut behind her.

"Babe, it's ninety-seven percent humidity out."

"I am well aware, as is my hair." Leah rolled her eyes upward as if she could see the frizz the weather caused. "And it's like the North Pole in here."

"Dramatic."

"Pretty sure the sweat that was rolling down me has frozen in place."

"Dramatic and hilarious. A twofer." Teddi took the plate from her and added a burger to each of the plates she'd doctored up on the kitchen counter. Buns, lettuce, tomato, onion, condiments, sweet potato fries. Two bottles of beer looked like they were part of a commercial, condensation running down the sides.

Leah snatched one of them up and took a swig, then shivered exaggeratedly. "Dramatic, hilarious, and *freezing*."

Teddi handed her a plate, leaned in close to her ear, and whispered, "Don't worry. I'll warm you up." A swipe of her tongue across Leah's ear punctuated that promise, and Leah shivered again, but for reasons that had nothing to do with the air-conditioning.

It was a Thursday night, and as had become their routine when they were together on a weeknight, they ate side by side on the couch while watching a show of Teddi's choice. Tonight it was an episode of *Dateline*. Leah watched her face as the story progressed. Teddi was riveted, and Leah's heart did that thing that had become a regular occurrence: It warmed and swelled whenever she looked at Teddi when Teddi didn't know she was being observed. The way she focused on the show, the way her chewing slowed down or sped up depending on what was happening. Little quirks of hers that Leah had been noticing and tucking away made her grin. And once in a while, like that night, Teddi would glance over and catch Leah staring.

"What?" she asked, her face flushing a pale pink.

"Nothing," Leah said with a gentle shake of her head. "I just love you."

Teddi leaned over and kissed her quickly. "Love you, too." Then back to the investigation on the screen.

"Thank God they found him guilty," Teddi said a little while later as they carried their dishes into the kitchen, rinsed them, loaded the dishwasher. "I was worried they might not."

"People are awful," Leah said as they returned to the living room.

"Well, not *all* people."

"Lots of them."

"You need to watch something full of love and happiness now?" Teddi knew her well, handed over the remote with a knowing expression on her pretty face.

"Yes, please." Leah switched the channel to a new romance that was premiering that night, then curled herself into Teddi. Reaching for the back of the couch and the fleecy throw that hung there and dodging three swipes by Lizzie before she got a grip on it, she feigned irritation as she muttered, "Middle of freaking July and I need a blanket on me." Teddi laughed and tightened her hold.

The movie turned out to be about a couple on the verge of getting married, and the comic relief was represented by a minor character who was their wedding planner. Teddi had a great time pointing out the inconsistencies with real life. "That's not what happens...Oh my God, I'd never do that...Seriously? She didn't charge for that?"

Leah laughed, found it amusing, and did her best to tamp down the niggling little voice in the back of her head that kept saying *Ask her*. She couldn't. It wasn't the right time. She didn't want to alter the mood. She was afraid of starting an argument. So many excuses why she couldn't bring up a subject that was important to her. Until the movie ended with the not-even-a-little-bit-surprising wedding. Also not surprising was the fact that she teared up.

"Aww, you okay?" Teddi asked, pulling Leah closer and kissing her head.

She nodded, collected herself, craned her neck around to look up at Teddi. "It was so sweet. Didn't you think?"

"I did, yes."

Leah sat up and looked at Teddi's face. "It didn't make you tear up, though."

A warm, tender smile. Teddi reached up and stroked Leah's cheek. "Honey, if I teared up at weddings, I'd have a bit of a problem, don't you think?" She arched an eyebrow with humor.

"Good point," Leah said and let it go.

For now.

❖

Something was up with Leah.

Teddi could feel it. It wasn't big, wasn't something that interrupted their conversations or interfered in their time together. No, rather, it was something that just kind of hung out in the background, like it was waiting for the right time to step into the spotlight, jump up and down, and wave its arms. Was it biding its time? Would it reveal itself at the most inopportune of times? And most importantly, had Teddi lost her marbles, thinking of a feeling or mood of Leah's like it was an actual living thing that hid and knew how to make decisions about timing?

A quiet scoff pushed through Teddi's lips, but Leah didn't seem to notice, which was good. It was Sunday and they were on their way to Kelly and Dylan's for dinner. Their wedding date was closing fast and Kelly's stress levels were high. Leah had suggested that maybe cooking dinner for guests was something she didn't need to do until after the big day, but Kelly had blown up at her. Maybe that's what was bothering her? If she had something she needed to talk about, she'd say so, right? If that slight shadow behind her eyes that darkened the bright green just a little was something important, Leah would bring it up. Until that happened, Teddi had to respect her right to privacy.

Yeah, but… Teddi closed her eyes for a moment. She'd respected Julia's privacy, too, and look where that had gotten her.

"Are you okay?" she asked Leah before she could stop herself.

Leah blinked several times as if she'd been lost and Teddi's voice had yanked her back to the driver's seat of her car. She shot a quick smile Teddi's way. "Yeah. I'm good."

The fact that she didn't ask why Teddi posed the question was kind of a clue that there *was* something bothering her. Obviously, she wasn't ready to share it.

Teddi left it alone, but it sat in the back of her mind, niggling at her and irritating her like a scratchy tag in a new sweater.

Kelly was both happy to see them and also a little bit on edge, but as she hugged Leah, Teddi could see her visibly relax. Leah was her calming force, and it made Teddi smile as she followed behind them through a small and charming living space and out the back door.

The deck was spacious and looked newly painted a deep, dark brown. A glass-topped table sat off to one side, circled by four chairs with brightly patterned cushions in reds and oranges. In the center of the table was a pitcher of what looked to be sangria and several glasses. Along the side of the deck, there were also two zero-gravity chairs side by side and then a grill on the opposite side. Dylan stood in front of it, scraping the grate with his grill brush. He turned to them and grinned a hello as Leah gave him a hug. Teddi did the same. She'd only met him once so far at one of the meetings, but she'd liked him instantly. He was a tall, handsome African American man with a demeanor that put you at ease the second you were near him. What he seemed to care about most in the world was that his fiancée was happy.

"Less than two months away," Teddi said as they took seats and Kelly poured them each a glass of sangria. "How are you guys feeling?"

Kelly and Dylan exchanged a glance, then Dylan shook his head and their tandem grins had a sheepish quality to them.

"Dylan is super calm." Kelly handed out the glasses, then flopped into a chair with a loud sigh. "I, on the other hand, am a hot mess."

"I'm sure that's not true," Teddi said.

A loud snort came from the vicinity of Dylan. Kelly scooped an ice cube out of the sangria pitcher and chucked it at him with an indignant "Hey!" Her face held a hint of a smile, though, and when she turned back to the women at the table, she shrugged. "He's right. I am edgy, to say the least." She took a big slug of her drink. "I knew it was going to be stressful, but *man*."

Teddi sat forward in her chair. Leaned toward Kelly. This was something she knew about. This was her forte. "Listen. Planning a wedding *is* stressful. There's no way around that. It's a ton of money and a ton of decisions and you're basically trusting complete strangers to keep their promises and get you exactly what you asked for exactly the way you want it and on exactly the day you deem. It's *a lot*."

"It's so much," Kelly whispered.

"I've been doing this for a long time, you know?" At Kelly's nod, Teddi went on. "What I have found over the years that helps the most for brides-to-be who are really feeling the pressure is simple. Much simpler than you'd think."

"Oh my God, please tell me. I'll do anything."

"You've got to choose your battles."

Kelly squinted at her.

"By that, I mean you need to decide what's worth your focus

and stress and what isn't. This is why you have me, you know." Teddi smiled widely. "Look at your list of things you needed to get done. You've checked off a good three-quarters of them, right?"

A nod from Kelly. Dylan had also turned and was watching the conversation, seeming to follow with enthusiasm.

"Okay, so the stuff that's left is no big deal. You have your list of what needs to be done and when. The invitations go out next week. You've got an appointment with the florist, and I'll be with you then. Your bridesmaids are in good shape with their dresses and shoes?"

"Yes." Kelly nodded. Drank some more.

"The groom and groomsmen have their suits all squared away?" Teddi turned to face Dylan, who nodded.

"Yes, ma'am."

Back to Kelly. "You found shoes?"

"I've narrowed it down to three pairs."

"Good. That's better than the nine you started with." Teddi winked to lighten the words. "Your dress is being altered as we sit here. Hair and makeup are lined up…" She let the words drift off and waited for Kelly to catch up with her.

"I'm in good shape," Kelly finally said, almost surprised by the sentence.

"You are in good shape," Teddi said, covering Kelly's hand with hers. "See? Take a breath, babe. Nothing to stress about." Watching Kelly's face relax, watching her look to Dylan and smile tenderly, was a satisfaction Teddi would never tire of. It was a part of her job that she loved. Taking away some of the stress and the worry from freaked-out brides-to-be was a major role, and Teddi had perfected it.

"Thank you, Teddi," Kelly said, her voice soft, as she stood and leaned over to hug Teddi.

"You're welcome." Teddi's eyes met Leah's over Kelly's shoulder, and for the first time in months, Teddi had trouble reading Leah's face. Her expression seemed almost shuttered, like she was only letting Teddi have a partial view of what she was feeling. She smiled at Teddi quickly, like she realized she needed to school her features, and it made Teddi uneasy.

The rest of the evening went fairly quickly and Kelly was in a much better place. The tension that had taken up residence on her face had moved out and found someplace else to live—at least until

September hit. They ate delicious steaks and roasted new potatoes that Dylan cooked on the grill like a pro. Teddi had made a salad with walnuts and dried cranberries and goat cheese, and the sangria flowed. Leah almost seemed to be back to her regular self by the time they got ready to go. It was clear to Teddi that she and her sister helped level each other out. Teddi loved her own siblings, but had never had the kind of tight bond Leah and Kelly had, and she found herself a bit envious. Still, though, it warmed her heart to watch them hug good-bye.

Leah had gone a little hard on the sangria, so Teddi drove them back to Leah's place, and Leah was quiet for much of the ride. When they got back to her house and were inside, she went to the fridge, cracked open a bottle of water, and leaned against the counter.

"Do you want to get married?"

Teddi blinked at her, utterly confused by such a weirdly random question. "I'm sorry?"

A half shrug. "It's a simple question. Do you want to get married?"

Teddi tried for a grin, went for light to level off the dark and heavy tone of Leah's voice. "Are you proposing?"

A sigh of obvious frustration. "No." Then a squint. "Yes. I mean, what if I was?"

Teddi had had enough, held her hands out to the side, then dropped them. "Leah, what is going on?"

"Why can't you answer the question?" A little louder than normal. Lots of blinking. Furrowed brows. Leah was obviously angry or frustrated or both. Teddi had never seen her like this.

"Because," Teddi said, keeping her voice level and not raising it, "it's a really random question, and you seem upset, and I'm trying to figure out what's going on."

And then Leah's demeanor shifted from irritated and slightly combative to just plain sad.

Teddi closed the distance between them, rubbed Leah's upper arms. "Baby. What is it? Please talk to me."

Leah swallowed audibly, sipped more water, didn't meet Teddi's gaze for what felt like a long time. Then, with a clear of her throat, she spoke. "Tilly said you told Jen that you didn't want to get married again. That once was enough."

"Well, yeah," Teddi said. The way Leah's eyes went wide and the flash of pain that zipped across her face told her she should've stepped a bit more carefully. "I mean…" She wet her lips, looked away. "My divorce was awful, Leah." Her words were a whisper. "I don't have good feelings around marriage."

"You're a fucking wedding planner." Leah said it much more matter-of-factly than Teddi expected.

"I am. I know. And I love my job. I meant that I don't have good feelings around marriage for me. Around *my* marriage. The end of it wrecked me, Leah. You know this."

Leah nodded. Slowly. Slugged some water from the bottle. When she turned her face toward Teddi and spoke, her voice was hoarse. "And a second marriage is out of the question for you?"

"I…" Teddi let the sentence drop off because she didn't know what to say. She didn't want to hurt Leah. She also didn't want to lie to her. "I don't really know that it's for me." She spoke slowly, carefully choosing her words. "It's not really something I think—"

"For God's sake, can you just answer the question, Teddi? Do you ever want to get married again?"

How did we get here? How had they gone from spending every available minute together, cuddled up to watch TV, dining with friends and family, to this heated argument? To that awful, filled-with-dread look on Leah's face? How had that happened? "I don't. No."

Leah flinched, almost like she'd been poked, and she nodded slowly. "I see." More nodding. "Okay."

They were good together. Teddi knew it. Leah knew it. They were *good*. So why couldn't they just keep going the way things were? Teddi opened her mouth to speak, to ask that exact question, but was stopped by Leah's upheld hand.

"I think…" Leah stared at the floor as if searching there for her thoughts. "I've had a bit too much to drink tonight, so I just want to think." She lifted her head, met Teddi's eyes. "I need to think."

In Leah's eyes, Teddi saw confusion, sadness, and a naked, raw pain that grabbed her heart and squeezed it. Hard. A lump formed that she couldn't seem to swallow back down.

"You should probably go home tonight," Leah said, surprising Teddi.

"What?"

"Yeah. I just need to be alone. I need to think. Please?"

It was the last thing Teddi wanted to do, but Leah's expression was pleading. Her eyes were so sad, and Teddi wanted to make that go away. "Maybe we should talk—"

"No." Leah's one-word interruption was firm, and it startled Teddi. "I'm not in the right frame of mind to do that. I need some time."

"You need some time." Repeating the line was the only thing Teddi could do. She had no idea what to say.

"Yes. Please." Apparently, there was something interesting on the floor, because that's where Leah was looking again.

What could she do but honor Leah's wishes? She could stay, sure. Try and force Leah to talk to her now. But there was something about her face, her demeanor, the tone of her voice that stopped Teddi from pushing. Something that told her maybe going—for now—was the best course of action.

"Okay." A whisper. It was all Teddi could manage as she gathered her things. Leah stayed in the kitchen, remained leaning against the counter. Teddi quickly kissed her on the temple. "Call me later."

An almost indiscernible nod.

Another beat. Two.

Teddi sighed quietly and let herself out of the house. The drive home didn't take long but felt awful. The knowledge that she was driving away from Leah, and the weird feeling that this was some kind of foreshadowing, sat on her heavily, like a lead vest, making it hard to breathe.

Something was about to change.

No. Teddi shook her head. That wasn't quite right.

Something *had* changed.

What was she supposed to do now?

CHAPTER TWENTY-FOUR

Ignoring Teddi's calls and texts was not a cool thing to do. Leah knew that. In fact, she hated doing it. But she just wasn't ready to talk yet. She hadn't quite sorted things in her head, and it was about to be a crazy busy week at work, which was maybe a good thing.

Teddi had called last night. To her credit, she'd given Leah a good three hours before doing so, and she couldn't bring herself to answer. Cowardly? Yes. But she just hadn't been up for talking. About forty-five minutes after she'd ignored the call, Teddi had texted her good night and told her she loved her, just like she had every night for months now.

Leah hadn't responded. Also cowardly. And kind of cruel, she knew.

She usually texted Teddi good morning, as her day started first, but this morning, she hadn't. She'd gotten right up—mostly because she'd been awake on and off all night—showered, dressed, and headed to work. A stop at Starbucks later and she was at her desk, one of the first people in that day.

A little after eight, a text came through from Teddi. *Good morning. Are you just not talking to me at all now?*

Leah sighed. She wasn't being fair at all and she knew it. Quickly, she typed back, *Sorry. Just super busy at work.*

The three gray dots bounced and bounced. Stopped. Bounced some more. Finally the text came: *Got it.*

An awful lot of bouncing dots for two words, so Leah knew that Teddi had typed and discarded several responses. That she was likely upset. Leah was being childish. She was being a little passive-aggressive. She needed to have a talk with Teddi. She knew all these things yet couldn't bring herself to do anything about them.

Teddi didn't want to get married.

Leah absolutely wanted to get married.

"What the hell, Universe?" she muttered into her empty office. Her intercom buzzed and the secretary let her know that her first appointment had arrived and was waiting in the conference room. Leah stood, gathering her paperwork for this particular case. *Okay, let's go talk to yet another person who hates marriage, shall we?*

Leah had grown skilled at turning her own crap off while she worked so she could focus on her clients. Compartmentalizing. And honestly? The busier, the better for her. Anything that could keep her brain occupied and not thinking about Teddi was more than welcome into her schedule, and that's how she looked at that particular day. She stayed busy. Too busy, really, but it was what she needed in order to get through. Teddi texted twice more throughout the day, but Leah couldn't bring herself to respond. Instead, she focused on the four clients she had meetings with, the ton of paperwork she needed to complete, and a sit-down with her boss to keep him abreast of her current caseload.

It wasn't until 7:15 that evening, as she sat at her desk answering email, that she was unceremoniously forced to deal with that crap she'd shoved into a box all day because Teddi walked right through her door. And if her determined steps, her furrowed brow, and the hands parked on her hips were any indication, she was angry. Rightfully so, Leah had to admit.

Leah braced herself, as she hadn't expected Teddi to just show up there. Though why she hadn't expected that was a mystery because, yeah, Leah had been kind of an asshole all day. Well. Not kind of an asshole. An actual asshole. And she suspected Teddi was about to tell her exactly that.

"Seriously?" Teddi led with that, and it was effective, if Leah was honest. She felt herself shrink a bit in her chair, slid her eyes to the left. Teddi closed the door behind her—didn't slam it, much to her credit— and crossed the office to take a seat in a chair in front of Leah's desk. "Have you just never been in a relationship before? So that this is how you think problems are dealt with? You send me away and then decide to pretend I don't exist for the next day?"

"I wasn't pretending you don't exist," Leah said, slightly embarrassed by the catch in her voice.

"No? That's what it felt like. You never don't answer my texts."

"I know."

"What the actual fuck, Leah?"

The curse got Leah's attention. Teddi didn't use the F-word often, another clue that she'd gone beyond upset to *really* upset. "I'm sorry." It sounded kind of lame, and Leah cleared her throat and tried again. "I'm really sorry. I just...our conversation has stuck with me."

"Totally allowed. But can you at least talk to me about it? Instead of acting like a damn child?"

Fair point. Leah took a moment. Okay, they were going to do this now. She gave one nod.

"Okay. Good." Teddi seemed to settle a bit more into the chair, folded her arms across her chest. "Talk to me. What's going on?"

"You don't want to get married." There. She said it. Maybe blurting it out like that wasn't the best approach, but she said it.

"No." No hesitation this time in Teddi's voice. No softness. Leah had obviously pushed her to the point of her being nothing but factual.

"I do. No pun intended." *I can play that game. I can be unemotional, too. See?* It felt awful, though. Instantly.

"Yeah."

A beat went by. There was no other sound discernible aside from the clock ticking on a shelf and Leah's pounding heart. The reality, which Leah thought had sunk in last night, apparently hadn't, because that's what it was doing right now. The woman she'd fallen head over heels in love with didn't want the one thing Leah had been anticipating her entire life. "But why not?" she asked, embarrassed by the crack in her voice.

Teddi must've heard it because her own voice softened just a tiny bit. "Because, Leah. I've done it, and it did not end well for me. I lost so much of myself. After my divorce was final, I vowed that I'd never put myself in that vulnerable a position ever again. I work too hard for what I have."

"But..." Leah couldn't understand why Teddi didn't realize there were options. "If you feel that strongly, then we just draw up a prenup. Something that says your stuff is your stuff, no matter what." Inside, she hated that idea, but she wanted Teddi to know she had choices.

"I don't want to do that." Teddi's eyes slid away, and she focused on the book shelf on the wall.

"Okay, that doesn't make sense. You don't want to get married because you don't like the idea of losing things you've worked for. But you don't want to create a prenup to keep that from happening. I don't understand."

"Why is getting married so important to you?" Teddi countered. Her dark eyes flashed and Leah could see the anger still simmering just below the surface.

"Because it's something I've always wanted. Don't you want a relationship to be working *toward* something? Growing? Instead of staying still? Stagnant? Marriage is that thing for me. Something I've always dreamed of. Being gay doesn't mean I don't think of picking a wedding gown with my mom and choosing just the right music and flowers and wanting to celebrate the intense love I feel for somebody with all my loved ones. Watching Kelly plan her wedding has only solidified it for me. I want to be with somebody who wants that, too. Who wants to share our love with all of our friends and families. Who wants to stand next to me, before them and before God, and promise to love each other for the rest of our lives, ask our loved ones to help us keep that promise. I've pictured it my whole life, Teddi. I picture it with you. Not tomorrow. Not next month. But one day in the not-so-distant future. I picture it with you."

Teddi simply blinked at her and looked like she'd been taken by surprise, which was fair, as Leah hadn't really talked about how very important marriage was to her and why.

Changing tacks, Leah went on. "Look, I can understand how you're kind of soured on the whole thing. I get it. As a person who sees divorce day in and day out, I get it. Your fear is valid. I understand it."

"Yeah?"

"Absolutely. So, why not just do the prenup and nip that problem in the bud?"

Another flash in those dark eyes caused Leah to sit back in her chair.

"Tell me something, Leah." Teddi stood. Began to pace the room. "What the hell is the point of getting married if I have to have legal paperwork drawn up to make sure you don't take half my business when this ends? What is the point? Why not just go on like we are? Is it so bad? Is it terrible that we don't have a piece of paper that says we're legally married?"

Leah had zoned out after one line of that, hadn't heard any of the rest. "When this ends?" she asked quietly.

Teddi turned to look at her. "What?"

"You said, *when this ends*. Like…are you expecting it to? Is it standard to you that this…*thing*…we have is just going to peter out eventually, no matter what? I love you, Teddi. *I love you*. Correct me if I'm wrong, but I'm pretty sure you love me, too."

"Of course I do." Teddi shifted her weight from one foot to the other, an obvious sign of unease.

"Just not enough to marry me. Because this will likely end anyway."

"I mean, there's no guarantee, right?" Teddi chewed on her bottom lip.

Leah stared at her for a moment. Seriously? Teddi wanted guarantees? "No. There isn't. Because this is life, Teddi. It's *life*. And it's worth it, even without guarantees. But if you've entered into this relationship with me assuming it will end at some point. With no faith…" Leah swallowed down the tears that threatened as she looked around the office, trying to find any shred of hope. Then she stared at Teddi until they made eye contact. "Is that what's happened?" she asked quietly.

Teddi blinked, swallowed, looked away.

Leah's heart cracked in her chest and she nodded slowly. "Wow. I see. Okay. I understand. So, then, let me make this easier on you and take care of that right now, okay?" With that, she crossed the room and opened the door. Held it for Teddi, who blinked in surprise. She looked like she had a million things to say, yet she said none of them. Instead, she stood, shouldered her purse, and continued to stare at Leah, who looked down at her shoes. She felt Teddi walk by her and through the doorway more than saw her. Felt the shift in the air. Smelled the scent of her body spray, coconut and lime, fresh like the summer. Listened to the click of her heels as she disappeared down the hallway and out of Leah's life.

Time passed. Leah stood there, lost track of how long. Finally, she closed the door quietly, crossed to her desk to sit back down in her chair, and laid her head back against it as the rush of sadness and remorse built and flooded her entire being. Elbows on the desk, she cradled her head in her hands and let the tears come. She ached, but she'd done the right thing. She couldn't be with somebody who never wanted to be married, who never wanted to take their relationship to the next level, who didn't want to be working *toward* something more. She'd done the right thing.

Hadn't she? And if she had, why did it hurt so much?

❖

As she drove home, Teddi wondered if Leah realized that she'd actually proven Teddi's point. That things didn't last. That everything was temporary. That getting married was stupid.

Okay, maybe that last one was a teeny bit harsh, but...

Leah had pretty much dumped her. Because she didn't want to get married. Was it really that big a deal? A wedding? Guests to witness you both being saps and promising something to each other that likely would not hold up? Yes, she helped people plan weddings. She saw the irony, of course she did; she wasn't an idiot. But more than fifty percent of marriages ended in divorce. Teddi wasn't making that up, it was a fact. Something a factually minded attorney should appreciate.

Why was it such a big deal? Teddi had dreamed about her own wedding when she was younger, too. She could admit that. Those visions from her teenage brain had certainly helped nudge her in the direction of her chosen career, she couldn't deny it. Getting married in a court house had been a matter of convenience, mostly, and marriage wasn't that big a deal to Julia—until it came time for her to claim half the assets. Then she'd been all about it. Teddi scoffed at the memory.

Once home, she poured herself a very large glass of white wine and dropped onto the couch in the living room. Exhausted. Wrung out. Flattened. That was how she felt as she sat there, remote in hand, and tried to find something to watch even though she was barely paying attention. A slug of wine went down hard and she absently wondered if something heavy and invisible was sitting on her chest, as she felt like it was hard to get a full breath. She sat forward, set her wine glass on the coffee table, and tried to focus on her lungs, even as her heart rate kicked up to hummingbird speed. Hand pressed to her chest. Edges of her vision going black. Her entire body suddenly flushed, and she felt like she might spontaneously combust as she ripped her top off and sat there in her bra, panting, wheezing, wondering if she was about to pass out.

It would be another twenty-four hours before Teddi realized she'd actually had her first panic attack in a very long time. Yeah, she was back to that.

Chapter Twenty-five

L eah hated the dead of summer. The heat. The bugs. The goddamn humidity. She just wasn't built for late August in the northeast.

A pool definitely helped. She took a seat on the edge of JoJo's and dropped her bare feet into the water, a sigh of instant relief pushing from her lungs. "Oh, thank God," she muttered from her perch at the shallow end. Watching JoJo's boys and several of their friends daring each other to do flips off the diving board at the other end of the pool, Leah leaned back on her hands. She closed her eyes, letting her head drop back so the sun beat down on her.

"Tell me you have sunscreen on your face." JoJo. Leah opened her eyes to the sight of a large margarita in a plastic glass right under her nose. JoJo sat down next to her, put her own feet in the water, and made a sound very similar to Leah's.

"SPF fifty. I promise."

"Good." They sat quietly, sipped their drinks, watched the kids. "How're you doing, kiddo?"

Leah shrugged. It was the best she could do.

"That good, huh?"

Both JoJo and Tilly knew the whole story. It had been nearly a month since Leah had tossed Teddi out of her office, and aside from a couple of uncertain texts, they'd had no contact. Which was for the best, Leah kept telling herself.

It didn't help.

"No contact?" JoJo had large sunglasses on, so Leah couldn't see her eyes.

A head shake. "Not really. Not since the texts early on."

"That you didn't answer."

Another shake of her head. After a moment of boys splashing and laughing, Leah turned to JoJo. "Do you think I made a mistake?" The question had plagued her for weeks now. She missed Teddi so much it was hard to breathe.

"Do *you* think you made a mistake?"

"Ugh. I hate when you do that."

JoJo shrugged. "I mean, it doesn't really matter what I think."

"Jo, you're my friend and you know me. I'm *asking* you what you think."

JoJo took a deep breath, then set her glass down and leaned back to mimic Leah's pose. "That's a tough call because I really can see both sides of the argument."

Leah nodded. She almost could, too. Almost. "I have always wanted to get married." She said it quietly. Almost wistfully.

"I know this about you."

"The thing is, I don't think I even knew how much I wanted it, how important it is to me, until I was told I wouldn't have it."

JoJo nodded, didn't say anything, kept her eyes on the boys while she listened.

"And in those moments of doubt, I think, *Was I too hasty? Did I give her a chance? What if she changes her mind?* And then immediately on the heels of that thought comes, *What if she doesn't?* I'm just not willing to put more of my heart and soul into a relationship that's never going to go any further." Anguish. It's what Leah felt every time she went through this whole thing in her head. "Is that selfish of me?" She looked to JoJo, one of her best friends in the entire world. What was it she expected? What did she want from her? Absolution? Agreement? A magic fix?

JoJo turned her way and laid a hand on Leah's thigh. "No, I don't think you're being selfish. I think you have to do what works for you."

It was vague at best. "I just don't think I could take it if we stayed in it for another year—or longer—and nothing changed. Like, what would we be working toward? What would be the point?"

"I mean…" JoJo lifted one shoulder, her attempt at nonchalance, Leah knew. "I guess the point would be loving each other? Building a life?"

Not the answer Leah wanted, and it sliced at her a bit. Before she could say anything, JoJo continued.

"But if you want something more, it's absolutely your right to say so. To hold out for it. There's nothing wrong with that."

Okay. Better. Not great, but better.

Leah blew out a long slow breath. "It would be easier if I didn't miss her so damn much. How did that happen? It was a few months."

"Seven. Seven months. That's more than a few."

"I guess."

"And you were in love. You *are* in love. That doesn't just go away. If it did, it means you weren't in love in the first place."

JoJo was right. Quiet reigned for several moments as they kicked their feet languorously and watched the kids play, empty margarita glasses set out of the way of the water.

"The wedding is only a few weeks away." JoJo made the statement. Asked nothing. But the question was clear.

"Yeah." Leah had avoided Kelly's last two meetings with Teddi, and her sister was less than thrilled about it. Leah had gladly given her opinions to Kelly at her house or at lunch or at their mom's or anyplace but Teddi's shop. "I'm going to need that time to gear up for the wedding day. I wonder if it will be easy or hard to avoid her." A bitter laugh followed.

"She'll be busy. And you'll be all about Kelly. It'll be fine."

Would it? God, she hoped so. Leah certainly wouldn't do anything to spoil the day for her sister. She could be around Teddi. She was a grown woman who had mastered many difficult things in her life. Spending a day in the same general vicinity with the woman she loved more than she'd expected to but couldn't be with should be something she could handle. She'd do it for Kelly.

"And you and Tilly will be there. You can keep me from losing my mind, right?"

JoJo gave a snort. "That might be a lost cause."

"Ha ha. You're hilarious."

"You'll have me and Rick and Tilly and Jen. We've got you, babe."

"I almost forgot about Jen." Another mirthless laugh. "So much for Tilly making an honest woman out of me when I turn forty." She grinned at JoJo to show she was just teasing, because she really did like Jen a lot, and Jen made Tilly happier than Leah had ever seen her. But that simply meant Leah was the only one left of the trio who was alone. Still. She looked up as she felt JoJo squeeze her shoulder with affection.

"I'm a little worried about you, kiddo."

The simple statement—and the concerned love in JoJo's eyes—made her own well up. Several blinks and a clear of the throat helped Leah pull it together. She covered JoJo's hand with hers. "Me, too," she whispered.

❖

Throwing herself into her work was the only thing Teddi could do to keep from going completely out of her mind. She'd expected to miss Leah, but not this much. Not so much that she had a hard time sleeping. Not so much that she couldn't eat. Not so much that her panic attacks became more frequent, to the point where she knew she should probably call a doctor about them.

Thank God fall was almost as busy as summer for weddings. The oranges, yellows, and reds of the leaves were a huge draw for brides-to-be. The weather could be fickle, but September was usually a fairly safe choice, and every weekend of the month was booked for Hopeless Romantic, with three of them being double. She and Preston were going to be running around like toddlers on too much sugar taking care of everything. But she wasn't worried. Preston was more than capable, and Teddi herself was happy to have so much to focus on that wasn't about her and Leah.

Of course, Kelly's wedding was this weekend.

"This is exactly why you don't get involved with anybody at work," Teddi muttered to herself as she used a box cutter to slice open a recent UPS delivery of accessories.

"I've told you that more than once," Preston said as he walked past her, a stack of plates in his hand. He was changing out the tablescape window display, replacing the summery one with a display of jewel tones for fall. Deep eggplant, slate blue, muted reds and oranges would all play a role.

"Same, same, same," said Harlow in a singsong voice as she sat at the table updating some of the photos Teddi had hanging around the shop.

Teddi dropped her head, let it hang as she took a deep breath. While her friends had been supportive enough and showed some sympathy, they were less than enthusiastic about it, and she realized in that exact moment that her patience had run out. Tears filled her eyes as she stood up and held her arms out to the sides. "Why are you guys acting like you're mad at *me* over this?" She'd hoped to sound firm and authoritative, but instead, her voice cracked and the eye-welling got worse. "*I* didn't break things off."

The glance that Preston and Harlow exchanged across the shop made one thing painfully clear: They had discussed this very subject with each other. And they had feelings about it, which was punctuated by Preston setting a plate down a bit too firmly. Then he turned, hands on his hips, and opened his mouth to speak.

Harlow jumped out of her chair, held a hand up his way, and he snapped his mouth shut. Teddi watched all of this happen like a spectator watching Ping-Pong.

"We love you." Harlow led with that, a clear indicator that Teddi wasn't going to like what followed, and she said as much.

"Ah. Okay. Positive reinforcement first. Preparing me for the blow." She shook out her arms like a boxer at a fight. "Okay. Ready. Hit me."

"I guess we just don't…" Harlow looked to Preston, then back at Teddi, seeming to walk on eggshells as she said, "We're not quite sure why you haven't fought to get Leah back."

Teddi blinked at her. Turned to Preston and blinked at him. Did Harlow really just say that? Was that really what her friends thought? She swallowed down her anger at them. "Fought to get her back? Did you guys miss the part where she said she couldn't be with me? When she threw me out of her office? 'Cause I'm pretty sure I mentioned that, but if I didn't, please say so and I'll recap."

Harlow scratched her forehead as she blew out a breath and seemed to take some time figuring out what to say next.

"Because you can't bend." It was Preston, and unlike Harlow, he was not walking on eggshells. In fact, he sounded pissed.

Teddi furrowed her brow at him. "Excuse me?"

"You can't bend." Preston shook his head. "Or you won't. I'm not sure which."

"I have no idea what you're talking about." Teddi really didn't. She needed more information. She needed to understand why the man who'd been her right hand and a most trusted friend was looking at her with such disappointment on his face, it made her want to cry.

Preston crossed the floor so he was closer to Teddi. His deep eyes bored into her as he spoke. "I have never seen you so happy as you were with Leah around."

A sudden lump formed in Teddi's throat.

"She was good for you. *Really* good for you." Preston had softened his tone just a touch.

"She really was," Harlow agreed.

"I know." Teddi couldn't deny it. It was the absolute truth. "But—"

"If you say you want different things, I will punch you in the face." The softness in Preston's tone had vanished. Teddi flinched at his words.

"Um, harsh."

"No, Teddi, you want to know what's harsh? Not bending a little bit and trying to meet the person you claim to love in the middle. That's harsh. Shutting somebody's dream down completely because it's not necessarily something you want—somebody you claim to love, BTW—is harsh. Not trying to find any kind of compromise so you can salvage an incredible relationship is harsh."

Teddi gaped at him, shocked by the anger of his words.

"You had something amazing, something many people never find, and you tossed it away because you can't step back from your own fears and look at the big picture for one damn second. If I had somebody who looked at me the way you two looked at each other…" The wind seemed to leave his sails then, and Preston shook his head, looked out the front window. "I just can't with you right now. I love you, but I just can't." He went back to his window display, leaving Teddi to continue to stare after him.

Silence reigned for a moment or two, the only sound the clattering of plates and chargers and silverware as Preston set his table. Teddi turned to Harlow, who simply raised her eyebrows and shrugged, clearly not about to contradict anything that Preston had said.

Spaghetti head. One of Teddi's brides had used the phrase once with Teddi when she was completely overwhelmed by all the decisions she'd had to make. She told Teddi she had spaghetti head, and the visual was perfect. Teddi had known exactly what she'd meant and she knew it now as well because that's what *she* was currently suffering from. Complete and utter spaghetti head. There was so much in her brain: Kelly's upcoming wedding, her own failed marriage, memories of how hard it had been for her to claw her way back to normal life. But mostly, her head was filled with Leah. Leah's face and her laugh and her body and her huge heart and how she made Teddi feel and the look on her face when she'd asked Teddi to leave her office and how empty Teddi's life had felt since.

There was no more conversation at that point. The phone rang and Teddi went back to her office to take the call, a vendor double-checking about what time the venue for Kelly's wedding would be open. She filled him in just as another call beeped through. That was likely how the rest of the day would go, prepping for the weekend's ceremonies. Which was good because Teddi was able to shelve the one question that plagued her, at least for now.

Was Preston right?

CHAPTER TWENTY-SIX

Kelly's wedding was equal parts emotional and beautiful, and it went off without a hitch. Leah had seen Kelly in her dress multiple times, right up until the moment they had to walk down the aisle. You'd think that would have prepared her for the sight of her baby sister, on their father's arm walking slowly down the aisle between rows of white chairs. Leah's eyes welled up immediately and she feared for the makeup that been so painstakingly applied to her earlier that day.

Stunning. It was the only word Leah could find to describe her sister. The dress was simple, with beaded stitch work and a long train, her bouquet of yellow, red, and orange flowers adding a splash of color. Leah cried silently, felt hot tears track down her cheeks. Makeup be damned, this was her little sister and she was beautiful.

It amazed Leah how quickly it all went. They'd been planning for more than a year. So much went into making one day as perfect as it could be. Just one day. And before Leah knew it, the ceremony was over, dinner had been eaten, the lights were down, and dancing had ensued. She sat at a table with her aunt and uncle and a glass of wine and simply watched as Kelly's teacher friends formed a conga line and chugged around the room, Kelly in the lead. Dylan stood off to the side watching. He'd been grinning like a fool since the morning, and when he looked at Kelly, Leah's heart ached. In two ways. It ached with happiness and joy for her sister, who now had a husband who adored her. And it ached for Leah herself, who'd had a woman look at her like that—a woman she'd given up on in the blink of an eye.

A woman who is right over there by the cake table.

Leah turned her chair so she couldn't see Teddi. She'd been fairly successful at avoiding her all day, aside from times when they had to communicate or be in the same room, and much of her process had involved shifting her view. It didn't help that Teddi looked amazing. Leah had never seen her dressed for a work wedding. She wore all black—an attempt not to stand out, Leah assumed—but on Teddi, with her dark hair and eyes and olive skin, a tight-fitting black dress was damn near the perfect outfit. She wore pumps, which surprised Leah, as Teddi was on her feet the entire time, but even now, as things were beginning to wind down, Teddi looked completely fresh, not a hair out of place, not anything remotely resembling a frazzled expression. Only smiles, calm words, instant solutions.

Damn her.

She hadn't tried to talk to Leah on anything other than a business level today, and for that, Leah was both grateful and irritated. She also knew she was being selfish and irrational, and she was annoyed with herself for all of those feelings. Thank God this was almost over because she was beyond ready to be done and go home. Back to her couch and her cat and her romance movies that were now nothing more than cruel fantasies. Nobody had ever been able to shake her love of rom-coms. Until Theodora Baker had sidled into her life and been tossed out of it.

"Hi."

Leah startled, and looked up into the darkest eyes, accentuated by dark, full lashes. Teddi's face was framed by all that bouncy, wavy hair, and Leah was both drawn in and pushed away by the beauty.

"Hi." That damn lump was back. Leah pressed her lips together in a straight line.

Teddi pointed at the empty chair next to Leah. "May I?"

Leah gave a curt nod. What was she supposed to say? No? She wasn't about to be rude at her sister's wedding.

"The ceremony was beautiful," Teddi said once she'd taken a seat, and while to anybody else she would have sounded perfectly normal and confident, Leah knew her well enough to hear the slight tremor in her voice. The hesitation. "Kelly looks stunning."

"She does. Everything went well."

A beat went by as the two of them watched the dancers.

"I'm really happy for them," Teddi said.

"Me, too." *God, this is painful.* Did it have to be? How did they get here? How exactly had this happened? And why? What was the point of the Universe handing her somebody like Teddi—somebody she clicked with like two puzzle pieces fitting together—only to turn around and take her away? Leah had spent weeks now trying to understand what she was supposed to have learned.

"I miss you." Teddi said it so quietly that between her low volume and the music from the DJ, Leah wasn't sure she'd heard correctly. When she ventured a glance in Teddi's direction, she knew she had. Teddi's eyes were sad, wet, and she visibly swallowed.

Leah had so much to say and at the same time didn't want to say anything. Not here. Not now. "Look—" she began, but stopped when Teddi held up a hand.

"No. No, I'm sorry. This is your sister's wedding. It's not the time or the place. I shouldn't have said anything." She stood and pushed the chair neatly back in to the table. Looking down at Leah, her whole expression softened. She reached out a hand as if to touch Leah's face, but seemed to decide against it and let it drop to her side. "But it was really good to see you today, Leah. You look beautiful."

She turned and walked away.

It felt final.

Leah understood suddenly that because the wedding was over, there would be no more need to see Teddi without making an effort. There were no more meetings. No more *I don't want to go, but I have to* trips to Hopeless Romantic. This was it.

Leah downed the rest of her wine in a huge gulp, set the glass on the table behind her, and felt everything in her simply deflate.

It felt final because it was.

❖

The aquarium was always busier on the weekends than during the week when Teddi usually went. But she needed the feeling, the calm it always brought her to sit and watch the sea creatures. She'd found a small bench in a tucked-away corner, and she sat there for a long while, watching the tropical fish in all their brightly colored neon glory swim past the glass.

Yesterday had been brutal. She could admit that now.

Turning the whole thing over to Preston had crossed her mind. More than once. But she couldn't do that to Kelly. She'd been with her every step of the way, and passing her off to Preston on the day they'd been working so hard toward would've just been cruel. Bad business, yes, but also a bad thing for a friend to do. And she did consider Kelly a friend now. Which was probably stupid, given the circumstances.

Leah had been...

God.

Leah had been beyond gorgeous. Stunningly beautiful. Yes, all eyes were supposed to be on the bride on her wedding day, but Teddi's focus had been on the maid of honor pretty much all day. She did her best to be subtle about it and Harlow only shot her a look once, telling her she noticed. But for the love of all things holy, the off-the-shoulder emerald dress? The way her hair was pulled back into a very complicated twist, a few strands hanging down to frame her face? The pride and love in her expression all day? Teddi had never seen a woman more beautiful in her entire life as Leah Scott was on her sister's wedding day. Seriously. Teddi'd had trouble taking a full breath for much of the reception.

She was glad she'd approached Leah, that she'd sat with her. It had been so hard to simply walk up and say hi. Ridiculous, really, because how hard was it to say hello? But Teddi felt like her skin was being taken off by a vegetable peeler, she was so nervous. Leah had allowed her to sit, which was more than Teddi had expected, so the fact that the conversation hadn't been long or in-depth or any of the things she'd intended didn't really matter. And it really hadn't been the right time to talk anyway. Teddi was proud of herself for taking her leave when she had. The sight of Leah's deep green eyes looking up at her in concern, uncertainty, and sadness was something she wouldn't be able to erase from her memory any time soon.

A bright yellow seahorse made his way by while a blue-and-yellow angelfish passed by him going in the opposite direction, and Teddi smiled, felt her stress level decrease by a point or two. She liked to think of the sea life as moving along on a road, heading to work or school or home, busily living their lives and paying zero attention to the brooding brunette human sitting outside their window.

The only reason she'd slept like the dead last night was because she was so tired. The night of a wedding was always like that for her. She would go, go, go nonstop from eight in the morning until after midnight that night, and when she got home, she'd simply fall into bed.

Sometimes, she didn't even undress. Last night had been like that—except she woke up at four a.m. and her mind filled with Leah.

She had to do something.

Nobody made her think like Leah. Wasn't that a weird thing to say? But it was true. First, about the dissolution of her marriage. Teddi had spent the better part of two years being bitter and angry and Leah made her see that yes, the end of any marriage was sad, but the split had been fair. Awful, but fair. It was a bump, an obstacle, but she'd gotten over it and had gone on with her life, and how amazing was that? Second, about marriage in general, specifically marriage for a second time. Well, to be fair, Preston and Harlow had also played roles, but the topic had been hanging out in Teddi's head for days now. Sometimes in the background, tapping at her with a gentle finger. Other times in the forefront and using a sledgehammer. And she certainly hadn't changed her mind and decided to jump into a second marriage. She was far from ready for that. What she had been doing, though? She'd been considering the possibility. And *that* was a big deal.

She had to do something.

But what? Because she very well might have blown it. For good. Leah had barely made eye contact yesterday and it hurt more than Teddi cared to admit. It had sliced her like a scalpel, deep and precise.

The blackbar soldierfish went by in a bright orange school, and Teddi watched them move as one. That's what she wanted. To move as one with somebody. No. No, not with somebody. With Leah. Only with Leah.

She had to do something.

She slid out her phone and sent two texts out, then blew out a huge breath and sat back against the wall behind her bench. A purpose. She had a purpose now. A goal. That simple fact relaxed her in a big way as she watched the marine life flit by the glass. It was possible she'd fail. It was possible that she really had blown it, that there was no fixing things. But damn it, she was at least going to try. And that would allow her to look at herself in the mirror each morning. Knowing she'd tried instead of run.

It was time to do something.

❖

"I hope you guys know how much I appreciate you meeting me on a Sunday. I'm so sorry to pull you away from your lives, but…" Teddi slipped her coat off and tossed it over the chair behind the front counter in Hopeless Romantic. She, Preston, and Harlow were all there. In fact, they got there before her and Preston had let Harlow in. They were waiting for her when she'd arrived from the aquarium, and the speed with which they'd dropped whatever they were doing and had shown up for her brought tears to her eyes. "I need your help."

Harlow crossed to the coffee area and popped a pod into the machine. "Anybody else?" she asked. At two nods, she readied two more.

Preston reached under the counter and pulled out an unopened bottle of Baileys, a gift from a client the previous month. "Seems like we might need this," he said, and Teddi surprise-hugged him, throwing her arms around his torso before he even saw her coming.

Once they all had coffee and Preston had poured a shot of Bailey's into each mug, they sat around the table. Preston sat back in his chair, his arms folded across his chest, and the casualness of his jeans and black Under Armour compression shirt took nothing away from how precisely good looking the man was. Harlow wore leggings and a long gray sweatshirt that said *Be Kind* on the front. Her hair was in a messy bun, and she sat forward, leaning her forearms on the table. They waited.

"God, I don't even know how to begin this other than to say I've been doing a lot of thinking lately." Teddi took a sip of her coffee, savored the sweetness of the Baileys, then cleared her throat. "About Leah. About me and Leah. About me. A lot about me."

Preston sipped, waited. Harlow's eyes never left hers.

"I want her back." There. She'd said it. She inhaled, then blew out the breath loudly and said it again just for the hell of it. "I want her back. I miss her so much, my entire body aches."

A grin had slowly grown and spread across Preston's face. Harlow looked like she was two seconds from a happy giggle—which came two seconds later, and she clapped her hands together in delight.

"It's about goddamn time," Preston said. "I didn't think you were ever going to get here."

"Was it yesterday?" Harlow asked. "Is that what did it?"

"Seeing her yesterday definitely gave me a nudge, but I've been rolling some things around in my head for a while now. And you guys the other day?"

Harlow grimaced. "We were hard on you." She sent a look Preston's way.

"No," Teddi said, her voice strong. "No, you were telling me what I needed to hear. I didn't want to hear it, but I needed to hear it." She turned to Preston, who hadn't said anything about that day, but the red in his cheeks told her there was an element of shame for him. "And you were right." Teddi reached across and squeezed his hand, silent forgiveness. "So. Here's what I know." She went on to tell them everything she'd concluded at the aquarium, the sum of all her thoughts of late mixed in with what it had felt like to see and be around Leah yesterday. "I realized at the end of last night that it was very possible I'd never see her again. With the wedding over, there's not really any reason we'd end up in the same place at the same time. If we wanted to see each other, we'd have to make it happen, make the effort." She gave one determined nod. "And I think that effort has to come from me."

"I think so, too." Preston sat forward and mimicked Harlow's pose of forearms on the table, hands folded. He squinted—his thinking face, Teddi knew.

"I'm not ready for marriage and I don't think Leah is either. But I need to find a way to tell her that I'm open to it. In time."

"And are you?" Harlow asked, her eyes searching Teddi's. "Are you truly?"

Teddi didn't hesitate, surprising both of her friends and herself when the grin blossomed across her face. "I am."

Harlow reached over, squeezed Teddi's hand with both of hers, and if her happiness had been written all over her face, it would've been in bright neon colors.

Preston clapped his hands and rubbed them together, apparently preparing to hatch a plan. "Okay, then. You're gonna need something major here."

"Agreed," Harlow said, her excitement palpable, her arms waving in enthusiastic animation. "Time to pull out the big guns. You need Bill Pullman from *While You Were Sleeping* bringing his whole family to the tollbooth."

"You need Piper Perabo from *Imagine Me & You* standing on a car in a traffic jam." Preston. At the startled look Teddi gave him, he shrugged and said, "What? I watch lesbian stuff sometimes."

Harlow laughed, then said, "Henry Golding from *Crazy Rich Asians* professing his love on a crowded airplane."

"God, that man is hot, steamy sex on a cracker," Preston said on a sigh.

"Oh my God, he so is." Harlow dreamy-sighed, too.

"Hey," Teddi said, snapping her fingers in front of them. "Come back from fantasy land. We're talking about me here."

"Right, right. I've got an idea." Harlow got up and hurried behind the counter, then returned with a pen and a small notepad. She sat down, turned to Preston, and then they were talking to each other. "We get her attention using what she loves: rom-coms."

"We?" Teddi asked, amused.

"You. You. You know what I mean. But we're going to need some stuff from the warehouse. And time to make it all work." Harlow jotted some notes; Preston read them, nodded, and added a few things himself.

Teddi picked up her coffee mug and held it in both hands as she sat back and watched her best friends hatch a plan to help her. God, she was lucky to have them. She listened as the idea came together slowly, each piece sliding into place with a click. As Teddi's eyes widened at the scope, Harlow smiled tenderly at her.

"Go big or go home, right?"

Teddi nodded, and when she smiled back at her friends, it was with a renewed sense of possibility.

I'm gonna get her back.

CHAPTER TWENTY-SEVEN

I hate you because you're tan." Leah punctuated the statement with a pout as she sat in Kelly's passenger seat.

"As long as you don't hate me because I'm beautiful," Kelly countered with a grin.

"I hate you 'cause of that, too."

"I don't believe you."

Leah smiled as they drove along Main Street and out of downtown toward the suburbs. Fall was in full force as November waited in the wings, ready to make an appearance. The color palette of the world had shifted from lush greens to cozy oranges, reds, and yellows. Leaves blew along the street, summer flowers bid farewell until next year, and the air held that scent of earth and wood and crispness.

"I missed you," Leah said as they sat at a red light. "I'm so glad you liked the cruise, though."

"Oh my God," Kelly said, dropping her head back and making a sound of intense enjoyment. "It was the best. I think everybody should take a cruise at least once. We need to get Mom on one. She'd love it."

"And you and Dylan…?"

"Had so much sex I think we scared the older couple in the next cabin." They laughed together as Kelly hit the gas and propelled them forward. "And how are you doing?"

Leah tried unsuccessfully to stifle her sigh. "I'm okay." She felt Kelly look at her more than saw it.

"Yeah?"

A half shrug. "I guess."

"Any contact since the wedding?"

"No." And Leah was disappointed by that. And also confused. Because she'd been the one to break it off. She was the one who cruelly held the door open for Teddi and told her to leave. Expecting any more contact than Teddi had already attempted was not only unfair, it was ridiculous. Still, she missed Teddi more than she cared to admit to anybody. Time had only eased the pain the smallest of amounts. It still hurt. It still squeezed her heart. She still remembered how it was with Teddi, still dreamed about her...

A subject change was in order. Now.

"Where are we going again?" Leah asked.

"I'm going to look at some school supplies I found on eBay. This woman has space in a warehouse at the edge of town, and she's trying to get rid of some stuff. I thought I might be able to use it."

"You're meeting a stranger in a warehouse at the edge of town at seven in the evening. That's not sketchy. Nope. Not sketchy at all."

"Why do you think I asked you to come?"

"You do get points for that."

"Duh. And I promise to take you out for a birthday dinner afterward."

"Ugh. I don't want to think about that. I have decided I don't want to be forty, so I'm not going to be."

"Oh, good. 'Cause that works."

"Shut up."

Another ten minutes and Kelly turned into a driveway that led to a large parking lot with a large array of buildings circling it, all of the gray, steel, industrial type.

"Okay..." Kelly squinted to her left. "There. Number nineteen." She pulled the door handle and got out.

Leah ducked her head to get a better look, but there wasn't much to see. A handful of cars dotted the lot, and lights were on here and there, but there was little activity. She got out of the car. Kelly was typing on her phone.

"She's in here." With a gesture for Leah to follow, Kelly started toward building number nineteen.

The gray steel door was closed, an outdoor light hung above it shining down in a pool of hazy yellow. A doorbell was mounted to the left, and Kelly pushed it.

"I feel like this is the beginning of a horror movie, Kel." Leah glanced around the lot, a weird feeling of anxious anticipation in the pit of her stomach.

"Would you relax?"

"Yeah, you won't be saying that when the masked serial killer comes at us with an ax." She shivered. "Tilly would love this." The sudden buzz of the door startled her enough to make her flinch, and Kelly pulled it open.

"Ready?"

Leah shrugged. "To be murdered and dismembered? I guess."

Kelly smiled and shook her head. "I think this will be much more pleasant."

"Famous last words."

They went in.

To their left was what seemed to be an office. There was a window looking out onto the rest of the space—which Leah couldn't see because the office was the only bit with any light. Its door was shut. There was a note taped to it.

Kelly pulled the paper off the door and read it aloud. "Follow the lights to the X. I'll meet you there." The second she finished, there was a loud click and one light overhead lit up. It wasn't bright, just bright enough to light their way. Leah still couldn't see into the rest of the warehouse area. Then another light about ten feet farther down also clicked on.

"Seriously? That's not creepy at all."

But Kelly wore a big smile and grabbed Leah's hand. "Come on. It's an adventure."

Another light another ten feet down the line clicked on, and now there was a clear path to walk.

Something about Kelly's demeanor—her big grin, the sparkle in her eyes—told Leah to follow her. So she did.

When they were standing under the third light, Leah looked around. "Okay. Where's the next one." She glanced at Kelly, who was still smiling. "You're not even a teeny bit unnerved by this? Really?" The next click was louder, and a big space suddenly lit up. Leah squinted, as it looked like a tollbooth of some sort. A large orange X made out of tape was visible on the floor in front of it. "What the hell?"

Kelly held up the note, waved it around. "It says to follow the lights and stand on the X."

Leah shook her head. "I don't know about this…"

Kelly tugged her by the hand. "Come on, Leah." At Leah's raised eyebrows, Kelly tilted her head to the side and said, quietly and simply, "Trust me."

Swallowing down the nerves and trepidation, Leah squinted at her sister, but followed her to the X.

"Okay. Stand on it."

"You're the one trying to buy stuff. This isn't for me."

Kelly grabbed Leah's shoulders and moved her until she stood on the X. "Yes, it is," she whispered.

The three lights that had led the way suddenly clicked off, and with a knowing grin, Kelly stepped backward until the dark swallowed her and Leah was left standing in the pool of light in front of what, yes, actually was a tollbooth. Nobody was inside, but Leah could see through the windows to the other side of it—and that's when a figure appeared, and Leah couldn't believe her eyes.

Teddi.

She stood on the other side of the tollbooth, like she was looking inside, gave a small wave. "Hi, Leah."

Leah blinked several times before remembering how her voice worked. "Hey." A soup of emotions ran through her body, her mind, her heart. First and foremost was how amazing it was to simply see Teddi in the flesh again. To have her standing no more than a dozen feet away. Of course, that was followed by utter confusion. "What's going on? What is all this?" She started to move, but Teddi stopped her.

"*No*. No, stay there. Please. And just hear me out. Okay?"

Something about her voice. Not pleading or desperation, really, but…Leah searched for the right word. Hope? Yeah, maybe it was that, and Leah was willing to let that glow, at least long enough to hear what Teddi had to say.

Also, she looked fantastic.

Leah could only see her from the waist up, but she wore a red sweater with a V-neck, and her dark hair was pulled back in a casual ponytail, random wavy wisps framing her beautiful face.

"Okay."

Teddi's relief was apparent, and a tentative smile bloomed across her face. "Thank you. So." She stood up taller, clasped her hands together. "The very first thing I need you to know is that I miss you.

So much. You have no idea. For two solid months, I've thought of you every single day. Wondered where you are, what you're doing, if you're okay, if Lizzie is okay…" Leah smiled at that. "You're the first thing I think about when I open my eyes in the morning and the last thing I think about when I go to sleep at night. So, some things haven't changed." She gazed down toward the floor as if gathering some strength. When she raised her head again, there was a new determination in her eyes that Leah could see even from where she stood. "The second thing I need you to know is that I have done a lot of thinking. *A lot* of thinking. About you and about us, but also about me. That seems to be a talent you have—making me delve into myself and really examine things that I've kept tucked away for so long…" With a grin, she tossed a token into the little receptacle of the tollbooth, which hit a vaguely familiar note for Leah, and the lights clicked off, plunging Leah into darkness.

But only for a couple seconds, as another light clicked on to her left. Before her was a lone car and nothing else. About ten feet in front of it was another X. Leah dutifully walked over and stood on it.

Teddi appeared from the darkness and Leah watched as she literally *climbed* the car until she stood on the roof.

"Wait." The proverbial lightbulb went off in Leah's head, and something very pleasant flooded her body. Was it that same hope she'd seen in Teddi's eyes? Pointing a finger back in the direction she'd come from, she asked, "Was that *While You Were Sleeping*?"

"Shh," Teddi said with a grin. "Don't interrupt me."

Leah held up her hands and laughed. "Sorry. Apologies. Continue, please."

"Where was I? Oh, right. The thinking. You, Leah Scott, are the only person in my entire life who somehow forces me to look inward. That's not easy for me, and I resented it for a while, especially after we broke up." Her voice softened. "Because I didn't like what I saw when I looked inward."

Leah swallowed, and her heart squeezed in her chest at the sad self-awareness on Teddi's face.

"But I've done some serious soul-searching. Which is horribly clichéd, I know, but still true, and I've realized some things." She cleared her throat, shifted her weight, looked down at Leah. "I've realized that letting go of the past is okay. That I'm allowed to do that.

That it doesn't define me or my life." A pause. "I have also realized that past performance doesn't indicate future success. Which I just heard and it sounds like something an ad for your firm would say in fine print." Teddi's chuckle was a nervous one, but Leah smiled anyway. "And most importantly. *Most importantly*, I learned that I do not want to be without you."

A loud click and Leah was plunged into darkness again. As she waited, her brain raced at breakneck speed. Teddi had put this together and she was using settings from Leah's favorite romances to punctuate her points—the car was obviously a shout-out to *Imagine Me & You*. It was brilliant and it was beautiful and it was working. Leah already felt herself slipping back toward her. She was afraid of that hope, but also? She wanted it. She craved it so badly, she could taste it, she could feel it sneaking into her brain, into her heart, wrapping around her like ivy. She stood still and waited until another light clicked on. Without hesitation, she moved to the X and scanned the scene. It was the inside of an airplane, or a section of it. Six rows of seats, two seats on each side, blue industrial carpet down the aisle and a doorway with a curtain drawn across it at the end. Leah waited and in a moment, the curtain was pulled aside and Teddi walked onto the carpet, hands behind her back, face earnest. Leah noticed that her upper lip was beaded with sweat. As she spoke, she took small, slow steps up the aisle.

"I love you, Leah. That's not news. And I know I acted like we don't want the same thing—no." She swiped a hand through the air. "No, I basically *told* you we don't want the same thing. But that's not true. Because what I want is to be with you." At the end of the aisle closest to Leah now, Teddi brought her hands out from behind her back. In them was a black velvet box.

Teddi got down on one knee.

And Leah gasped softly.

"I know it's way too early for marriage. We have things to work through. Things to discuss and so much more to learn about each other. There's nothing more in my life that I would rather do. I want to spend the rest of my days with you, Leah. And until we reach that point where we decide we're ready to take the next step—and we will—I am giving you my heart." She opened the box slowly. Inside was the most gorgeous necklace Leah had ever seen. A thin silver chain sparkled in the light, supporting a silver heart encrusted with what looked a hell of a lot like diamonds to Leah.

"Oh my God." Leah brought her fingers to her lips, shock, disbelief, joy, hesitation all warring within her. But along with them was the biggest emotion of all. Love. Big, bold, all-consuming. She loved Teddi. She'd never not loved Teddi.

"Leah?" Teddi's voice was soft as she knelt in front of Leah and held up the box toward her. "Can we try again?"

There was no question, and Leah knew it. If she was being honest, she'd known it the second the tollbooth had lit up. She reached down and cradled Teddi's face in both hands. "Yes," she whispered. "Please. Let's do that."

The smile the erupted on Teddi's face—and that's what it did, erupted, like joy exploded—was the most wonderful thing Leah had seen in months. Teddi stood and Leah wrapped her arms around Teddi's neck and kissed her. Soundly. Thoroughly. With every ounce of love and happiness she was feeling in the moment.

"Here." Teddi stepped back slightly and took the necklace out of the box. "I seriously almost bought a ring."

"You did not." Teddi's hands under Leah's hair, fastening the necklace, were trembling.

"Swear to God."

Necklace fastened, Leah leaned back so she could look Teddi in the eye. "You've really changed your mind about getting married?"

"I've changed my mind about getting married to you." Teddi brushed a lock of Leah's hair off her forehead. "I don't want to be without you, Leah. Ever. These past couple of months have been horrible. I missed you so much I didn't know what to do."

"Me, too."

"I know it seems fast and it's a big change, but give me time to show you. Okay?"

Leah ran her thumb across Teddi's lips. "I will give you anything you want. Don't you know that?"

"I do now." As Teddi leaned down for another kiss, a voice boomed through the warehouse.

"Can we come out now?" Kelly.

"We?" Leah asked as lights clicked on and several figures emerged from the office they'd passed on their way in. Not only was Kelly there, but accompanying her were Tilly, Jen, JoJo, Harlow, Preston, and Leah's mother. Leah's eyes went wide and she gaped at them as they all gathered around, hugged and kissed her and Teddi. "Oh my God, where did you all come from?"

"Do you think this all just set itself up?" Preston asked with a grin.

Harlow had her camera and snapped a photo of Leah and Teddi as they stood close, her face colored with delight and happiness.

"What is this place, anyway?" Leah asked.

"I rent space here," Teddi explained. "Remember? I think I mentioned it during one of Kelly's first meetings with me. It's where I keep all my supplies for weddings. Tables and chairs, arbors, tents, décor, stuff like that. I'm lucky enough to know some of the other folks in this industrial park who had the things in their storage spaces that I needed to make these scenes." She shrugged like it was no big deal, but Leah understood the scope of it, the magnitude of the effort she'd put forth to make this all happen just right.

"I can't believe you did this," she said quietly.

"I would do anything for you, Leah." Teddi hugged her close and pressed a kiss to her temple. "Anything."

"Mom?" Leah asked, as she noticed her mother's eyes were wet. She held out a hand to her. "You okay?"

Her mother came up to her, wrapped her arms around both Leah and Teddi. "I'm just so happy." She pulled away, laughing and crying at the same time, and laid a hand against each of their cheeks. "You two are meant for each other. I'm so glad you see it, too."

"We do." Leah looked up at Teddi, at the absolute sheer joy on her face, and she knew this was it. They were going to be okay. Not only that, but they'd get married. Not today. Not tomorrow. But it would happen. Leah knew it, felt it with every fiber of her being. And even though she didn't think her smile could grow or her happiness could burn brighter, they did. Because Leah finally had what she'd always wanted, and she would make Teddi her wife one day.

And those romances that she'd loved so much, the ones that had saved her from the fighting and the heartbreak of her parents' split, the ones that salvaged her sanity when she dealt with bitter divorces and the end of love on a daily basis, the ones that her friends loved to tease her about, tell her she was a hopeless romantic because they were unrealistic and far-fetched? Turned out she'd been right and her friends had been wrong all along, because guess what? Leah was about to get *exactly* what all those movies promised.

Leah was finally getting her happily ever after.

About the Author

Georgia Beers is an award-winning author of nearly thirty lesbian romance novels. She resides in upstate New York with her dog and cat, a wide array of plants, and at least the desire to learn how to cook. When not writing, she watches too much TV, explores the world of wine, and dutifully participates in spin class. She is currently hard at work on her next book. You can visit her and find out more at georgiabeers.com.

Books Available From Bold Strokes Books

A Love that Leads to Home by Ronica Black. For Carla Sims and Janice Carpenter, home isn't about location, it's where your heart is. (978-1-63555-675-9)

Blades of Bluegrass by D. Jackson Leigh. A US Army occupational therapist must rehab a bitter veteran who is a ticking political time bomb the military is desperate to disarm. (978-1-63555-637-7)

Hopeless Romantic by Georgia Beers. Can a jaded wedding planner and an optimistic divorce attorney possibly find a future together? (978-1-63555-650-6)

Hopes and Dreams by PJ Trebelhorn. Movie theater manager Riley Warren is forced to face her high school crush and tormentor, wealthy socialite Victoria Thayer, at their twentieth reunion. (978-1-63555-670-4)

In the Cards by Kimberly Cooper Griffin. Daria and Phaedra are about to discover that love finds a way, especially when powers outside their control are at play. (978-1-63555-717-6)

Moon Fever by Ileandra Young. SPEAR agent Danika Karson must clear her werewolf friend of multiple false charges while teaching her vampire girlfriend to resist the blood mania brought on by a full moon. (978-1-63555-603-2)

Serenity by Jesse J. Thoma. For Kit Marsden, there are many things in life she cannot change. Serenity is in the acceptance. (978-1-63555-713-8)

Sylver and Gold by Michelle Larkin. Working feverishly to find a killer before he strikes again, Boston homicide detective Reid Sylver and rookie cop London Gold are blindsided by their chemistry and developing attraction. (978-1-63555-611-7)

Trade Secrets by Kathleen Knowles. In Silicon Valley, love and business are a volatile mix for clinical lab scientist Tony Leung and venture capitalist Sheila Graham. (978-1-63555-642-1)

Entangled by Melissa Brayden. Becca Crawford is the perfect person to head up the Jade Hotel, if only the captivating owner of the local vineyard would get on board with her plan and stop badmouthing the hotel to everyone in town. (978-1-63555-709-1)

First Do No Harm by Emily Smith. Pierce and Cassidy are about to discover that when it comes to love, sometimes you have to risk it all to have it all. (978-1-63555-699-5)

Kiss Me Every Day by Dena Blake. For Wynn Jamison, wishing for a do-over with Carly Evans was a long shot; actually getting one was a game changer. (978-1-63555-551-6)

Olivia by Genevieve McCluer. In this lesbian Shakespeare adaption with vampires, Olivia is a centuries-old vampire who must fight a strange figure from her past if she wants a chance at happiness. (978-1-63555-701-5)

One Woman's Treasure by Jean Copeland. Daphne's search for discarded antiques and treasures leads to an embarrassing misunderstanding and, ultimately, the opportunity for the romance of a lifetime with Nina. (978-1-63555-652-0)

Silver Ravens by Jane Fletcher. Lori has lost her girlfriend, her home, and her job. Things don't improve when she's kidnapped and taken to fairyland. (978-1-63555-631-5)

Still Not Over You by Jenny Frame, Carsen Taite, and Ali Vali. Old flames die hard in these tales of a second chance at love with the ex you're still not over. (978-1-63555-516-5)

Storm Lines by Jessica L. Webb. Devon is a psychologist who likes rules. Marley is a cop who doesn't. They don't always agree, but both fight to protect a girl immersed in a street drug ring. (978-1-63555-626-1)

The Politics of Love by Jen Jensen. Is it possible to love across the political divide in a hostile world? Conservative Shelley Whitmore and liberal Rand Thomas are about to find out. (978-1-63555-693-3)